the hate date

AN ENEMIES TO LOVERS ROMANCE

KAYLENE WINTER

Clover

I sink down into the oversized chair in my living room. Stare at my phone in disbelief.

What the actual *fuck*?

My heart thunders as I press the button to repeat the video. Call me a masochist. Call me an idiot. Call me devastated.

Call me anything you want, but I *have* to see it again. Just to be sure.

Yep. It's my bedroom. Yep. There he is. My husband, Harrison Finklestein splayed naked across the pure-white linens on our three-hundred-thousand-dollar Hästens Grand Vividus custom bed.

His cock is flush against his belly. His black-brown eyes widen as the camera gets nearer. He licks his lips. His thick, black eyebrows furrow. The camera pans down to his hand stroking his erection. Yuck.

When did the dark hair on his fingers get so visibly bushy?

"Stop fucking around, we don't have much time," Harrison snarls.

The angle changes abruptly. A shard of glass pierces my heart. There she is. My best friend since I moved to Los Angeles, Solange Brown, who pouts then smiles widely into the lens. Her pearly-white veneers gleam, reminding me of shark teeth. She holds her phone out wide so I get a good view of long, blonde extensions brushing against her perfectly round silicone double Ds. I watch her straddle my husband and impale herself on his bare cock.

Harrison groans, "Shit, Solly. Your pussy is like fuckin' heaven."

She giggles.

Then the screen goes black.

I toss my phone on the couch in anger. I *want* to throw it against the wall and watch it shatter.

I'm not stupid, though. No matter how much this hurts—and it fucking hurts so badly I can barely breathe—I can't risk losing incriminating evidence. Because I'm divorcing my husband. No question. The iron-clad prenup I signed is void if either of us cheats, so...

I stare out the window. Attempt to process. Try to come up with a plan. My brain is so jumbled, I have no idea how much time passes. All I know is at some point, despair takes over.

How could they do this to me? I trusted them both implicitly. Solange and I have been friends for so long. Harrison and I have been married for almost a decade. I've never detected an iota of attraction between them.

Or so I thought.

Omigod. I'm going to be sick.

The betrayal is overwhelming.

Tears stream down my face. How could Harrison have been sleeping with my best friend behind my back without me knowing about it? My mind whirls. Trying to figure out if I missed any of the signs.

God. I trusted her with him. *Implicitly.* I confided so much about our relationship to her.

Now, I feel so fucking stupid. Naïve.

Harrison has always been somewhat controlling. A bit of a pompous ass at times, sure. But in the decade we've been together I've never known him to be *dishonest.* The man prides himself on integrity.

Which is *rich.*

If I'm brutally honest with myself—which is important if I'm going to survive this—our story is a true Hollywood cliché.

By my early twenties, I'd been acting for a while and had some success dabbling in pop music. We met at one of my concerts. He was charming, rich, and fifteen years older than me. I got caught up in a whirlwind romance. Never, in my entire life, had someone focused their energy on me in that way.

It was intoxicating.

So, when he asked me to marry him and start a family, I said yes. A few months later, when he complained about my work schedule, I gave up my career. For him. So I could support him the way I thought he was supporting me.

It's funny how the years sneak up on you. The kids never happened—he kept wanting to postpone "one more year" because I was still young. To keep from being bored, I immersed myself in charity work, which fulfilled me on many levels and kept me busy. We never fought. He always showered me with gifts and public displays of affection.

I wasn't overwhelmingly happy, but I loved him and was content with my life.

Comfortable.

For the most part, I thought we had a decent relationship even if our love life has always been a bit—meh. Well, at least for me. He, on the other hand, bragged about my blow jobs to anyone who would listen, much to my embarrassment.

But, I guess that was a lie too.

Because it never, ever—not once—occurred to me that he'd cheat.

Oh *God*. This is really happening.

I take a deep breath. No matter how much this sucks, I'm no weakling. I can't let them get away with this.

I *won't*.

After I stop crying, I take a deep breath, wipe my tears and vow not to shed another tear for Harrison.

He doesn't *deserve* my tears.

I get up. Grab my phone from the couch. Locate the video and save it to my private Dropbox. As a backup, I email it to myself. A girl can't be too careful.

Retreating into the bedroom, I open the safe and gather my jewelry and pack it in one of my small Louis Vuitton suitcases. I fill the rest of my luggage with designer clothes and shoes, my toiletries, cosmetics, and skincare products. Load my belongings into my Cayenne Turbo GT.

Next, I head into Harrison's home office, log into our bank account and transfer five hundred thousand dollars into my personal account. I'm able to locate a folder of our important documents and upload copies into the Dropbox. It takes a while, but I'm patient. Diligent.

It feels good to take charge. I *like* being in charge.

Glancing at my phone, I see I've missed a text from my soon-to-be ex-husband reminding me to be ready for a dinner I'm supposed to attend. Apparently, he has some bigwig financiers he's trying to woo for his next investment project.

Fuck that.

Let him take *Solly*.

Once I've taken care of business, I sit at the kitchen counter with a full glass of Harrison's most-prized bottle of wine, a 2015 Hundred Acre Vineyard Cabernet Sauvignon Reserve. I'm admiring the dark garnet color of two-thousand-dollar grapes swirling around in my crystal goblet when the door opens and footsteps approach.

"What the fuck, Clover?" Harrison stands before me with his hands on his hips. "You're not ready? We're going to be late."

I casually grip the glass of wine and hold it out over the stone floor. "I'm not going." I deliberately drop it and the fine crystal shatters in a puddle of red liquid.

Harrison storms over to me. "Are you *crazy?*"

"No. But, I think *you* are." I swipe the bottle with my arm, sending it crashing to the ground where it explodes.

Harrison looks horrified. "What the hell are you talking about?" he hisses.

"I *know*." My voice is quiet. Lethal.

He doesn't get it. His face is red with anger. "Know *what?*"

"I know about you and Solange. I hope you have a happy life together because you and I are through." I stare him dead in the eye. Cock my head.

Harrison wilts but recovers quickly. "Sweetheart, no. I'd never do that to you." He reaches out to touch my arm.

I yank away from him, disgusted. "I don't want to hear it. She recorded a video and sent it to me. I saw her riding your dick with my own eyes. There's nothing you can say. I told you cheating was a hard *no* for me, and it still is."

Harrison looks at me, his eyes blazing with fury. "You can't do this to me. You'll leave with nothing. You're a lazy washed-up actress, one-hit wonder. I'm the best you'll ever get."

I laugh bitterly. "That's where you're wrong, Harrison." My voice is cold as ice. "I was someone long before I met you *and* I'll be just fine without you. This is *your* loss, not mine."

With that, I hop off the stool, grab my purse and keys and walk out the door. Hurriedly jump in my car and head to the Chateau Mormont, where I've booked a suite for a month to sort out the mess of my life.

It's not the first time I've had to pick up the pieces and start over.

But, after this latest debacle, I'm determined it's going to be the last.

I'll never play second fiddle to a man again. Especially one who is rich, powerful, and controlling. Arrogant, entitled assholes aren't capable of truly loving someone. From what I've experienced, they expect you to drop every one of your own dreams to support theirs and thank them for the opportunity.

Never. Again.

God. I'm *so* done with him. With anyone *like* him.

I'm making some big changes. I'm not sure what I'm going to do or how I'm going to do it, but I'm giving myself one year to figure it out.

Chapter One

Eight Months Later

I wake up to the annoying sound of my phone buzzing.

Groggily, I reach over to grab it from where it's charging on the nightstand. It's Madison, aka "Mazza" Green, my longtime agent. A woman who'd actually forgotten she represented me when I called a few days after I split up with my ex.

Shit. I hope it's not more bad news. Not before Christmas. Auditions have been few and far between. I can't even land a commercial to save my life these days.

For a brief moment, I contemplate ignoring the call. Except, while I'm comfortable financially for the time being, I'm certainly not going to turn down the possibility of work. I might as well find out what she wants. I tap the talk button and put her on speaker.

"Babe," she coos. "I've got some good news. Unexpected news, actually."

I sit up in bed, the sheets pool around my waist. "Oh, yeah? What is it?"

"Veronica Miller reached out. She wants to take you to lunch." Mazza sounds baffled.

"Huh." I'm also a bit confused. I knew Ronni Miller many years ago when I had a supporting role on *Hawaiian High*, the teenage drama she starred in before her breakout sitcom, *She's All That*, took the world by storm.

"Word on the street is she's casting a new show." Luckily, Mazza always has the inside scoop. She just doesn't usually use her knowledge to help get me parts.

Could there be a role for me? Clearly, Ronni's going to star in whatever show she's involved in. Maybe she wants me to play her sister. Or her BFF. Something inside me sparks. Is this what I've been waiting for? "That's amazing! When? Can you send me the script?"

"Next week. I'll send you the details. No script," Mazza answers efficiently.

"Oh. Okay." A cold read. I can handle that. "Thanks, M. Appreciate the call."

As we hang up, I can't help but smile. A wave of gratitude washes over me. I'm so glad I answered the phone. I didn't anticipate getting back into the acting game would be so difficult. I've never been a superstar, but a couple chart-topping pop hits meant I never had a problem booking jobs.

Until I got married and gave it all up.

Unfortunately, the decade-long break has made me invisible to a new crop of casting agents who have no idea who I am. My one-year get-your-shit-together deadline is looming.

It's time to get moving. I've been through the stages of grief. I've wallowed and mourned. Lamented and raged. I have a therapist. Girls' nights with the friends who haven't abandoned me. Spas. Wellness retreats. I've done it all.

It seems I'm finally in the acceptance phase. Even though it's been rough, I've come to realize the goddesses were smiling down on me, timing-wise, when I learned the truth about my marriage.

The video of Harrison and Solange was my ace in the hole to retaining a large portion of my wealth. Our divorce was uncontested. Swift. My pre-nup was upheld. I kept all of the assets that were mine before we got married, which means our house is titled in my name. So is the Porsche. All of my belongings. Jewelry. Designer clothes. Oh, and five million dollars in cash.

So, for now, I'm good.

Thank God. A few weeks later, Harrison was indicted for some stuff that happened with his work. His assets were frozen. I'd likely be in dire straits if I hadn't caught him when I did. We'd still be married and everything in our joint accounts would have been seized, including what belonged to just me.

Except... *Shit*. Is that why Ronni wants to have lunch with me? To talk about Harrison? I seem to remember she was using his firm at some point.

Don't think that way.

Right. No reason to go down that rabbit hole.

Yet.

I manage to push the thought out of my mind. The next week is a blur. I work out like a madwoman for a couple hours a day. Massage. Facial. Spray tan. Mani-pedi, Wax. Teeth whitening. I've got to go into this lunch believing I can land a role, whatever it is. Looking my best is mandatory.

Act *as if*, and all that.

By the time I stroll into the Palm in Beverly Hills, I'm feeling myself. Casual white suit. Gold jewelry. Minimal makeup, except I've rimmed my aqua-blue eyes with black eyeliner. My long, dark hair is wound up in a stylish knot.

I've still got it. I *think*. At the very least, I look like I belong in this industry hot spot. The restaurant's host even does a double take before he leads me past the Hollywood mural to a booth in the back where Ronni is already seated.

"Clover, you're dazzling." She jumps up and hugs me tightly. "Divorce looks good on you."

I take in her petite frame, long, reddish hair and spectacular green eyes. As usual, she's flawless. "Didn't you just have twins? I can't believe it."

"Oh, it happened. Believe me. It takes a village to get me to leave the house these days." She beams and scoots into the booth, gesturing for me to sit across from her.

Once seated, I can't help but fidget. I decide to address the elephant in the room head-on. "I was surprised you reached out, considering."

Ronni looks me directly in the eye. "You aren't responsible for what Harrison was involved in. I'm fine, by the way. It didn't affect me or my husband."

"I didn't know he had ties with Kircher. He knew how I felt about that man." I look down at the napkin I clutch tightly in my hand. "It makes me sick. I'm so sorry."

A few months before my divorce, the entire Hollywood foundation was rocked when the *LA Times* did an expose on Don Kircher, our former showrunner on *Hawaiian High*. His misogynistic ways were brought to light by none other than my lunch date, and he's facing many years in prison for all of his misdeeds.

It's why my ex is going down too. I recently learned he played a huge role in Kircher's notorious—and highly illegal—poker nights.

Ronni shakes her head. "Of course you didn't. This whole thing is mind-blowing. For too many years I was obsessed with stopping Kircher's web of sexual assault. I never realized how tangled it was. Or how dangerous. Thank God the *LA Times* did such a good job uncovering everything. I hope it helps make the industry more accountable."

"*Right*." I snort. "Others will take their place in a heartbeat."

"Not if I have anything to say about it." Ronni smiles and reaches across the table for my hand, which surprises me. It surprises me even more that I give it to her. "He didn't hurt you, did he? Please say he didn't."

I gulp. An unconfirmed rumor on the set was Kircher made Ronni have sex with him on her eighteenth birthday and then he fired her. A month later, Ronni's best friend, who played her love interest on the show, committed suicide. *Hawaiian High* was canceled and we all lost our jobs.

It was a dark, dark time. One I try avoid thinking about. "Uh..."

"No," she whispers, her eyes filling with tears.

I shake my head. "He never did anything to me. I promise. I guess one good thing came out of playing the cute, chubby sister. All he did was constantly criticize my weight. Not great for my self-esteem, but I was never an object of his desire. Thank God."

"You have always been the sweetest, most beautiful soul." Ronni's grip on my hand tightens. "I hate he made you feel less than."

"I was lucky," I sigh. "Wynn's death hit everyone so hard, but what you've done to try and make those assholes pay is unbelievable."

Ronni's eyes fill with tears. "It haunted me. I didn't want to leave him, but I had no choice when I got fired for *not* sleeping with Kircher. Everything I've done to expose that bastard is because of Wynn and for all of us who didn't have a voice. We didn't deserve how we were treated. I don't want anything like what we went through to ever happen again."

I squeeze her fingers with mine, grateful to hear the rumors about her were false. "I wondered why you'd put yourself on the line like you did. It was brave."

"I nearly lost everything. If it hadn't been for my husband, I'm not sure I'd even be here today." Ronni's eyes go dreamy. I get it, she's married to one of the most gorgeous men on the planet, Grammy award-winning Less Than Zero's bassist, Connor McGloughlin, who comes complete with a sexy Irish accent.

I extricate my fingers from hers and take a sip of water. "Well, I'm glad we could catch up. I hope this gives you some closure."

"Closure?" Ronni's nose scrunches up in confusion.

"Isn't that why we're having lunch? Complete your *Hawaiian High* chapter now that Kircher's in prison?" Might as well say it, this lunch isn't about a role.

Ronni laughs. "Oh, Clover. I knew you'd be perfect."

"For what?" I tilt my head.

"The lead in the new show I'm doing for Netflix." She picks up the menu and casually peruses it as though she didn't just give me the comeback offer of a lifetime.

I sit slack-jawed for a beat before I manage to eek a word out, "*Me*? Why aren't you the lead?"

"So you *do* know about the show." Her eyes sparkle. "I planned to star in it. After the babies, the network didn't think I'd be camera-ready given our expedited shooting schedule."

This infuriates me, and I let it show. "*Ronni*. Let's not mince words. I'm distinctively larger than you are. No one's casting a size ten woman as a lead. I may hate it, but it's true."

"Trust me. I've avoided too many delicious carbs for years to stay thin. This industry is brutal on a woman's self-esteem no matter what size we are. In this instance, I'm realistic. I've been on television for years. The public has a certain perception of me and what I look like." Ronni shrugs and leans back.

I can't help but shake my head. "Sizist *bullshit*."

"It's okay...well, not okay but the reality is my body hasn't fully bounced back yet. While I could push the issue and probably win, somehow I don't find myself caring anymore." Ronni's eyes shine. "I'm in love. I have two adorable babies. This is my chance to take my career to the next level, but I've never been on this side of the business."

My mind whirls with excitement. Anticipation.

"It's going to take all of my focus because I want this show to be groundbreaking," Ronni continues. "Plus, I'm not in the headspace to play this character. Which is why *you*, my dear, are perfect. I need you. I can't produce, direct, and act with twin babies to take care of."

I don't say anything. I can't. This is the most unexpected and incredible opportunity I've ever had.

When my silence goes on too long, Ronni taps the table with her perfectly manicured nude nail. "You're awfully quiet. What do you think? Do you hate the idea?"

"They've cleared me?" I squeak, anticipating her to say she hasn't run it past them yet. I'm not going to get my hopes up if this is still up in the air.

"Yes. Of course. Kris Blakely, my producing partner, and the network think you're perfect." She can't help but show her excitement. "It all came together when I showed them the interview you gave to *People* last month about your divorce and new philosophy on dating. I believe the exact word was, 'genius.'"

I'm shocked yet again. Genius? What the heck? "I guess I should ask for some details. How would casting me be so genius?"

Ronni giggles. "Well, let's see. You'd be playing a gorgeous woman who's divorced from a cheating asshole. She's decided that her taste in men sucks. In her attempt to get back in the game, she makes a pact with herself to only date men who are the opposite of who she's usually attracted to. Hilarity ensues."

Without thinking, I clap my hand against my mouth. My eyes couldn't be wider. I'm literally stunned silent.

Again.

Ronni is patient. She waits.

"Wait, so it's essentially, um, a show about my life?" I breathe out when I'm able to talk again.

She slaps her hand on the table. "I swear, Clover. I've had this idea written down for a couple of years. It's like the timing of all of this was meant to be. Please say yes."

"Omigod. Yes!" I shimmy in my seat. "Yes. Yes. Yes. *Thank you.* It's an incredible offer."

The rest of lunch goes by in a blur as Ronni fills me in on the script and accelerated timeline for shooting. We leave with her promise to have a contract for me by the end of the week. If the terms are acceptable—and let's face it, the odds of me turning it down are zilch—I'll be heading to Vancouver BC to start filming in a couple of months.

For the first time in nearly a year, life is definitely looking up.

Chapter Two

A Few Weeks Later

My black Bentley Flying Spur Mulliner pulls up to the sleek, glass building off Wilshire Boulevard.

Ordinarily, I don't usually handle the changing of the guard when I take over a distressed business. Today, however, is special. It requires my personal touch.

"Please wait for me here. I won't be too long," I address my regular Los Angeles driver-slash-security detail, Victor, who nods his understanding.

As I exit my car, I button the jacket on my bespoke Cad & The Dandy navy linen suit and slide on my Bulgari sunglasses. It's a short hundred yards or so to the entrance, but I deliberately take my time.

I even stop to tie the laces on one of my custom Berluti loafers, resting my foot on the edge of a large pool where a mermaid sculpture spouts water from her mouth.

Oh, I'm certain everyone who's still working at Eminence Partners has their nose pressed to the window twenty floors above me. I'm expected.

Feared.

As I should be. I'm about to take charge.

Pushing through the front door, the security guard seems to be expecting me. I like that. He shows me to the elevator bank. Once inside, I check the time on my phone. Seth King, my best friend and general counsel arrived an hour ago. I love sending my surly, take-no-shit advisor in ahead of me.

It keeps everyone on edge.

The doors open into the reception area of Eminence, once the most-trusted money management firms for the worldwide elite. Up until founder Harrison Finklestein screwed everyone by using client funds to back illegal celebrity poker games. Finklestein was in cahoots with famed movie director, Don Kircher, who's in jail for some misogynistic shit that puts Harvey Weinstein to shame.

Finklestein's going to rot in a cell next to that asshole, I'll make sure of that.

"Mr. Jacoby," a tiny girl with an oversized dress and glasses addresses me shyly. "I'm Maria. We're expecting you. Everyone's set up in the back conference room. Mr. King is already here. Can I get you a coffee? Water?"

Impressed by her professionalism in the face of the shitstorm that's about to descend upon this office, I refrain from intimidating her too much. She could be useful at some point. "It's Joar. Rhymes with 'door.' And, I'm fine. Thank you. Please just show me the way."

I follow her down the hall, which is curiously lined with expensive original artwork on one side and huge portraits of the partners on the other. These fuckers sure spared no expense on the art, which I understand. Convincing the richest people in the world to allow them to handle their money requires putting forth a certain image.

What the fuck is up with the portraits though? It's like they're leaning in to the tired, old stereotype that middle-aged white guys are the only people qualified to manage money. Not a person of color or woman in sight.

Idiots.

"They're in here." Maria stops and gestures to a room where four of the real-life versions of the portraits are seated around a large, oblong table.

Seth, who is seated at the far end, stands when I enter. "Gentlemen, let me introduce you to Joar Jacoby."

Three of the men greet me politely. I don't remember any of their names but why bother? None of them will likely be here tomorrow. No need to clog my mind with insignificant details of dead men walking.

The other man is Finklestein. A man I haven't seen since I was twenty-one. He glares at me petulantly.

"Harrison. It's been a few years." I take a seat and lean back in my chair. Scan the room indifferently until my eyes land back on the man whose life is about to get a whole lot worse. "When does your trial start? I swear, it couldn't happen to a more deserving asshole."

Arrogantly, he pounds his fist on the table. "How *dare* you."

Ignoring his outburst, I take my sunglasses off and chew on the temple tip. He stares me down, but I'm patient. When his eyes dart away, I hold a finger up. "You're no longer in charge here. Get a good look, you won't be back."

His eyes widen. "Um..." he mumbles, clearly caught off guard.

"I'll see you out." Seth stands and moves to Harrison's side.

Finklestein sneers at him. "I'm not going anywhere. *I'm* the founder and CEO of this company. I didn't have anything to do with Don Kircher's business. I'll be *vindicated*. There's no way I'll let that asshole—" he points at me "—take away the company I built from the ground up. Not a fucking chance."

His three cronies look over at me, clearly at a loss for what's about to go down.

"Seth?" I gesture at my lawyer. "You might as well show them."

While Seth pulls out folders for each of the men, including Finklestein, I dial Victor and speak quietly but firmly, "Send security up. We're in the back conference room. I need about five minutes."

"What the fuck is this?" Finklestein screeches when he reads the resolution Seth handed him. "*My* board assured me there would be no changes to management until I sorted all of this out. This is an outrage. I'm calling my lawyer."

"Do your best. I can assure you, it's over." I keep my face neutral. I might be a shark, but I'm not a gloater. Gloating is for insecure failures.

Harrison jumps up and storms over to me, sticking a pointed finger in my face. "It's *never* going to be over. Someone like *you* will never take over *my* company. It'll be over my dead body. Don't you forget it, you bottom-feeding loser."

Ah. And there it is. I knew he'd go low, it took much less time than I thought. Twenty-six years ago, Harrison and I were roommates at Yale for one semester during our freshman year. His path was Skull & Bones, my path was scraping my way through undergrad by working three jobs. An age-old story, except he stole my English paper and turned it in as his own without my knowledge.

He probably figured it would be his word—backed by his family's generous donation to the school—against mine, backed by nobody.

I was, after all, a boy who was abandoned by my parents and grew up in the foster system. A kid who just so happened to be incredibly gifted with an insanely high IQ. Focused and determined to change my lot in life after being shuffled around from family to family. Someone who managed to get a full-ride scholarship to one of the most prestigious universities in the United States.

Unfortunately, I confided all of these things in my roommate, believing I'd finally found a new friend other than Seth. My naiveite allowed him to take advantage of me.

Ruin me. For no good reason whatsoever.

If it hadn't been for my astute professor who went to bat for me with the dean, I would have been expelled. Instead, Harrison was suspended for plagiarism. I finished college, graduating with honors. But, for the rest of my years at Yale, Harrison and his "brethren" didn't make it easy on me.

Not even a little bit.

The worst was when they started a crazy rumor about me having herpes which, because of who they were, took on a life of its own. It didn't matter that I was a virgin at the time. I was so mortified, I didn't so much as ask someone out on a date let alone find an opportunity to have sex. I finally lost my virginity at twenty-three, during my second year of my MBA program in NYC.

They say what doesn't kill you makes you stronger. I'm living proof. The experience fundamentally changed me. Hardened me against getting close to people. Made me more determined to become so successful and powerful no one would ever mess with me again.

I've succeeded. Beyond even my own wildest dreams.

Don't let anyone fool you—being wealthy is fantastic. When you have as much money as I do? You *can* do whatever the fuck you want. I've come a long way from being a destitute kid stuck in the foster system. Harrison, on the other hand, is still the same old shithead he ever was.

"It's already done." I gesture to the security guards who have appeared at the door. They enter and I flick my gaze to Finklestein. "Your access has been suspended. Your computer and phone confiscated. These gentlemen will escort you from the building. As far as any personal belongings you may have, someone will arrange to get them back to you after a thorough audit of the books. Have a nice day."

Finklestein sputters and squirms as he's dragged from the room.

For the next few days, Seth and I pore over financial reports while my IT team does a forensic deep dive on the computer files. It's tedious work, but it's necessary to get a clear picture of the company's financial viability.

As the week wears on, I get a sense of the incredibly tangled web of relationships that has contributed to Eminence Partners' troubles. There are shady business deals with unscrupulous clients, questionable investments, and a host of other issues. But one thing stands out above all the rest: Harrison Finklestein's ex-wife, Clover Callahan.

Clover conveniently divorced Harrison just before his scandal broke, and she made off with millions of dollars in assets that, in my humble opinion, rightfully belong to the company. As far as I'm concerned, anyone who could stay married to a creep like Finklestein for a decade is complicit in his misdeeds. No question. This is a blatant act of theft, and the thought of it makes me furious.

"What do you intend on doing?" Seth taps a finger to his nose. "It certainly *appears* she's involved in this mess."

"I'm not sure yet." I scroll through her Instagram feed as Seth goes back to reviewing some documents.

I'm vaguely aware of who she is. A washed-up B-list actress who had a couple of random pop hits a decade ago. What I didn't remember is that she's absolutely jaw-droppingly stunning. Long, silky black hair.

Wide-set eyes that are so many shades of aqua they have to be contact lenses. She's voluptuous, with creamy, golden skin. Pouty lips that, if circumstances were different, I'd love to see wrapped around my cock.

Yeah, she's definitely my type.

Except for the fact she's probably a fucking criminal.

Her latest post is a duck-pout selfie with A+ list actress, Ronni Miller, who is *truly* a class act. I've never met her, but last year she put her entire career on the line to expose Don Kircher's reign of casting-couch terror. The man is, thankfully, going to spend the rest of his life in jail because of her efforts.

The caption reads, "*Hawaiian High* besties reunited at last. Guess who's in Vancouver BC? Me! I'm back in business, bitches. Playing the lead in Ronni's new show. Stay tuned!"

Huh. I'm surprised at the connection, but it infuriates me even more. My gut tells me that woman was definitely in on the scam with her ex. *Fuck*. Clover probably led her husband to Kircher. Ronni Miller could be one more of Harrison's victims. I'm going to get to the bottom of it. That's a promise.

"Add Canada to my schedule." I turn my screen to show Seth the post.

He smiles. "She's smokin' hot. That's the wife?"

"Yep. As luck would have it, Ronni Miller's new series is filming at our facility in Canada." I waggle my eyebrows. My company owns J&M Studios, a multimillion-dollar production facility just outside of Vancouver, BC. If Clover Callahan thinks she's going to escape unscathed, she's got another thing coming.

"Good call. Finklestein put this entire company at risk with his shady dealings. If his ex-wife is part of it, we've got to know." Seth nods.

I scroll further through her Instagram feed. The gorgeous woman gives off a decidedly girl-next-door vibe but has a body of a burlesque dancer. It's easy to understand why Finklestein married her. "The team needs a few months to complete the audit. After I check on things in London, I'll head to Vancouver BC. Will you arrange for a P.I. in the meantime? I want to know her every move."

"No problem." Seth winks at me. "She seems to like rich men. Maybe there's one more way to stick the knife in."

I tap her picture with my finger. "Nah. I don't think it's wise to go there with this one. But, maybe I'll change my mind once I've met her."

A smile emerges for the first time in a few days.

I'm no angel. She's definitely someone I'd ordinarily hit up.

Who knows? Maybe this part of Finklestein's takedown will be even more fun than I originally thought.

Chapter Three

One Week Later

I love Vancouver, BC.

Until we started rehearsals a few weeks ago, regretfully, I'd never been in Canada, let alone British Columbia. It's my loss. If I didn't know better, I'd think I was somewhere in Europe. There's a vibe here. A *very* cool vibe.

Not to mention there's so much to do.

The city is filled with skyscrapers but is sparkling clean. Cosmopolitan. People are chic and always moving fast. The shops are upscale but also quirky. World-class restaurants abound. I'm not super outdoorsy, but even I've biked around Stanley Park. Spent an afternoon or two at the Granville Island Public Market.

Don't even get me started on how stunning the setting is. The city is essentially built on an island in between Vancouver Harbor and English Bay. Everywhere you look has spectacular panoramic water views. The North Shore Mountains overlook the city, providing a dramatic backdrop to the gleaming high-rises.

The surrounding areas are just as magnificent. Before we started shooting, I tagged along to the Whistler ski resort with Ronni, her husband Connor, their twins, and nanny. I didn't ski, but sure enjoyed the hell out of shopping for cozy sweaters, stocking up on maple syrup, and drinking artisan hot chocolate.

Who knew that was even a thing?

The downside—and it's a big one—is how much it freakin' rains. My God, it's a relentless gray drizzle some days. Almost like you're in the middle of a cloud that's constantly leaking.

Not today though. It's nearly sixty degrees and sunny. Considering it's my only day off for the next two weeks, this morning I took a long walk along the waterfront. Now it's time to day drink and get some dating advice from my self-appointed gay husband, Paxton Price.

I'm waiting for him at the Coal Harbor Cactus Club, sipping on their signature bellini drink, a frozen concoction of rum, peach schnapps, sparkling wine, peaches, and sangria. My God, it's so delicious. And dangerous. Two or three of these and I'll be hammered.

Hmmm. Maybe that wouldn't be the worst thing. I'm determined to lean into my new single-life and live each day to the fullest. I've never been naked wasted before. This afternoon is as good a time as any.

"Clover. There you are." Pax, as stylish as can be in black slacks and a gray sweater, swoops into the room and sits next to me at the bar. He points at my drink and gestures to the bartender. "I'll take one of these."

Quickly, I slurp the last bit of slushy goodness from my martini glass and blurt out, "Me too."

"Easy, girl." Pax shakes his head. "If we're going to be BFFs, you've got to let me catch up."

Pax is Ronni's personal assistant. I met him on set and he and I hit it off immediately. I've been nervous about putting myself out there, so he promised to help me with a dating plan. I'm ready to get my groove back. It's been nearly a year since I've had sex, and my hoo-ha is getting dusty.

"I'll sip this one slowly," I promise as the bartender sets the drinks in front of us.

"Okay, spill. Why the *hell* have you been celibate for a year?" Pax rests his chin on his palm.

I sigh, regretful I told him such private information last week. He won't let it go. "Cheating husband. Disintegration of my friendship. Loss of my so-called friends after the divorce. Working on myself. *Rebuilding*. Blah. Blah. Blah." I wave my hand in the air.

"Nope. Those are *cliches*, not reasons. Try again." Pax narrows his eyes.

"Fine." I pout. "How about I have terrible taste in men. I don't trust myself to pick a good guy."

"Why would you want a good guy? You don't want to settle down. Get yourself some dick, girl." Pax rolls his eyes like it's the easiest thing in the world. It probably is for a guy with his confidence.

"The thought of getting involved with another controlling, manipulative man like Harrison makes me sick to my stomach. At the same time, I don't want to be alone forever. I want to find someone who respects me and treats me as an equal." I sip my drink and look to him for, I don't know—approval?

Pax considers me for a second. Looks me up and down. "So, you're looking for another husband."

"No!" I recoil.

He raises an eyebrow. "Sure sounds like it."

I grab my phone and scroll through one of the dating apps I signed up for a couple days ago. I've never used them, but I'm willing to give it a try. "I'm going to sign up for an app. What do you think? Plenty of Fish? Tinder? Bumble? eHarmony?"

"No. No. No. *No*." He takes my phone and places it face down on the counter. "You're starring in a new series. You can't do that anymore."

Shit. He's got a point. I nod in understanding. "Raya? Ugh. I don't think the celebrity dating app thing is for me. I just want a regular guy."

He buries his head in his hands and mumbles, "Clover, what am I going to do with you?"

"*What?*" I scrunch my nose. "How am I going to meet anyone? I'm on set all day..."

I'm cut short when Pax presses his palm to my mouth. "Shush. We need to work on your game. Do you see the way dudes look at you? Every day, wherever you go, men practically worship the ground you walk on. Tell me you know this." He removes his hand. Holds my gaze until I break eye contact from the intensity of it all.

"Stop. I know you're just trying to help me, but don't lie. No one looks at me that way. Especially now that I'm pushing forty." I take a deep pull of my peachy slush.

Pax spins my stool to face him. "You're thirty-two years old. You're hot *and* you're going to be even hotter when this show comes out. Grow some self-esteem, woman."

Now it's my turn to roll my eyes. "Look. Ronni gave me this role, and I'm grateful. She told me her vision: I'm the girl next door. The chick who every woman relates to yet is destined for the most *epic* romance. It's what the show's about."

"Do you hear yourself?" His brow furrows. "This show is your life. You've joked about it to the entire crew. What did you say your foolproof plan is?"

"First on the list is to revive my career. Hopefully this show will do it for me. Second, I'm embracing every day to the fullest. If I want to make out with someone, I'm going to do it. For the first time in my life, I'm going to learn what makes me happy. Finally, I'm never dating another guy who wears a suit." I emphasize each item on the list by holding up a finger.

He sucks in his lips, pondering. "As far as the second and third items on the list, my recommendation is you try some guys on for size, if you know what I mean." He flicks his eyes to his junk and back up at me. Waggles his eyebrows.

My drink is nearly empty and I'm feeling a good buzz. "You think I should chat up a guy and take him home with me?"

"I think you should open your eyes. See yourself how others see you. It will all fall into place." He cups my cheek with his palm. "Don't look now, but there's one hot MF checking you out. He's behind you and to the left."

Even I have enough game not to turn around and stare at him. Instead, I slide off my barstool, grab my phone and purse and point to the front of the restaurant. "I'll make a quick trip to the ladies room and have a look. Be right back."

I confidently stride past the bar toward the dining room and sneak a glance in the general direction of where Pax said the dude was sitting.

Holy friggin' moly.

My heart stops. As do my feet.

Pax wasn't kidding. A man with tousled, longish, dark hair cropped short on the sides is buried in a menu. He fills his white T-shirt to perfection, I swear I can see each defined muscle in his arms and chest. His olive skin is smooth. He's got a square-cut jaw with a hint of stubble. As I get closer, I see he's a bit older than me from the sprinkling of silver throughout his sexy mane.

His eyes, cast down to peruse food choices, snap to mine as I walk past. They're incredible. A truly distinctive shade of blue, no—violet.

It's like I've been zapped with a jolt of electricity.

Right to my core.

He's caught me gawking, so it's all I can do to keep my feet moving and pretend I'm not affected. This perfect specimen of a man is so completely out of my league it's not even funny.

Then something unexpected happens.

He smiles at me. Tips his head, even.

Oh, this guy's a player and I know exactly what this means. He's giving me an opening to go talk to him. My mind races with potential things to say. Funny anecdotes. Witty self-depreciating comments. I could even admit the truth: I want him to do wicked things to my body right here.

Right now.

In the four seconds I stand gaping, a million possibilities of how to approach him and what to say run through my mind.

In the end, I do nothing because fear takes over.

As does my flight instinct.

Instead of hitting the ladies room, I hustle myself right out the door, leaving the gorgeous man and Pax behind.

Chapter Four

Earlier the Same Day

I'm seething.

Harrison Finklestein is, quite possibly, the stupidest shithead I've ever come across. My team has spent the past few weeks auditing each and every client file at Eminence Partners and reconciling all financial records. The business is salvageable. Under my corporate umbrella, it will bring hundreds of millions of dollars of revenue into my portfolio.

This won't happen overnight, unfortunately. It will take months to turn the business around completely. We need to rebuild faith in the company. Shift things away from the Harrison era. To think so many celebrity elite entrusted their life savings with the fuckwad...*Jesus.*

It blows my mind. The man skimmed money from his clients' accounts and no one seemed to notice.

He scammed every last one of them, the poor, trusting idiots.

Clover Callahan, on the other hand, is smart. Although there is nothing overtly tying her to his operations, my gut tells me there's no way she and her ex-husband weren't in cahoots. And, I trust my gut. Implicitly. It's gotten me to where I am today.

My theory is Harrison and Clover devised the poker games as a way to distract authorities from delving further into his financial management business. When Kircher was exposed by Ronni Miller, their quickie divorce allowed them to put millions of dollars of property obtained from his client's stolen assets into Clover's name.

Before Finklestein's involvement was revealed months later.

He's under investigation for his participation but, even if he's indicted and then convicted, it's just the tip of the iceberg. No one but my team knows the extent of his illegal activities. Evidence we've uncovered will put Finklestein away for life.

Meanwhile, I believe Ms. Callahan is sitting on—conservatively—twenty million dollars in assets. Real Estate. Jewelry. Designer clothes. Cash. Not nearly enough to pay back all of the money her husband took, but it's a start.

If there's one thing I can't stand, it's a thief. As far as I'm concerned, she's as guilty as her ex-husband. This situation is personal to me. One way or the other, I'm going to make the people Finkelstein scammed whole again. His ex-wife is just one part of my plan. Make no mistake, I want that money back and I'll do whatever it takes to get it.

I gaze out at the sparkling waters of Coal Harbor from my suite at the Fairmont Pan Pacific. My entire afternoon has been spent buried in the documents Zed, my private investigator, compiled about Clover's background and current situation. Honestly, there's not much to go on. She's been doing mostly charity work and attending events with Finklestein since the wedding.

My phone buzzes. It's Zed. "Yeah?"

"Thought I'd let you know, she's a couple blocks away from you at a restaurant called The Cactus Club. Having drinks with Ronni Miller's PA." His voice is gruff and unemotional. He's a "just the facts" kind of guy, which I appreciate.

"Interesting," I say, spotting the restaurant from my vantage point at the window. "Stick close. I'll be there in a few minutes. It's time for me to observe her in person myself."

I'm still wearing a ten-thousand-dollar suit, so I hastily change into a simple white T-shirt and jeans. I don't want to draw attention to myself today and I certainly don't want Clover to notice as I watch her from afar.

Within fifteen minutes I'm seated at a corner table near the bar where I have the perfect, covert vantage point to observe Clover sip some sort of fruity frozen drink and chat with the PA-guy who's gazing at her adoringly.

God *damn*.

I did not expect this.

Clover is transcendent. Pictures could never do this woman justice. She faces away from me but is positioned at an angle where I have an excellent view. She wears a black V-neck sweater tucked into tight pink pants that hug her round, juicy ass. Her long, black hair gleams like glass. Graceful fingers tipped with long, white nails gesture wildly. The PA dude says something which causes her to laugh heartily.

A lyrical, musical thoroughly delightful sound.

I've been with hundreds of coveted women in my forty-seven years on this planet, including models, royalty, pageant winners, CEOs and actresses. So, I consider myself a connoisseur of gorgeous women.

But...I've never been so instantly attracted to someone in my life. She's beyond beautiful. Physically, it's a no brainer. Holy shit, though. Her magnetic presence draws me in. This woman has an "it" factor that pulls everyone around into her orbit. A quick glance around the restaurant proves my point. Both men and women stare in fascination.

I'll admit it. I've never been so enchanted by a woman I haven't met. Easily a half hour goes by before I realize I've been thoroughly engrossed in all things Clover Callahan. Like every other googly-eyed asshole in this place.

I practically have to force myself to remember I hate everything this woman stands for.

I'm here for a *reason*.

Add one more.

I want to *fuck* her. No question. Good God, to bury my face in those soft tits. For a brief moment, I allow myself to imagine spanking that plump ass as I'm pounding into her from behind. How I'd wrap her long hair around my wrist as she deep-throats my cock.

For fuck's sake. It occurs to me it's the second time I've fantasized about a woman I've never even spoken to giving me a blowjob.

This time, though, I'm hard as a pole. In public.

Goddammit. I'm taking back control of my faculties. There'll be none of that. Not with her.

Not a fucking chance.

I pick up the menu. Decide I might as well grab a bite while I'm here. It'll give me something to do other than ogle the woman I'm supposed to be here to destroy.

Out of the corner of my eye, I see a flash of pink. My entire body tingles as if I can sense Clover approaching. I keep the menu tilted up to hide my face. Though I'm acutely aware of her getting nearer, I try my best to keep my eyes focused on the entrees.

It's no use. When I feel prickles of heat skating up my neck, I can't help but look up.

My eyes lock with hers. One beat. Two beats. Three. Electricity shoots between us. My scalp tingles. My cock stands at full attention.

I want you.

It happens without me even thinking about it. My lips have a goddamn mind of their own. I fucking *smile* at the beautiful creature staring a hole through my head. Salivating like she wants to devour me.

That look is all it takes for me to get sucked into her vortex.

Until a horrific thought takes hold. Does she recognize me? Did her ex tip her off?

Time stands still as I analyze the situation. My stupid grin freezes in place as our eyes stay locked. Her face reddens. She looks down. Back up at me again, shyly this time.

Hold on. There's not an ounce of recognition there. She thinks I'm interested in her. She's merely considering if I'm an option.

I relax immediately. I can handle this situation as easily as breathing.

Her obvious attraction has me reconsidering my options. Perhaps I'll indulge in the "easier" way to get information out of Clover Callahan. The more *pleasurable* way.

Oh, I like where this is going. So much. I tip my head and angle my neck slightly in invitation.

Come here, little bunny.

She freezes. Oh, hell yeah. I'm the fox and she's my prey. Her nipples poke through her shirt like little bullets. Her entire body shudders and she takes a tentative step forward. Bites her delectable lip. *Yessssss.*

Except she picks up the pace and rushes past me like a flash out the front door.

Shit!

I'm on the phone to Zed in a heartbeat. "She left, follow her," I demand and hang up.

Confounded, I pick up the menu again. Set it down.

Dammit.

I'm genuinely discombobulated.

I. Do. Not. Get. Rattled.

Not over a woman. It's never happened before. It's not happening now.

"*Fuck it,*" I mutter to myself. Pull out my wallet and toss a hundred-dollar bill on the table even though I haven't ordered a thing. Grab my phone and head toward the front door where Zed is waiting.

He stubs out a cigarette and points toward the buildings up the hill. "She jumped in an Uber and headed that way. Probably back to the Sutton Place Hotel. That's where the cast and crew are being housed."

It's a blessing in disguise. Her disappearing act gives me the perspective I need. I have an important call with Tokyo in just under an hour. The last thing I'm going to do is chase this woman around the city. This shit with Eminence Partners has taken up too much time as it is.

"Well, go keep an eye out. I have work to do. Call me if anything I should know about happens." I dismiss Zed and start toward my hotel.

On my short walk back to the Fairmount, I decide to get real with myself. First, the way I'm drawn to her is dangerous. Second, I'm making this business with Eminence Partners *too* personal. Third, I don't *need* to be here. If this were an ordinary acquisition, my corporate integration team would handle the transition and I'd let Seth worry about getting the money back from Clover.

For fuck's sake. It's what I should do now. It would be easy to call for my jet, head back to my headquarters in New York and return to business as usual.

I'm going to stay, though. Might as well admit it.

Thankfully, I'm a master keeping my priorities in line. Staying focused. Keeping my feelings out of the mix. Now that I've identified my own weaknesses, I can work around them. Keep them in check.

I'm leaving for Singapore in a few days anyway. Until then, I'll hang around the studio to get a read on the situation. My presence won't seem out of the ordinary—I have every right to be there. I *own* the goddamn place.

If she recognizes me, it'll be because I'm the handsome man she locked eyes with at The Cactus Club. I'll flirt with her. Maybe take her to dinner with a nice bottle of wine so she'll let her guard down. I'll figure out what her involvement is. Where the money is.

Then lower the boom.

If somewhere in-between all of this we happen to get naked?

That'll just be an added bonus.

Chapter Five

A Few Days Later

The working title of the show is *The Essential Hunk List*, but Netflix has decided to change it to *The Boyfriend Experiment*. We're a few weeks into filming the mockumentary style dramedy. My character frequently speaks directly to the camera and has various confessional interview segments which will be woven into the scenes.

The entire production is first class. The cast and crew are fantastic. Ronni is, well, perfection.

I'm in absolute heaven.

My character is Jenna Lewis, a thirty-something woman, married to a doctor who leaves her for one of his residents. On the day her divorce is finalized, her best friend, Sunithra Jones, challenges her to date outside her comfort zone. They come up with a list—called Essential Boyfriends—which details the types of men Jenna has never been with before. She's not allowed to get serious until she works her way through the entire list.

I've been pleasantly surprised at how smooth everything is going on set. Apparently, Netflix wants the series to premiere later this year, so we're working double-time to finish principle shooting. We've filmed most of the scenes between Jenna and Sunithra. Now, we're working through the dates with the "boyfriends" and my confessionals.

The pace is insane, but also invigorating.

I can't help asking myself—how is this my life? Last year I was essentially a failed actress-turned-stay-at-home wife. Now, I'm starring in the single-most-anticipated series this fall. One that could absolutely be based on my own life.

Insanity. All of it.

"Clover, ten minutes." A production assistant knocks on the door to my dressing room.

Vivi, my makeup artist, powders my nose and spritzes me with setting spray. "You're gorgeous."

I slide off my chair and undo my robe. I'm wearing tight black jeans and not much else. Vivi helps me into a gorgeous candy-pink corset with a tiny floral detail. "Holy crap, that's tight." I wince when she tugs and ties the laces.

"Oh, but it makes your boobs even more spectacular." Vivi waggles her eyebrows. "I'd give anything to have natural tits like yours."

Blushing, I check myself out in the mirror. I must admit, this little corset is especially magical, even if my girls are dangerously close to exploding out of it. I toe on the sky-high pink stilettos, which complete my outfit. Twirl around. Damn. I look scorching hot, if I do say so myself.

I'm nervous, though. Today we're filming potential boyfriend number one: the computer nerd.

On my way out, I pop a cinnamon mint in my mouth and teeter to the elevator across the hall. The sound stage where we're filming my next scene is on the bottom floor of the facility. I'm casually scrolling through lines on my phone when the door opens. Distracted, I take a step inside just as a man rushes out.

We collide and I'm knocked flat on my ass with a distinct thunk.

"Shit. I'm sorry. Let me help you up." The man's voice is deep, gravely, and commanding. His biceps bulge under the cotton fabric of his black Henley.

I glance up at his face and can't believe what I'm seeing. It's the delectable guy from The Cactus Club. Here. At the studio. "Um. No, I'm okay," I manage to eke out. I'm *shook* at the sight of the man I've fantasized about for the past few nights when I turn on my trusty little bullet vibrator.

"Uh. You might need to—erm—adjust your top." He flicks his eyes to my chest.

When I look down, I'm completely mortified. My girls have let me down. Both brown nipples peek out above the lace of the corset. "Oh God!" I slam my palms across my breasts and twist around to shove them down where they belong. Once they're hidden underneath the fabric, I push myself up off the ground and stand facing away from him.

"Are you okay?" The man's stern voice is in direct contrast to the gentle grip on my elbow.

I paste on a smile and turn, determined not to appear rattled. Or let him know I recognize him from the other day. "I'm fine. Just a little embarrassed. I do need to run though, now I'm late for my call time."

"I'll go with you." He regards me curiously. "To make sure."

His violet eyes sparkle, but there's an intensity in his gaze. I feel it all the way through my body. "No, really. I promise I'm good. Only cast and crew are allowed on set."

"Ah." He doesn't break eye contact. Just peruses me, like he's cataloging every inch of my body. Unabashedly.

It's all I can do not to shudder. This man is sex personified.

Gah! I manage to break eye contact and press the button for the elevator. While I wait for it to arrive, I stare at the doors, unsure of what to say. This guy has me tongue-tied and I don't even know him.

Thankfully, he's quiet too.

When the door opens, he follows me in and stands close, but not close enough to make me uncomfortable. "I recognize you."

Surprised, I look over and up. He's easily a foot taller. My assessment of him the other day holds true. He's not old, just older than me. His hair is spectacular. I notice the stubble on his face is dusted with a few silver hairs as well.

Sexy. Sexy. *Sexy*.

He still doesn't smile but wears a somewhat pleasant expression. A *knowing* expression.

He's seen your tits, Clover.

Oh, right. He's an ordinary dude. It's no wonder he got back on the elevator with me. "Oh?"

"The Cactus Club. That was you, wasn't it?" he challenges.

Crap.

I could deny it, but why? "Uh, *yeah*. I thought I recognized you."

"Why did you run out that day?" He squints. Lifts a finger to smooth an errant hair on my forehead. His touch is like wildfire, burning a path down the side of my neck to my core.

I step back like I've been singed. "Um... I had to be somewhere." My voice comes out high and breathy.

He leans back against the rail as the elevator doors close and we begin our descent. "You said you're due on set. Are you an actress?"

"I am." The words feel strange, considering this is my first job in over a decade.

He nods. Clasps his hands. Doesn't break eye contact. Waits.

I don't elaborate because in my experience, guys either think what I do is frivolous and want to be my savior—like Harrison—or that I'm easy lay—like everyone else I've ever dated. I don't want to know which side of the fence this guy falls on. "You?"

"I built this place." He nods to the tool caddy on the floor next to him. I've been so lost in his magnetic eyes, I didn't even notice.

But...this is good. "Oh, so you work here?"

"You could say that." He doesn't smile. He *smolders*. Still eye-fucking me like he can't help himself.

Which, I understand, because I'm eye-fucking him too.

I can't help *myself.* This man is delicious.

We reach the bottom floor and the doors open. Somehow I manage to tear myself away from the grip of his stare. I rush out without saying a word, wincing at my lack of manners. The man has me all bewildered. He makes me want to flee.

I don't have time to ponder it further though because I'm already late as it is.

I push through the doors into the bustling studio. Ronni and her producing partner, Kris, are huddled together with the camera operators, so thankfully they're not quite ready. Pax isn't on set, unfortunately. He's going to lose his mind when I tell him what happened.

As I take in this afternoon's scene, which is set in a restaurant, I spy the actor who's playing my date, Miles, pacing back and forth by the table where we'll be sitting. He's mouthing his lines. Priding myself on professionalism, I know I owe him an apology.

"Hey, I'm Clover, sorry I was running a few minutes behind. I had a slight wardrobe malfunction." I hold out my hand to the red-haired actor who wears thick glasses, a bow tie and a suit that is slightly too tight. All by design, of course. Underneath it all he's very handsome.

His eyes nearly pop out of his head when he sees me—and my tits. "Eddie Bannon." He grips my hand a little too tightly, eyes fixated on my cleavage.

"Should we run our lines until they're ready?" I wince and pull my fingers from his, gesturing to the table. "I thought the dialogue was hilarious."

"Okay." He sits without pulling my chair out for me first.

God, no manners. Just like real life.

We go through the scene where the know-it-all nerd tries to school my character about fine dining. I'm pleasantly surprised. What Eddie Bannon lacks in manners he makes up for in acting skills. By the time we run through it once, Ronni is ready to film. We nail the dialogue during the first take.

Except for the last two lines.

Which I flub completely when I notice the carpenter all the way in the back. Standing there. Violet eyes boring a hole into me. I try to regain my composure. "I'm sorry, should we start from the top?" I direct my question to Ronni.

"No, I'm good with this take. Just go back to where Jenna says, 'Oh, please.'" Ronni gestures to the two of us.

I suck in a breath, keep my eyes focused on Eddie. I will not let the gorgeous carpenter affect my work. Not when I've been handed an opportunity of a lifetime. I center myself and pop immediately back into character.

Jenna: "Oh, *please*. I can appreciate good food without being a pretentious snob about it, Miles."

Miles: "I wouldn't call it being a snob, I'd call it having a refined palate."

Jenna (speaking to the camera): "I'd call it 'operation order a pizza and watch cat videos on YouTube.' Anything would be better than spending another minute with this guy."

"That's a wrap." Ronni claps her hands. "Well done both of you. Clover, head back to wardrobe. Let's burn through a few of the confessional clips tonight, if you're up for it."

I glance back to where the carpenter guy was standing. He's gone. A wave of disappointment washes over me. "Of course, sounds good."

On my way back to my dressing room I look around for him, half-expecting that he'll be waiting for me.

No such luck.

I guess it's for the best.

Something tells me he's way too much for my fragile heart.

Chapter Six

Early Evening, The Same Day

I've been rock hard most of the afternoon picturing Clover Callahan's tight, puckered nipples poking out of her sexy pink lingerie top.

I'd preplanned running into her earlier today, but I did not anticipate knocking her down like a brute.

Although, I can't say I'm sad about it. The nip-slip was the best thing that's happened to me in…years?

Not going to unpack that shit right now.

While our encounter was short, I learned three things in such close proximity. First, I didn't imagine it—she's wildly attracted to me. Second, she's terrified of that fact, as evidenced by how fast she ran out of the elevator just like she did at the restaurant. Third, the delicious combination of her desire and fear makes me want to fuck her into oblivion.

Even more than I did before.

The overwhelming attraction I felt at the restaurant was *definitely* not a fluke.

She's a force of nature. Few people I've come into contact with possess the "it" factor Clover exudes from every pore of her body. It's the type of allure that causes men to lose every ounce of their willpower.

To give up power and concede control.

To sign over millions of dollars of their assets.

She's met her match in me though. I *am* impenetrable. Careful. Diligent.

I won't succumb to her charms.

Not a fucking chance.

I loathe women like her. Users. Climbing up the ladder on the backs of others.

For the past couple of weeks, I've known exactly where to find her and where she'll be at any point during the day. An updated copy of her call sheet is emailed to me every morning. When she's not at work, Zed keeps me up to date on her whereabouts.

It's been surprisingly easy to keep track of Ms. Callahan. She rarely leaves the hotel. Aside from the day at

The Cactus Club, she doesn't hang out at bars or venture more than a block or two from her hotel. Doesn't seem to interact much socially with the cast and crew, though she's kind and thoughtful on set.

I chalk it up to her trying to keep a low profile. Probably for good reason, if my suspicions prove to be correct. Her ex-husband's misdeeds are, after all, all over the trades. She obviously doesn't want to call attention to the fact she was once married to the bastard.

Anyway, I couldn't resist ducking in to watch her scene earlier today. Admittedly, the woman has talent. She's friendly. Engaging. Flirty, even. A good actress, obviously.

I didn't stay long, though. The last thing I want is to be conspicuous. Raise the little bunny's hackles. As far as she knows, I'm some rando she saw at a restaurant who happens to work here.

Which is precisely how I want it.

What I do is none of her goddamn business.

Until I get the money back, whatever she does is *mine*.

But, given *very* recent events—as in the past twenty-four hours—I certainly don't need to micromanage the situation. I have people to handle shit like this when

I have better things to do. Like negotiating a lucrative, billion-dollar media acquisition that fell into my lap.

An opportunity which has changed my priorities. Tomorrow, I'll be in Singapore to close the transaction, which speeds up my timeline here in Vancouver BC considerably.

So...tonight's the night.

Clover is currently in her dressing room two floors below my office. The entire facility is deserted except for the two of us. Ronni Miller left ten minutes ago. The crew shortly thereafter. I've choreographed this perfectly. One more "chance" encounter and I should be set up perfectly to get some information from her.

I'm ready to put this Eminence Partners mess behind me and move the fuck on to bigger and better things.

My phone lights up with a text from Zed: *She's on the move.*

I text back: *Cool, I've got this from here. You can go.*

With that part done, I grab my tool bag and step outside the office. Zed parked the elevator on my floor to ensure I can ride with Clover alone. I get in and press "G." The way I figure it, if I can talk Clover into having dinner with me, I'll turn on the charm and see what she'll spill.

I'm still here for one more night, after all. Even though my plans have changed, it's certainly worth a try.

If not, so be it. I'll be on my merry way first thing tomorrow morning. Once I leave, Seth will take over as he probably should have in the first place. I'm still kicking myself for allowing myself to get too personally invested in this matter.

Uncharacteristically, I might add.

The elevator door opens to the floor where the dressing rooms are located. Clover teeters into the cab wearing those ridiculously high pink pumps, looking utterly exhausted. For fuck's sake, she wears essentially the same outfit she had on earlier today, with a pink jacket thrown over the flimsy pink bra top. "Oh, it's you. Elevator guy." Her eyes widen when she recognizes me.

"I could have sworn I was The Cactus Club guy." I shrug as the doors close behind her. "You going out?"

Clover nods. "Yeah...um, no. I planned on meeting my friend Pax for a drink, but now it's a bunch of the crew. I'm peopled out so I just texted him to cancel."

"Peopled out?" I've never heard of such a thing.

She closes her jacket in front of her cleavage. "Yeah, I know it might seem weird. I've been on set with everyone all day and I've had to be 'on.' Hanging out with Pax is easy, but I'm not up for a big group. Looks like it's sweats, room service and a good book for me tonight."

"What a shame. You're all dressed up with nowhere to go." I turn toward her. It's the perfect opportunity to convince her to grab dinner in a nice quiet restaurant. Who knows, maybe I'll get another nip-slip if I'm lucky.

Her eyes meet mine.

Zing.

God, we have *chemistry.*

She licks her lips, staring at me like I'm filet mignon. "*Ha ha.* It's been a long day. My scenes were a little emotionally taxing so..."

"I'm JJ." I hold out my hand, not sure why I dropped my foster care nickname instead of "Joar."

She places her hand in mine with no hesitation. "Clover."

"I won't make a loser joke about it being my lucky day." I wink.

She cocks her head sassily. "Good, then I won't have to roll my eyes all the way back into my head."

Well, well...she's a little firecracker.

"Oh-kay...point taken. How about I make up for my cheesy one-liner by taking you to dinner?" I fix my gaze on her. Nod my head slightly in the universal "I want to fuck you now" sort of way.

Her entire face pinkens. Like I've surprised her. She looks around and word vomits, "Oh...um...oh, uh...gosh. Um. That's so nice. Um. I don't really know you..."

Suddenly, the elevator comes to a jolting stop. The lights flicker but stay on. Clover shrieks, clearly panicked. I realize we're still having a friendly handshake when she crushes my fingers like a vise.

It takes me a second to process what just happened. Are we stuck here? Is the elevator broken? How will we be rescued?

Shit.

Now I have to totally switch gears. This stupid incident throws a huge wrench in my strategy, but I'll adapt. I always do.

Protector. That's my play.

"Hey." I gently loosen the grip of her soft, supple fingers from mine. "It's going to be fine. I'm here with you."

Clover wrings her hand free. Wraps her arms around herself. "It's not *fine*. I'm claustrophobic. The idea of being stuck in this tiny space with a stranger is my worst nightmare."

I clasp her shoulder. Stare into her frightened aqua eyes. "Clover, you *are* fine. I'll buzz for help, don't worry. Let me help you sit down so you can take some deep breaths. I promise I'm not a serial killer."

She shivers but allows me to guide her to a seated position. When I get her situated in the corner of the elevator cab, I turn to examine the panel. Find the intercom button and press. It buzzes but no one answers. I try three more times to no avail.

"Omigod. We're going to die in here," Clover cries softly. She's balled up in the corner, arms wrapped around her knees.

I crouch beside her. "We're not going to die. It's all fine. I'll call for help."

Except, when I reach into my back pocket for my phone, it's not there. Standing rapidly, I slap my front pockets, back pockets, and then dig through the tool caddy. Nothing. *Godddammit.* I know exactly where it is.

On my desk upstairs.

Fuck.

She watches me through watery eyes. Whimpers when she realizes that I don't have my phone.

"Clover, listen to me." I kneel, point at her tote. "Do you have your mobile with you?"

After a beat what I'm asking sinks in. She nods. Tilts the bag. Rustles through and pulls out her phone, which is encased in a pink, glittery cover that you'd expect a twelve-year-old girl to have. She clicks the side button to turn it on, then her face crumples. Her clicking grows frantic until she throws it down on the ground. "It's dead. It's fucking dead. We *are* going to die here."

Ignoring her panic for a moment, I grab the phone and press the button. Try a hard reset. Nothing.

Fuck.

I flop down to sit beside her. "Well, unless one of has a smart watch, it looks like we might be stuck here for a while. I stand by my promise we won't die, though."

She holds up her bare wrist wistfully. My own watch—a Cartier—is in the hotel safe. Not that it would have helped in this situation. "Ah, well." I lean back against the wall. "Try not to worry, we're okay. Someone will find us."

"When?" She buries her face in her hands, then peeks up at me.

I'm a tactical guy, so I consider the reality of our situation. The buzzer doesn't work. We don't have a way to call someone. Security won't need the elevator unless they catch something on their cameras, so it's unlikely they'll find us tonight. "Let's not worry about it. How about we pretend we're at The Cactus Club having dinner and chat for a while?"

Despite the circumstances, I can't look a gift horse in the mouth. I couldn't have planned this better—Clover Callahan is my captive audience for eight to ten hours, give or take. No need to *actually* spend my money to wine and dine this beautiful thief. In her emotionally vulnerable state, she'll be an open book to whatever I ask.

"It's going to be okay." I take her hand and clasp it between mine to reassure her. "Tell me something about yourself."

She's still trembling, her voice comes out wobbly. "What do you want to know?"

"Well." I fix my eyes on hers. "Did you always want to be an actress?"

Clover keeps eye contact with me. "I've never told anyone this before, but no. It was my mom's idea. She's the one who wanted me to be on television."

Huh. Interesting. Not what I expected.

"Why?" I lean into her, just a slight touch.

"I don't know." She puffs out a breath of air. "It's all I remember. Throughout my childhood, she took me to auditions. Commercials. Music Videos. Movies. You name it."

"How unconventional. It sounds kind of cool," I encourage, hoping to elicit some insight into her motivation to marry Harrison.

She shakes her head. "Mostly not. I didn't like acting at first. I wanted a more traditional childhood. It didn't happen, though. When I was thirteen, I landed a huge part and ended up moving on my own to Hawaii." She sees me tilt my head quizzically and almost telepathically answers my unspoken question. "The show was *Hawaiian High*. That's where I met Ronni Miller."

"I remember that show." I know a lot about her back history, including this, though my team did not uncover the she'd been shipped off on her own at such a young age. With Kircher, no less. I resist a shudder. "I was a little older than the demographic for that show, so I can't say I watched it."

Clover shifts away to face me. "How old are you?"

"Forty-seven," I say without hesitation.

"Ah. That makes sense." She bites her lip. "I'm thirty-two."

"Just a baby," I tease, unable to stop myself from tucking her black hair behind her ear.

Again.

Her face tilts up to mine. "You're distracting me, aren't you?"

"Whatever do you mean?" I smile down at her like she's the sweetest dessert I've ever seen.

She is.

"Getting me to talk about myself keeps me from freaking the fuck out." Her plump, pink lips press together.

As I look back at her, all of the energy from our earlier elevator experience zings and zaps between us. I forget, for a moment, that she's my nemesis. "Is it working?" I say quietly, never taking my eyes from hers.

"Yes."

Chapter Seven

Seconds Later

I stare at this man, JJ, who seems to be utterly perfect. We're sitting so close together, I can't help but admire his sculpted physique. Bulging biceps. Golden-brown arms with a smattering of dark hair. His square jaw, cleft chin. One small dimple.

He smells like heaven. Like the forest. Leather. A knight in shining armor, maybe.

And those eyes. So expressive. Soulful. I've never seen a violet color so vivid. Against his sooty, dark eyelashes, it almost looks like he rims them with eyeliner. His eyebrows are neat and sculpted, but not groomed.

And that hair.

Good God. My heart is pounding. I'm scared as hell, yes. Confined space and all, but...

There's something about JJ that draws me in. Makes me feel safe.

I haven't reacted this way to someone...hmmm. Ever?

And it's not just because he's so devastatingly handsome. It's something bigger. I haven't been with many men, but I have an idea what this is. Maybe, just maybe, I felt it back at the restaurant when I first saw him. The second our eyes met it was like an invisible strand connected me to him in some intrinsic way.

I'm beginning to think he feels it too, although it's hard to know for sure.

Is this what it's like when you meet your person?

No. Wait. How crazy do I sound?

Do I seriously think some carpenter from Canada who, by the way, I flashed this morning is my soulmate?

I'm clearly delusional. Probably from filming too many scenes about this particular subject today.

He just wants to see my tits again.

Yeah.

That's totally what it is.

"Clover?" JJ waves his hand in front of my face.

I shake my head vigorously. "Sorry. I spaced out for a second."

"Stay with me." He cups my cheek. "I'm not a big fan of enclosed spaces either."

Unwittingly, I lean into his palm. "I'll try."

We sit in silence for a few moments staring at each other. His hand remains against my face until he lowers it and rests it on his jean-clad thigh. His gaze drifts to the doors of the elevator like he's thinking hard about something then returns his attention back to me. "You're nothing like I thought you'd be."

"What?" I'm surprised. Also a bit confused. Did he know who I was? How? I've been away from the public spotlight for years.

"That came out wrong." He leans back and extends his legs in front of him. Crosses his arms over his chest. "You're obviously beautiful. It's no secret I'm attracted to you. It's just...when I realized you were an actress this morning. Well, I guess I had a preconceived notion..."

I roll my eyes, though inwardly I'm squeeing because he just admitted he digs me. "Oh, I've heard it all. Trust me."

"No. Not like that. I didn't think you'd give a guy like me a second look." He reaches over and encircles my wrist lightly. Squeezes. "*That's* what I meant."

As flattering as that is, I consider what to say. There's a fine line between flirting and honesty. Although, being stuck in an elevator catapults us up a few levels, so I go for truth. "I don't date much. I got divorced last year. Let's just say all wasn't what I thought it was in my marriage. I was blindsided by—so much. I've become a little protective of my heart."

"Oh?" I could swear his face lights up.

I'm over Harrison, but I'm still reeling from the betrayal in our marriage. His business. Everything. I hate that I've become so skeptical. Closed off. I'm working through it in therapy, but it's hard. I'd love to be carefree and open again.

Maybe I'll give it a test drive tonight.

"When Ronni offered me this role, it couldn't have come at a better time. I hadn't acted in over a decade. I was ready to make a comeback. It was time to take my life back after...everything." I finish my thought out loud.

He nudges me with his shoulder. "Ronni Miller, huh? So, she's cool."

Aaaaand...test drive over.

"Very." I narrow my eyes. Look away. Move my arm to release the grip he has on my wrist.

"Hey. Hey...I didn't mean anything, Clover. I don't give a shit about celebrity stuff. But, you'd have to live under a rock not to know her." He cocks his head. Seems sincere. From the tone of his voice at least.

It's true. Ronni Miller is and always will be America's sweetheart. I may be skittish, but he's got a point. I decide to take his word for it, though I keep my gaze pointed at the elevator doors. "Fair enough. She's definitely cool. One of the fiercest women I know. She's also smart, talented, and I'm lucky she gave me this job. I don't know where I'd be without her."

He doesn't respond. We sit in silence for a bit, giving me time to think.

Lord. Overreaction much? My freak-out certainly killed the mood. Any chance I had with this guy is dunzo. Probably for the best. One second I have myself convinced we're soul mates, the next I'm sure he's got ulterior motives. Time to slow my roll. I might be catching feelings, but I'm not about to make another stupid mistake.

"I hope I didn't fuck things up." JJ's words shock me. It's like he read my thoughts and he was having the same worries.

I roll my head toward him to find he's watching me. "Well, we don't know each other. There's not much to fuck up, is there?"

He dips his chin. Shakes his head. "I disagree. We're *getting* to know each other. Tell me what happened with your husband."

"Well..." I think of how to say what I want to say. Inadvertently, I scrunch my nose. Decide to just tell it like it is. "I found a video of him screwing my best friend. Divorced him. Learned a lot more about shady things he was involved in. Ran like hell. End of story."

"Huh. That sucks." JJ purses his lips and stares straight ahead. Like he's thinking hard about something.

A few minutes pass. Finally, I nudge him with my shoulder. "What?"

"You're not over him." He raises an eyebrow in question. "Did I nail it?"

I narrow my eyes in frustration. "*No*! You're not even close. He's an asshole on so many levels. I didn't realize how much I *wouldn't* miss him until all of this happened. My ex-BFF on the other hand? That was a bitter pill. You expect bad behavior from powerful men like Harrison. I did *not* expect it from a girlfriend. Did I mention that she was the one who texted me the video?"

"God. I'm sorry." He reaches over and takes my hand in his. Looks at our clasped hands and up at me. "This okay?"

"How long have you been a carpenter?" I answer his question with a question but make no move to pull away. His soft, warm grip feels too good. No one's touched me this way in...forever.

"Huh?" He looks puzzled, then looks over at his tool caddy. "Oh... No. You got the wrong idea. I own this studio. That's what I meant earlier when I said I built it."

I'm shocked and my mouth falls open to prove it. "What?"

He shrugs. "Assumptions."

Point taken.

At the very least, his comment gives me perspective. I can't expect from him what I don't give back. I relax a bit more and allow myself to take comfort in our newfound connection.

"You're not married, are you?" Feeling a bit naughty, I reach over and grab his other hand to check for a ring. What I don't anticipate is this position has me leaning over him in my corset top. I'm inches away from a full-blown motorboat. Talk about giving mixed signals. Apparently, I'm the queen.

He tries desperately not to look down my top. Instead he wiggles the fingers of his left hand. "Never married. No kids. No time. Workaholic."

The energy between us buzzes.

He bores a hole into my soul with those hypnotic eyes.

"Clover," he practically growls.

"JJ," I whisper.

"What are we doing?" He reaches for my waist. Tugs me closer.

I tilt my head up. He leans down to meet me, slanting to press his lips against mine. Soft. Pliable. Velvety.

A feeling of rightness consumes me.

My mouth opens and I let him in. He sucks on my tongue to lure it into a dance with his. We tango. Rhumba. Waltz. At some point, I climb aboard and straddle him to get closer. I chalk it up to the fact I've never kissed anyone with such intensity. Expertise.

It's an all-encompassing devouring, which feels like possession.

We continue this way for a while until my lungs are on fire and I must come up for air.

Or, get my bearings.

Either way.

"That was..." He cups my ass. Squeezes.

"Intense," I whisper. "Best. Kiss. Ever."

There's something about him that is so magnetic. It's more than chemistry. It has to be.

He raises his knees and scoots me back a bit so I'm leaning against them. Using his thumb, he swipes my lip gently. Studies me. Smiles. "Best. Kiss. Ever."

"You don't have to say that, JJ." I feel shy. Exposed.

His hands grip my waist. Work their way down to my hips. I sigh happily.

"There's nowhere I'd rather be." He sits up. Presses his forehead to mine. "I never say anything I don't mean. Trust me on that."

It's all I can do not to nuzzle him. "This is getting a little..."

"Heated." He latches his lips on to a sensitive spot behind my ear. Licks. Nips.

Each swipe of his tongue feels like a liquid inferno. My pussy aches with need. I know in this moment I'm going to live my life to the fullest and fuck this guy. Right here in the elevator. Cameras and all.

And I don't care.

Chapter Eight

Same Time, Different Perspective

I'm out of control with desire.

Clover tastes like sunshine and peaches. One kiss wasn't enough. I find myself exploring every inch of her mouth. Lost in a frenzy of discovery. When I cup her face and move her where I want her, she whimpers and presses against me. My cock is weeping, straining against my jeans. It wants her as much as I do.

I've got to end this madness. I'm letting it go too far.

"Intense." Her voice is faint but definitive. Her eyelids, which are half-mast, blink dreamily. "Best. Kiss. Ever."

Whoa.

I did not expect that.

She's *sincere.*

In this instant, I realize I've gone about this all wrong.

Maybe you've got her all wrong.

Although I didn't go through with the carpenter ruse, Clover still thinks I'm someone else. A person who is me, yet a mere fraction of who I am. Or what I'm capable of.

Yeah, I've got to stop this. Immediately.

I may be ruthless, but I'm not a liar.

Jury's still out on whether she deliberately took Eminence Partners' client money, but my gut tells me I've misread the situation. She's not trying to hide anything. She hasn't lured me in like some poisonous black widow spider. Her confession about being left on her own in Hawaii as a teenager is heartbreaking.

Ditto about her cheating asshole of a husband. *And* best friend.

This woman is sweet. Vulnerable. Despite the fact people who were supposed to be the closest to her let her down repeatedly, there doesn't seem to be a nefarious bone in her body.

Or are you telling yourself that?

My desire for this woman is something I've never felt before. Something dormant inside is now awake. Alive. Which is terrifying and also useless. By this time tomorrow, I'll be on a plane to Singapore.

Still, I might as well admit it. There's no chance we're getting off this elevator without fucking. None.

Before I go there with her, I can't be a hypocrite. I've got to be honest.

Don't I?

Creating a bridge with my knees, I grip her waist and shift her back against them to move her ass away from my dick. God, she's fucking beautiful. Her lips are puffy. Her eyes are half-mast, as if she's drunk from our kisses. Good thing I repositioned her, I didn't think it was possible to get harder than I already am. I was wrong. My cock is attempting to drill a hole through these fucking jeans.

I touch my thumb to the skin above her lip, which is a bit red from my stubble. Tell her the truth. "Best. Kiss. Ever."

"You don't have to say that, JJ." Clover blushes all over, even her chest.

I want to pull her top down to savor her milk-chocolate nipples. Instead I slide my palms to her hips. I sit up and press my forehead to hers. "There's nowhere I'd rather be." Her face squinches a bit, as if she can't believe what I said. "I never say anything I don't mean. Trust me on that."

This seems to placate her. "This is getting a little…"

"Heated?" I ask as I bury my face in her neck. Kiss up to her ear. Suck. Nuzzle. Bite her earlobe. Lick her until she squirms in my lap.

Her legs wrap around my waist. She squeezes her thighs against my hips. Winds her arms behind my neck and threads both hands through my hair. I continue my sensual assault on her neck and guide her hips as she writhes and grinds against me.

"God, keep doing that," Clover keens.

"Clover," I pant, kissing my way back to her lips. "Should we slow this down? I think we both know where this is going, but I don't want you to regret it."

Her fingers are already unbuckling my belt, though. "For once in my life, I want to live a little. So what if we don't know each other. Maybe that's okay. Maybe we were meant to be here in this moment. Just this once. Let's not overthink what's happening here."

"Okay. As long as you're fine with what *this* is. It's important I'm honest with you if we're going to have sex. I'm leaving town tomorrow." I grip each of her wrists to stop her from touching my dick. I make deliberate eye contact because I don't want her to catch feelings.

I'm fully taken aback when she slams her lips against mine, seeking and finding my tongue. I release her wrists and she instantly gets to work on the button and zipper of my jeans. "I live in Los Angeles, JJ. Let's be real about what this could ever be. I'm okay with one memorable night in an elevator with a sexy stranger."

"Well...I'm definitely in. It looks like I'm going to eat *you* for dinner." I kiss her nose. Nudge my cock against the heat of her core. "I can smell your sweet pussy and I'm starving."

Her eyes squeeze shut with pleasure. "Omigod," she moans. "Do you really talk dirty like that?"

"Oh, Clover, you have no idea." I tip her chin so she's looking at me without distraction. "Are we doing this? I need to hear you say yes."

She nods. "Yes. I have a feeling you're going to be an amazing lover. I want *everything*."

With her consent and preordained praise, I can resist no longer. In a flash, I yank her top down.

Holy fucking Jesus. I take in the most luscious, creamy breasts I've ever set eyes on. The quick glimpse this morning didn't do these beauties justice. I cup them with my palms. Thumb the puckered, brown nipples. Squeeze. Press her breasts together and swipe my tongue over the tips one after the other. Nip them lightly. Blow. As I worship her tits, Clover's fingers are once again buried in my hair. She scratches my scalp and arches against me.

"Let's try and make this more comfortable." Reluctantly, I pull away and move her out of my lap. Take off my shirt and lay it on the floor. Shimmy my jeans off.

"Here." Clover hands me her jacket and pants. I toss them down on our makeshift bed with the rest of our clothes.

I stand, peel down my final item of clothing, black boxer briefs. Throw them in the corner. My cock proudly rests against my stomach as I turn to take her in.

Her arms are crossed to cover her bare breasts. Her sexy top is around her waist. Panties—if you could call them that—are a wisp of a black lace thong hugging her voluptuous hips. As she stands before me, Clover bites the tip of her index finger, staring at my dick with trepidation.

"You're going to take every inch of this long, fat cock in your tight little cunt, aren't you sweetness?" I pump myself, rubbing pre-cum all over the tip.

Her eyes widen with shock. "Uh...I'm not sure it will fit."

"Oh, I'll fit." I stand before her. "I'll get you ready. Lie down."

Clover gulps but doesn't move. She watches me stroke up and down my length. Squeezes her thighs together. Her nipples are like bullets.

Holy hell, this is going to be the best fuck of my life. I know it in every cell of my body.

"I *said*, lie down. Don't make me ask you again." My voice is firm, not loud, as I gesture to the floor.

She kneels, her face level with where I'm fisting myself. The crown of my cock is millimeters from her lips. She looks at me, questioning. "You'll taste me later. It's your turn now." I gesture for her to lie back on our clothes.

"Okay, this is all new to me. I haven't been with anyone since..." She sits back on her heels.

I press my finger against her lips. "I don't want anyone else in here when you and I are fucking, Clover. If you're unsure about this, we can stop. But, know this, I draw a hard line at you talking about another man when my tongue, cock, and fingers are going to make you come so often you'll never be the same."

"*Oh*..." Clover squeezes her eyes shut. Her entire body shudders. She leans back and slumps over. Shoves her fingers down the front of her thong. Presses her thighs together and whimpers.

I'm astounded. Did she just…"Clover? Are you okay?" I kneel beside her, placing my hand on her hip.

"Uh-huh." She nods. Bites her lip.

I lean onto my hip, pressing my cock against her thigh. Hook the side of her thong with my index finger. Pull it down her legs. Holy God, she's bare. Her finger, tipped in pink, circles her clit. Mine joins hers. Together we massage her little nub. "Tell me the truth. Did you just come?"

"I…uh." Her face reddens with embarrassment. She still hasn't opened her eyes.

"Look at me." I push on her soft belly so she's lying on her back. She watches when I rip her thong in two and throw it on top of my briefs. "That was the hottest thing I've *ever* seen."

She shakes her head and looks away. "It's mortifying."

I lie down next to her. Flick my finger back and forth on her clit, which pokes out between her pussy lips. "No, it's sexy. Let me get you there again. Open your legs."

My cock digs into her thigh when I scoot closer. I cradle her head with my free hand so she's resting in the crook of my neck. "Relax, baby. I've got you." I kiss the side of her head. Lick and lave the spot that drove her mad earlier.

She melts into me. I dip my finger into her drenched channel and spread her juices everywhere. Lubricate her little nub. Circle. Circle faster. I can tell she's on the brink again. Clover's hips undulate. Buck. "Oh... Oh... Ohhhhh..." She seizes. Her stomach muscles tense. Her face is in rapture. "Omigod. Omigod. *Omigod*," she chants.

"Fuck me. I've got to taste you." I trail my tongue down her neck. Pay her phenomenal tits a bit of attention, then her belly. I can wait no longer though. I shift so I'm kneeling between her legs. Spread them apart with my palms. Bury my face in her heaven.

One taste and I'm addicted.

Every single plan I've made over the past few weeks is forgotten.

Clover Callahan has *literally* brought me to my knees and I haven't even fucked her yet.

Before this night is over, I'll have signed over my entire empire.

And I won't regret a thing.

Chapter Nine

Seconds Later

I'm having an out-of-body experience.

I've been transported to another dimension where I, Clover Callahan, am brazen, sexual, and multi-orgasmic.

I never want to leave.

Whether it's JJ's age and experience or just the chemistry between us, my body responds to this man. I'm leaning up on my elbows, watching his talented tongue and lips lick and explore every single inch of my pussy. A pussy which, until this night, has sadly never been worshipped so thoroughly. He seems to intrinsically know exactly what pressure to apply. When to lick. Suck. Swirl. Nibble.

Ohmyjesus.

I shudder when he inserts one, then two long fingers inside me. Rubs high against my inner walls in time to the suction of his lips. Just when I thought I couldn't get any wetter, he hits a spot that makes me clench so hard I explode with another orgasm.

This is the *third*.

How is this possible?

He grins up at me, his entire face drenched in my essence. "You are delicious. I think you're more than wet enough and ready for my cock."

I can't say anything, I'm a satiated noodle. Who wants more of whatever this man can give me. Including his play-by-play dirty talk.

In contrast to earlier when I was freaking out about getting stuck in this elevator, now I never want to leave.

"Condom?" I manage to eke out.

He pats the floor where his jeans are. Takes out his wallet—at least now I know what was digging into my butt cheek—opens it and holds up three connected foil packets. "We're covered."

"Let me." I push myself to a seated position. I'm still not convinced he'll fit, but I want to ride the most magnificent dick I've ever seen in real life like nothing I've ever wanted before.

Laughing, he leans back against the wall of the elevator. Reaches up to hold on to the handrail. His cock rests against his eight-pack, thick and long. The tip hits just past his belly button. He's well groomed, nearly hairless. "I'm all yours."

"Holy moly, JJ." I kneel between his knees, admiring his physique. I run my fingers along the indents of his abs. The man is a wall of muscle. He could be a sculpture in Italy, with a much bigger dick. I want to lick him like an ice-cream cone. "Are you sure you don't want a blowjob first?"

His eyebrows raise in surprise. "Oh, I do. Later. For now, I want you to impale your sweet cunt on my cock. When you adjust to my size, you're going to ride me hard and fast. I want to see your gorgeous tits bounce while I fuck you like an animal. How does that sound?"

Uh...may-zing.

Ohmyfuckinggod. Who is this guy?

"Climb on, sweetness." He holds my waist to help me straddle him.

JJ watches as I rip open the packet. I'm so nervous, I fumble and nearly drop it, but manage to recover and take it out of the foil. I hold the tip, squeeze, and roll it over his length.

That's when shit gets real.

"Let's start like this." He grips his sheathed cock and drags it along my seam. Back and forth, hitting my over-sensitive clit with each pass.

I can't help myself when I reach up and pinch my nipples between my thumbs and forefingers. Each time that magnificent dick hits my sweet spot, my nipples tingle and ache. Soon, I'm bucking against him, my juices trickling all over him. "Don't tease anymore. I'm ready, JJ."

"Okay, let's go slow." He angles the tip inside me.

I'm incredibly lubricated, but I'm only able to take a couple of inches before it's too much. I reach down and fist his cock, taking over so I can control the pace. "Will you play with my nipples?" I moan out a breathy request.

"Jesus, Clover." He obliges and rolls and twists my puckered buds with his fingers. "You're fucking stunning with my cock partway inside you. Your hard little clit is quivering. Your tits are what dreams are made of."

His dirty talk and manipulation of my nipples make me gush. I'm able to take more of him, but still not every-thing. I've never been with anyone this huge before. I'm so full. It burns a little, but it also feels incredible. "I'm sorry, JJ. I need..."

"Relax, sweetness. Just breathe. Let me help you." He releases one nipple and pinches my clit. Hard. Rubs it. Flicks it until I'm screaming with the pleasure of another intense orgasm.

I bear down when it rages through my body and just like that...he's all the way in.

I gaze down at our joined bodies in wonder. He does the same thing. We both look at each other at the same time.

"You're in." I smile.

"Told you I'd fit." He lightly rests his palms on my hips, his fingers sneak around to cup my asscheeks. "You're so fucking tight. You fit me like a glove. I could live inside you, babe. How does it feel for you?"

"You're a lot," I answer honestly. I don't want to stop, but I'm stretched so wide it's slightly uncomfortable.

JJ reaches up and strokes the side of my face. Presses his thumb against my lips. My tongue darts out for a taste and he pushes it inside my mouth. "Suck," he demands. "Suck my thumb like you're going to suck my cock later."

"Ohhhhhh," I moan with an intense desire that confuses me. He's bossy. Explicit. I love it. So, I do what I'm told. I suck and lave his thumb like it's my job. There seems to be a method to his madness, soon my hips undulate of their own volition. It loosens me up and my body adjusts in no time.

He pulls his thumb from my lips. "Good girl. Sexy, sexy girl."

He thrusts up into me from below, just once. Hits a spot so deep within me I can't help but cry out. "Again. Do that again."

"Oh, Clover. To see your beautiful face right now." He drives his cock into me over and over. "I love being able to give this to you."

JJ's hands encompass my hips and ass again. Just as he promised, he sets the pace. It's fast. Frenzied. I'm just along for the ride as he bounces me on his cock. My tits jiggle. His eyes flick back and forth between where we're joined and my breasts, like he can't decide which he'd rather focus on. His handsome face is blissful.

As for me, I'm a blithering, wailing mess of ecstasy. The tip of his cock keeps rubbing against a patch above my G-spot that sends me into some sort of insane oblivion. I'm coming and gushing, dousing us with my wetness.

"Holy shit, I'm gonna come so hard, baby. I can't hold off another minute." He winces and jerks. His eyes squinch when he throws his head back against the floor and holds me still as he pumps out his release.

I flop down on top of him, breathing heavily, my ear against his heart. It's beating wildly. His palms rub up and down my back and along the backs of my thighs, which cradle his torso. His cock twitches inside me. I can't move. "I've never come so many times in such a short period of time," I mumble against his chest.

"Damn shame." He tenderly rolls us over, then sits up. Grips the top of the condom and pulls out, tying it off and tossing it on top of our underwear. Lies back down, cuddles me to him and soothingly pets my head.

I sigh heavily, wondering if I'll regret what just happened.

Right now, I don't.

"I loved when you talked dirty. It turned me on so much." I sigh against his chest.

"Past tense?" He kisses my temple.

I'm confused. "Huh?"

"We're not done, Clover. Let's rest for a bit. Next go round, I want you to lick my balls and then suck my cock all the way down your throat. When I'm so hard I can't take it anymore, you're going to hold on to that handrail while I bend you over and fuck that greedy little pussy from behind. We're going to watch all of it in the mirrors on the wall." JJ's voice is confident but quiet.

My entire core throbs in anticipation, but we lie contentedly entwined for a long while.

"You're extremely commanding." I look up at him while I trace the outline of his nipple with my nail. Owning a production studio is a cool gig and all, but he's exudes a lot more power than is necessary for this type of operation.

He watches me closely. "I like to be clear with my intentions."

"You do a good job. Now all I want to do is suck your cock." I kiss his chin playfully. Snake my hand down his stomach and grip his shaft, which is already hardening.

He growls and thrusts his hardening dick into my fist. "Good, that's all I want too."

"Impressive. Seeing how you're a few years older than me, I thought you'd need a bit more time to recover." I pump him more vigorously.

"You're a dangerous woman, Clover." He grips my face with both hands and pushes me down toward his stiffening length. "I have a feeling I'd walk around with a permanent erection around you."

I kiss each plane of his abs on my way down to the prize. Press his strong legs apart with my palms. "I have a feeling I'd like that view."

Taking as much as I can in my mouth, I savor his masculine salty-sweet taste. His eyes are heavy with desire as he watches me lave and lick his balls and then suck him to the back of my throat. Just like he said I would.

"You're unexpected, sweetness, and I don't surprise easily." He twists my hair around his wrist and forces me to look at him. "Now, keep up what you're doing, you give world-class head."

I do what I'm told.

And I *love* it.

Chapter Ten

An Hour Later

Everything I thought I knew is fucked.

We've been stuck in this elevator for easily eight hours. That puts us at four, maybe five in the morning. Crew start arriving around seven, so we should be found soon. My private jet is scheduled to depart around ten, but I have enough wiggle room to bump my schedule a few hours if need be.

Why do I wish we could stay in this elevator forever?

Why didn't I tell Clover the entire truth?

I know the reason. I'm not going to see her after we get out of here. It's a damn shame, too.

If only circumstances were different.

Ms. Callahan is currently tucked under my arm dozing. I can't blame her. I've fucked her in every position we could manage in this space. All three condoms used. We've explored every part of each other's bodies.

In between we've talked, joked, told each other funny stories about our lives.

Kissed.

I went down on her again.

She gave me another blowjob.

We fucked some more.

Essentially, we've done everything except talk about seeing each other again. She still has no idea who I am. Why I'm really here.

I hope she never finds out.

In the span of one sex-filled evening in an elevator, this gorgeous woman has won me over. From what I know now, there's no way she knew what Harrison was up to.

Clover is everything pure and good.

Well, except for sex. I believe I've met my dirty-talking match. Plus, she's insatiable. My equal in every way. I'm not the type of guy to settle down with just one woman, but if I were...

"Get some sleep, JJ." Clover wraps her arms around me. Her plump breasts press against my chest. We're still naked. At my insistence. My excuse is it's warm in these close quarters, but really I want to be able to slide inside her again whenever I want.

I'm pretty sure she feels the same way.

Because despite her request for me to sleep, we can't resist touching and exploring each other. I cup her head and pull her in for a kiss. She opens her mouth to let me in. Our tongues tangle and twine and we wind each other up again. "I want to be buried inside you again. You're like a drug."

"Didn't we run out of condoms?" She blinks up at me and then sits up. "Wait. Hand me my tote."

Lazily, I reach over and grab the pink bag. She takes it from me and begins rummaging around. "Voila!" She holds up a strip of condoms. "Gina, the prop supervisor, gave these to me the other day after we filmed a scene. We're back in business."

"They're regular size, Clover. Too small for me." I grin, messing with her a bit. I'm willing to be a little uncomfortable for another slice of her heavenly pussy.

Her face crumples. "Darn."

"Come here, baby." I pull her onto my lap. Tear off a condom, roll it on. It's snug, but workable. I swipe my finger along her slit, she's slick but not wet enough for my liking. "Spread your legs wide for me."

She obliges without question. Leans back into me like we've been lovers for years. Like she's home.

Clover stretches her arms up and loops them back loosely around my neck, causing her tits to jut out. I cup her breasts and pinch her nipples hard. Smooth them with my thumbs. She writhes against me, wedging my cock against her ass. I dip my fingers into her honey and slip them inside. Pump and spread her arousal up to her clit. Circle slowly. I already know her body so well. Soon, she's dripping down my legs.

"Turn around, baby." I help her face me. "I want to look at you while we fuck."

She shifts position and grips my face. Kisses me deeply. As we devour each other lazily, I guide myself inside her and wind my arms around her back. Our bodies are pressed together, not an inch of space between us.

I can feel our heartbeats sync, we're that close.

That's when the realization hits me. Somehow, in the space of a crazy evening being stuck in a goddamn elevator, my heart has grown full. I'm not going to make her any promises tonight, but when I'm done with my transaction in Singapore, maybe I'll come back for her. Try to make a go of it. Sweep her off her feet and make her mine.

Fuck. I cannot catch feelings for her. I *can't.*

"You're thinking awfully hard." Clover smooths the hair from my face. "Do we need to pick up the pace? I like it when you're right here with me. Telling me the things you're going to do to me. Or what you want me to do to you."

I cup her ass and thrust hard into her. "Okay, then, how about I fucking love feeling your hungry cunt swallow my cock whole."

"There he is." She giggles, her melodic laugh fills the cab which smells like sex and sunshine and leather. Our combined scent permeates the air around us. I want to bottle it up like cologne.

Wrapped in each other, our bodies move in tandem culminating in another explosive climax. We fall splayed on our backs side by side. Chests heaving.

"So, what's in Singapore, if you don't mind me asking?" Clover's hand sneaks over to touch my forearm. I like the connection. A lot.

I steel myself to answer truthfully but evasively. "It's confidential—under NDA, but its lucrative."

"Ooooh. Sounds fancy." She throws her free arm across her eyes. "Did I tell you about the rules I made for myself after the divorce?"

"Rules?"

She rolls over and boops my nose. "Well, more like guidelines for a happier life. One of them is to never date a guy in a suit."

"Well, that seems closed-minded of you." I chuckle, but her comment lands. I'm not the guy she's looking for.

She strokes my inner wrist with her finger. "It is. I've just had bad luck with powerful men. Figured I owe it to myself to date men who are the opposite of the type I'm usually attracted to. So I can find someone to make me happy."

"Clover, are you trying to ask me something?" I roll toward her. Splay my hand on her waist.

She scoots closer so we're chest to chest again. Nestles against my neck. "No. I don't think so. I guess I'm just trying to live in this moment. Enjoy this perfect night with you. We're running out of minutes, JJ. We might not see each other again."

I tug her close. Squeeze her with my entire body. I'm about to say something when the elevator jerks and springs to life. We both stare at each other for a beat, wild-eyed and paralyzed before we spring into action.

Like teenagers caught in bed by their parents, Clover and I frantically try to get dressed. I manage to get my boxer briefs and Henley on. She, on the other hand, isn't so lucky. I manage to jump in front of her when the doors open, but the three security guards who stand there stare at us like the naughty teens we are. Clothes spilling out into the foyer.

"Give us some privacy." I point to the hallway. "Make sure no one is in the vicinity for at least fifteen minutes."

They gape at me unbelievingly.

"*Please.*" I put on my most authoritative CEO voice.

They do as I've asked. I tug on my jeans. Clover manages to pull herself mostly together, except for the pink bra. Her face is beet red. "Can you help?"

"Of course, sweetness." I kiss her shoulder and she shows me how to tighten it.

She drapes her jacket over her shoulder. "Thanks, JJ."

We stand there. Neither of us speak. Our eyes meet, then flick around the cab.

I spy the four used condoms and pick them up. "I'll get rid of these."

"Thank you." She's slipping away from me before my eyes.

I hold out my hand. "Come with me."

"No, I don't think that's best." Her shoulders slump. If she's feeling how I do, we're both flustered from our time in elevator utopia being so abruptly cut short.

I wiggle my fingers. "Just for a few minutes."

She sighs and takes my hand. Dips to pick up her tote and I lead her down the hall to the production office. No one is here. I glance at the clock, it's five in the morning. I'll still have plenty of time to catch my flight.

When the door shuts behind us, I wrap her in my arms. Lean down and kiss her. "Last night was my favorite night I've ever had. That's the truth. Thank you."

"Mine too." She smiles brightly.

"Everything that happened in that elevator was real." I grip her face in my hands. "You know that, don't you?"

She glances away.

"Clover?" I move my head around so she's forced to look at me.

Her aqua eyes blink up at me. "It feels real. Now that we're free, I also feel unbearably sad that you're leaving. How did you go from being a stranger to my lover in a matter of hours?"

"Life is funny, isn't it?" I press my lips to hers. We kiss slowly. *Finally*. "I'm going to think about this night for the rest of my life."

Clover runs her knuckles lightly along my cheek. "I will too, JJ."

We break apart. She watches me as I gather my things. "You heading to the airport?"

"I am." I close the latch on my laptop bag. "I've got to stop by the hotel first."

She tilts her head. "Hotel?"

Shit. Shit. Shit. Shit.

"Did you think I lived here?" I'm an asshole, through and through. I led her to believe I was a local. In my defense, when the night started out I was repulsed at the thought of Clover stealing Eminence Partners client money.

Now I'm halfway in love with her.

Yet, we aren't on a level playing field.

I've touched, kissed and fucked every part of her body and she doesn't even know who I am.

I'm ashamed. This is not the man I want to be.

"Of course I did." She's hurt, it's obvious. "I guess I shouldn't be surprised, though. It's not like we know each other."

"Clover..." I move toward her.

She holds up a hand then turns and moves toward the door. "It's okay, JJ. I'm a big girl. We're nothing to each other, you don't owe me anything."

"That's not true," I call after her.

She turns, her expression serene. "Last night was… I don't have words. I've never felt so sexy in my life. It was a gift. I will always remember it. And I'll always remember you. I hope your business meeting goes well."

"Clover, wait…" I reach for her. "Don't go, not yet."

"I have to get back to my hotel and shower. Take a power nap. I'm due on set at noon." She's at the door. "Goodbye, JJ."

I don't even bother to answer her.

For the first time in my life, I'm not in control.

I fucking hate it.

Chapter Eleven

Three Weeks Later

Today's my last official day on set.

I'm not even sad because we're getting another season.

I'm excited for my next phase. I've been asked to play a supporting role in an indy film. The director has a buzz, so I'd like to accept. One of my old music producers wants me to go back into the recording studio. Opportunities abound.

No thanks to my useless agent, Mazza.

Ronni advised me to wait until I get new representation and then get a career plan together. I think she gives good advice.

Meanwhile, though it's taken a couple weeks, I've come to terms with what happened on that magical night in the elevator.

No exaggeration, the experience changed my life. For one, it put a final nail in the coffin of my marriage. It also made me realize I won't ever settle for anything less than the kind of connection I had with JJ.

Even the passing thoughts I had about destiny, blah, blah blah. We were trapped. Of course I'd blow things out of proportion. So *what*. I'm truly at peace with reality. We both knew it was one night. With no strings.

That's why I was able to let my guard down.

I had nothing to lose. I let go of my inhibitions. Indulged in a real-life romantic fantasy of being stuck in an elevator with the hottest man I'd ever seen in real life. The situation was straight out of one of my beloved romance novels.

I wanted JJ to make love to me—*no*.

I wanted him to *fuck* me.

Hard. Ruthlessly.

And he did. He fucked me like he couldn't stand it when his cock wasn't buried inside me. He ate me out like he couldn't survive if he couldn't taste my pussy. He painted me with his come. He shoved his dick down my throat.

He commanded me with his filthy, sexy, talented mouth.

And, for the record, every woman should have at least one night with a man who is hell bent on making her come seven times in the span of eight hours. Or was it eight?

I'm just sayin.'

I've never experienced something so erotic.

Fucking an enigmatic, older stranger, who was more in tune with my body than my own husband ever was, is the best thing that ever happened to me.

I now know how it feels to truly feel desired.

Coveted.

Cherished.

So no. I wouldn't trade that night for anything. JJ helped me discover what my body was capable of. He gave me pleasure unlike anything I ever knew was possible.

It was a fantasy come true. A night that could never have been planned. It was fate.

And then it was over.

The second he let it slip about not living here in Vancouver, I knew I had to bolt. I didn't want the truth of our circumstance to creep in. I didn't want to feel ashamed or regretful of what happened.

It nearly didn't work.

When I left JJ that morning, I drove straight back to the hotel and crashed for nearly four hours. After a much needed shower, I got dressed in fresh clothes. then promptly freaked out so bad I nearly missed my call time.

Call it self-preservation, but I was scared to go back to the studio. Convinced everyone would be tittering and whispering about me being found naked in the elevator with the owner of the studio. I envisioned whispers from the crew about us fucking like crazed bunnies.

I mean it was true but...

Knowing the hottest night of my life would be reduced to petty comments and memes—cringeworthy. To say the least.

Except, when I went back, no one seemed to be remotely aware.

I've not heard a peep. Not then. Not now.

JJ somehow took care of things. Made it disappear. In the continuation of my fantasy, his parting gift was sparing me the embarrassment and humiliation of the gossip mill.

I'm startled from my thoughts when someone knocks on the door to my dressing room. I glance at the time. I still have an hour before I'm due on set. "Yes?" I call out.

"Clover? It's me. Can I come in?" Ronni pokes her head in.

I wave her in. "Of course. I'm just going over my lines. It's not every day you do a romantic scene with your boss's husband."

Ronni cast Connor McGloughlin, her giant Irish rockstar of a husband to play one of my love interests on the show. We've spent a few hours with the intimacy coordinator and are ready to shoot a scene that makes it look like we're kissing, but it's the magic of showbiz.

"He says he's ready." She plops down on the small sofa adjacent to my makeup station. "I think he's going to be great."

I laugh at the understatement. "Great? He's going to have a new career. That accent. Sense of humor. Good looks. He's the whole package."

"You're probably right." She chews on the end of a pen and squints at me.

"What?" I turn to the mirror and check my face. Then my teeth. "Is something wrong?"

She rests her chin on her palm. "I've been meaning to ask you. You seem lighter. Happier. Something's different about you. Are you seeing someone?"

"No!" I say too quickly and spin around to face her. I want JJ to be my perfect secret. Like Rose and Jack from *Titanic*. "I'm just being low-key. It's the first time in forever I'm doing something for myself. It makes me happy."

She cocks her head. "Try again."

"Honestly, I'm waiting for this shit with Harrison's indictment to die down before I start dating again," I lie through my teeth. "I'm sure you know he lost his entire company a couple of months ago to a media venture capital firm that seems to be scooping up a bunch of entertainment-related businesses."

"His shit is not your shit. You know that don't you?" Ronni tracks my movement around the room.

I slump in my vanity chair thinking about the one remnant of my time with my ex that's bringing me down. "I know, but I was married to him for so long. I see my name pop up in blogs. Linking me. Speculating. It pisses me off when they think I was part of it. For fuck's sake, the house we lived in was bought with the money I earned from my music."

"Women always take the brunt of it." Ronni shakes her head sadly. "Men always get off easy."

"Facts." I sigh heavily. A guilty man blaming the victim. Same story. Different day.

"But, back to you. When you're ready to date..." Her eyebrows knit. "Connor has a couple of cute brothers that are still single."

Since the sex marathon, I've thought a lot about what I want and when I want it. The first year of my marriage, I was on tour. Supporting the singles that were charting while trying to find new acting opportunities. Harrison hated it. He belittled my career. Insisted I didn't need to work. Begged me to quit and support him while he built his company, which he insisted would be more stable for the family we were going to have.

The family that never materialized.

"I was a fool to get married to a man like Harrison." I stand and grab the wardrobe bag to get dressed. "The red flags were all there, but I know better now. I'm sticking to my guns. My next relationship will be with someone who is loving. Kind. Creative. A true partner. Someone I can trust. No more emotionally stunted CEO-types. Every one of them I've met have egos so big there's no room for me."

"I wouldn't know.." Ronni laughs and takes the empty bag after I pull out my outfit. "I've only been with actors and musicians. Although, they come with their own special type of ego."

I can't help but laugh. If only the public knew that most of Ronni's public relationships were not what they seemed.

A serious but poignant thought consumes me. "God, Ronni. You know what? No matter what, I'll never give up what I love for a man. Ever again."

"Good. I always thought it was such a shame you quit acting. You're one of the most talented women I know. You have no idea how happy it made me when you agreed to do my show, Clover. It means the world." Ronni gets up and hugs me.

I hug her back tightly. "Your offer came at the perfect time. I always loved acting but hated auditioning."

"Same." Ronni looks at me knowingly. The auditions for *Hawaiian High* were traumatic. Abusive. Exploitive. It's why Kircher is in jail.

"Well, on a lighter note, I better get ready to fake-kiss your husband." I give her a goofy grin, complete with googly eyes. No need to dwell on a shitty time in both of our lives.

Ronni moves toward the door. "Have fun. Don't worry about me, I'm being serious. You guys will be great." She waves and slips away.

<hr>

Four hours later, and we're wrapped. Connor was professional and amazing. The scene went off without a hitch. Ronni seems happy.

I'm not released to leave the city just yet, but I've decided to pack up while I wait. Pax and I are having goodbye drinks tonight, so I have that to look forward to.

"Thanks for letting me borrow your man, Ronni. If you don't need me this afternoon, I'm gonna head back to the hotel." I sneak up behind her for a side hug. "Wouldn't it be great if they cast your hubby opposite my character next year?"

She bites her lip. "Oh, I'm not so sure he'd be down."

We chitchat for a bit until her business partner, Kris, interrupts and she excuses herself. Perfect timing, I cannot wait to pack. I'm ready to go home. I give the two of them a wave, spin around and make a move toward the exit.

I nearly don't recognize him because of the perfectly tailored, expensive gray suit he's wearing.

But the violet eyes are a dead giveaway.

"Clover." JJ smiles and holds his hand out to me, revealing a five-hundred-thousand-dollar Patek Philippe 5078G-010 Grand Complications watch.

A watch I'd recognize anywhere.

Because it's the gift I gave Harrison on his fortieth birthday.

Chapter Twelve

The Same Day

I didn't plan to stay away for this long.

When I left for Singapore three weeks ago, my plan was to get in and get out. Return for Clover.

Then the deal went to shit. I managed to put it to bed last night. Three weeks of eighteen-hour days, numerous threats of litigation, screaming, yelling, then finally acceptance and closure. No one loves it when my company takes over their business. Eventually, though, they always give in.

What other choice do they have?

Rather than the traditional celebratory dinner that invariably ends up with ten-thousand-dollar bottles of wine and a nighttime of debauchery, I skipped it. Hopped on my jet and headed to Vancouver, BC. Didn't bother changing. Didn't bother gathering my belongings from my presidential suite at the Marina Bay Sands. My people are taking care of that for me.

I couldn't wait another minute to see her. Time was not my friend. I didn't want to risk the show wrapping and her leaving the city before I could get back.

After much contemplation, I've realized how important it is for me to tell her everything. From the beginning. Although I never outright lied to her, she needs to know the truth. While I had my reasons for wanting to trick her, I feel sick about my deception.

A feeling that grows more and more each day.

Bottom line: Clover deserves better.

If I'm going to pursue a relationship with her—and I am—we can't have any mistrust between us.

From the shadows, I watch her film a scene with Ronni Miller's rockstar husband. It takes every ounce of willpower I have not to barge over and pull her away. Smash that asshole in the face. I fucking hate seeing her kiss another man.

Hate it.

She's mine.

Clover is so, so beautiful in a turquoise dress, which brings out her eyes. Gold bangle bracelets dangle from her graceful wrists. Her nails are painted a bright berry color. Her long, black hair is curled in soft waves and floats around her perfect, cherubic face. She wears more makeup than usual—for the camera—but she's dewy. Radiant.

Lickable.

Oh, I'm going to ravage her before this night is over. I adjust the bulge in my pants. If I'm not careful, I'll come just thinking about it.

So, I wait.

When the scene wraps, she stays behind and animatedly chats with Ronni while, unbeknownst to her, I watch. Patience is not my strong suit. Considering how many weeks I've been buried in work with only my fist to fuck at night, all I want to do is get naked with her.

Sink my cock into her hot, wet heat.

I'm giving her just a few more minutes before I drag her into our elevator and...

She's on the move. I step out from the equipment I was standing—not hiding—behind. She looks at me, confused.

"Clover." I extend my hand.

She stares at my wrist, dumbfounded.

I reach for her, but she recoils. "Where did you get that watch?"

Shit.

I forgot to take off her ex-husband's watch.

Total. Fucking. Mistake.

Or, maybe not. I'm here to give her the entire story, after all.

"I came here to see you. There are things I'd like to tell you..." I try again to reach for her.

She narrows her eyes. "Oh. My. *God.* You fucking asshole. You work with him, don't you? Are you *following* me? I know he doesn't have any access to money. Did he pay you with that watch?"

"Clover, no!" I shake my head. "It's nothing like that."

Isn't it?

"Then tell me what the *fuck* you're doing with his watch. I gave it to him as a special birthday gift," she seethes.

How the fuck was I supposed to know that? Clearly, there's sentiment attached. I decide to try a different approach. Sterner. More authoritative. She loved when I gave her orders in the elevator. "Clover. Calm down. I came back for you. We never exchanged numbers. I want to take you out so let's grab dinner and I'll tell you about the watch. And..."

Her horrified look tells me I missed the mark.

"Listen to me, JJ." She stabs her index finger at me. "Despite what happened in that elevator, get this straight. You do *not* own me. You do *not* tell me what to do. And you do *not* under any circumstances...*ever*...Tell. Me. To. Calm. *Down*."

My mouth opens to answer but she presses her palm against my lips. "Shut it. I want you to answer the question I asked you."

I nod in resignation. Looks like I'm giving her control. She removes her hand.

"Yes. He gave it to me as payment," I answer honestly. "He stole millions of dollars from his clients. I'm getting it back."

She looks at me as if I've grown two heads. "What. The. *Fuck?*"

Out of the corner of my eye I see her, too late to wave her off. Kris Blakely, Ronni's producing partner walks up beside us. "Joar! You're back. How was Singapore?"

"Joar?" Clover looks between me and Kris.

"Clover, haven't you met Joar Jacoby? He's the Founder and CEO of Jacoby International. The media conglomerate." She hugs me. "How was Singapore?"

I keep my eye on Clover when I answer. "Successful."

"He just took over Gigante, the biggest media group in the country," Kris mock whispers to Clover then turns to me. "What brings you back to your small-potato production facility?"

For fuck's sake.

Clover smiles sweetly. "So nice to meet you, *Joar*. Wish I could stay and chat, Kris, but I have somewhere to be."

"Thanks for your hard work today." Kris waves at her as she walks away.

Shit.

It's not like I can just run after her.

Can I?

"She's beautiful, isn't she?" Kris watches me watch her walk away.

My head snaps back to look at Kris. I don't owe her shit, but I'll try to be polite. "She is. Are you happy with the show?"

"Oh, mark my words, next year at this time that girl is going to be a star. Again." Kris smiles widely the lowers her voice to a stern demand. "Keep your grubby little hands off her. I know how you blow through women. She's not the one for you."

If only she knew that my grubby hands had touched every inch of her gorgeous body.

Or...maybe not.

"None of your concern." I fix her with my most intimidating look.

Kris shakes her head. "Oh, but it is. Clover has been through enough. If it weren't bad enough that her husband cheated on her, now she's facing backlash on social medial. Insinuation she's associated with all of his bad deeds. Typical. Blame the woman for the shit the man did. Gives people a reason to let him off the hook. Just look at Ronni. She's still dealing with the aftermath of Kircher."

"What do you mean by that? I'm genuinely interested." Not just because of Clover. Or Ronni. Kris is a woman I've encountered for years, and I respect her success. Her perspective.

"Joar, let me ask you something. Why were you here and why are you suddenly back?" She tilts her head, deliberately responding to my question with one of her own.

I gulp. Not quite sure how to answer. "Well..."

"Don't think just because it hasn't been publicly announced yet I don't know Jacoby International took over Eminence Partners." Kris crosses her arms. "Is Clover aware of that connection?"

I scrub my forehead with my hand. "I came back to tell her."

Understanding and slight disdain spreads across Kris's face. "And why would you feel compelled to do that?"

My stomach drops to my feet.

She knows. She fucking knows.

Then I recover. So the fuck what? Kris Blakely is not my boss. I don't need to tell her anything.

"That's none of your concern." My jaw sets. I glare at her.

"Oh, yes it is. Anything that happens on my set, on my show concerns me. So, how about I tell you, *'JJ.'*" Kris uses finger quotes when she spits out my nickname. takes a step back and assesses me. "A media mogul comes to Vancouver BC to 'check' on his little production facility. Except, the real reason he's here is to confront the wife of a man who stole millions from the company you just bought. Why? Because just like every other man, you've jumped to the conclusion that she got away with something."

I mumble, "Not exactly."

"Your face says everything, Joar. The details aren't important. The bottom line is you were in town for Clover. And your intentions were not pure." Kris stabs her finger toward me.

"Fine." I concede. "At first, I was here because I thought she took the money. I don't anymore." I toss my head smugly.

Kris bursts out laughing so hard that she clutches at a concrete post. Throws her head back and loses it again while I stand there oblivious to what is so goddamn funny.

"You seriously thought Clover Callahan would steal? From whom?" Kris wipes her eyes.

I shake my head. "You know I can't tell you that."

"It doesn't matter. So, would you like to tell me about the elevator?" Kris smirks.

The mike drops.

She wins. I'm speechless.

"Don't worry. I took care of it. Erased the footage. Paid off the security guards. Leave it to a woman to protect another woman's honor." She kisses me on the cheek and strides away before looking over her shoulder and winking. "You're a good man, Joar. Get your shit together, sell the stupid watch and stay away from Clover. Oh, and nice cock by the way."

She leaves me standing there alone with my jaw firmly implanted on the floor.

Chapter Thirteen

Half Hour Later

I t took longer than I thought.

JJ—Joar Jacoby—the man who took over Harrison's company and exposed his fraudulent ways, pounds on my dressing room door.

If I'd been smart, I would have left ten minutes ago and come back tomorrow. I'm not smart though. Or maybe I am. Ugh. I think seeing him again, just when I'd made peace with what happened that night...

I'm shook.

I'm also beyond livid. In fact, I don't think I've ever been so mad in all my life. Even after Solange and Harrison betrayed me.

This situation gives me the *icks*. Joar Jacoby deliberately used me. He knew specifically what he was doing in the elevator...he seduced me.

I feel violated. *Hurt.*

Why would he do it?

A bigger question is, once I found out, why didn't I bolt? Am I a glutton for punishment?

No, the truth is, I want him to explain. Apologize. Make sense of things. Redeem himself.

I'm so tired of this. Can I trust any man?

"Clover, let's talk." JJ—Joar—speaks calmly and authoritatively through the locked door.

Taking a few cleansing breaths, I mentally prepare to face him, then slump down into the sofa. I'm emotional. Crushed. Because I know my entire fantasy of him has blown up in my face.

He bangs on the door again. "Clover, I know you're there. I can sense you. Open up, sweetness."

That's what does it. His term of endearment from our night in the elevator sets me off.

Sets. Me. Off.

I fly across the room. Fling open the door. "What do you want, *Joar*?"

"I know you're mad..." He holds his hands up in surrender as he walks into my dressing room. A contrite look on his face.

Why do men say that? And why do they always wear that hang-dog expression when they do?

And why does he have to be so goddamn sexy? In that tailored gray suit. His hair all disheveled like he's been raking his fingers through it. Stubble for days.

That mouth. Those lips. Those *eyes*.

No!

I shake my head in disgust. Storm back to the couch. Sulk against the cushions. Pull my knees to my chest. Take a deep breath to gather my wits. "The groveling is unbecoming. Please communicate with me like a man. Not a naughty boy who got caught sneaking candy."

"Uh..." He raises his eyebrows. Looks around. "Candy?"

"Tell. Me. Why. You. Are. Here." I pound my fist in my hand with each word.

He shrugs like it's no big deal. "I came for you, Clover."

I shake my head. "Nope. Don't lie to me. Don't fucking deflect. Not today. I want to know why you were here *before*?"

"Same reason." He moves toward me and sits on the edge of the couch. The energy between us is confusing. Disturbing. Sparks fly all around. "I came for you."

His violet eyes capture mine. Plead with me.

Mine glare back at him because he's destroyed my respect and trust and yet my pussy is soaked. It disgusts me that I want him to throw me over the back of this couch and pound his thick cock into me so hard I won't be able to walk for a week.

Which makes me even madder.

I manage to keep my composure. Controlling my emotions gives me power. "So, let me get this straight. My husband owes you money. You think I have it. You befriended and fucked me under false pretenses because..."

"*Ex*," he growls.

I'm taken aback by his arrogance. "*What?*"

"He's your *ex*-husband." He leans toward me, his familiar scent of leather and pine nearly turn me into putty. "It's true. I thought you might have assets that belonged to his company. I wanted them back to pay back the clients he stole from."

The air is so charged it crackles. We stare at each other. My traitorous brain goes into overdrive. My pussy contracts, as I imagine his hands cupping my breasts. His lips laving that spot behind my ear. When my mind drifts to his magic fingers expertly circling my clit, I have to shift in my seat so I can clench my thighs together. Jesus. Do I really need to stave off the impending orgasm that's building at just the *thought* of having sex with him again?

"Clover," he whispers and moves over to me. Palms the back of my head and pulls me toward him.

I want to resist.

But, I can't.

Joar drags his nose down my cheek until our foreheads touch. He sucks on my lower lip. Kisses all around my mouth until I have no choice but to let him in. Our tongues war as we frantically shed our clothes. Within moments nearly everything is in a pile on the floor.

Except for the final barrier.

Which Joar eliminates. He peels off my panties and kisses my belly. Presses my legs apart and hooks them over his shoulders. Licks the hollows of my legs. Works his way toward my center. I claw at his head, trying to move him to where I need him, but he commands, "Place your hands above your head and grab the arm of the sofa. Do. Not. Let. Go."

I do as I'm told, much to my chagrin.

Yet, my chest heaves in anticipation. I want him more than anything I've ever wanted in my life in this moment. How can I resist?

But, how can I think this way? This man is a liar. A control freak.

He's wearing a fucking *suit*.

His mouth engulfs my pussy. He spreads my lips wide with his thumbs to hold me open, gorging on me. Licking up my juices. Fucking me with his tongue. Sucking on my clit. Nipping at it. Relentlessly, expertly going down on me like I've never experienced in my life. Except for that night...

My pussy spasms when he slides two long fingers inside me and massages my G-spot. I cry out when he flutters his tongue on my swollen nub. Holy hell, I see stars. Then the stars explode. I jackknife and buck when the orgasm hits me. I'm wild. Uninhibited.

Free.

Except, I'm *not*.

I'm still holding on to the goddamn arm of the couch. Just like he ordered.

Life is so cruel.

I can't go any further.

"JJ—Joar—get off me." I squirm out from under him. "I can't do this with you."

He kneels back, his magnificent cock juts out temptingly. Stroking it deliberately, he rubs the liquid leaking from the tip around his crown with his thumb. "What do you mean? We're *meant* to do this."

I reach for my dress on the floor and use it to cover myself. "No. *We* aren't."

"Oh..." Deflated but compliant, he leans over, snags his boxer briefs and slips them on. "I guess I read it wrong." Buries his face in his hands.

"You *lied* to me." I pull my dress over my head and pull on my panties. "I can't be intimate with someone who deliberately deceived me. Not again."

He rolls his head to look over at me. "You know me better than most people in my life. I shared things with you in the elevator that no one else knows."

"God. You would say *anything*," I scoff at his reference to whatever superficial shit we talked about that night. How can I believe any of it? "Tell me the truth. Am I that good of a lay?"

He whirls toward me. "Don't demean what happened. You know we shared something special. Something...important. You can't tell me otherwise."

"Oh. Poor *Joar.* Did you catch feelings for me?" I taunt. I'm being an asshole. A hurt asshole.

He winces. "Ouch. Okay, maybe I was right all along."

"Right about what?" I move toward my vanity to brush my hair, but mainly to remove myself from temptation.

Joar sighs heavily. "Never mind. I swear to you. I didn't plan on..." he gestures to his clothes still laying on the floor. "...this."

"And yet, here we are. I still don't have answers. Tell me the *truth.* Not your version of it. Not halfway. Be honest." I lean against my makeup table.

He straightens up. Looks me in the eye. "Fine. I thought you were in on the scam. You appeared to make out like a bandit in the divorce. He signed everything over to you, meaning we can't go after any of his personal assets to pay back the people he stole from. You own everything of value. Surely, you can see how that looks..."

"*Really?*" I'm shocked senseless. "How did you come to learn all of this?" I've been called many things over the years, but a scammer is definitely not one of them.

"It's how I do business. I learn everything. Then I came up here to see for myself. And I learned you are not who

I thought you'd be." His smile is genuine. "The opposite, actually."

"You had me followed?" I can't look at him anymore. This is next-level shit. Stupid, powerful, entitled asshole men.

"Yes."

"Did you know I'd be at The Cactus Club?" I flick my eyes toward him, but don't risk catching his gaze.

"Yes."

"You knew where I've been staying?" I squeak. "When I'd be on set. Everything?"

"Yes. Everything," he admits.

That's it. I'm done.

My heart ices over entirely. I walk to the door and hold it open. "Please, go."

"Clover..." he starts but I hold my hand up to stop him.

"No. Don't speak. Let me tell you something. Women were not made to be trifled with by men like *you*. Stalked. Mind-fucked. *Lied to*." My voice is quiet, but firm and deadly. "Hooking up with you that night was spectacular, I won't deny it. But I will not abdicate my self-worth or put my mental health and safety at risk, *ever* again. I do not need some rich, self-important blow-hard in my life who thinks he can work me over like a fucking puppet and sweet talk his way into my pants. Been there. Done that."

He's shocked.

So-fucking-what. I'm serious. I couldn't detest someone more if I tried.

"You hate me." He manages to clue in.

When I don't respond, he puts the rest of his clothes on. Slowly. Deliberately.

And I watch him. God, I can't tear my eyes away. He's the finest specimen of man I'll ever see, which makes this situation so much more disappointing.

Until he takes how I'm looking at him the wrong way and moves toward me like a panther.

Good God. The audacity.

I hold my hand up. "Stop. I *do* hate you. I hate everything you stand for. You think you can charm me? You can't." I gesture for him to leave. "Do not call. Do not text. Do not contact me again."

He stops in front of me. "I flew sixteen hours to get here just to apologize. To tell you the truth. Isn't that worth something?"

"Only if you were a good human to start with, which you're not." I look at the floor to avoid any ambiguities of how I feel. "Arrogance can only get you so far. With me, it gets you nowhere."

"You know what? *Fuck* this, Clover. You win," Joar snarls. I feel him brush past me. "For the record, I don't need to prove myself to you or anyone. I'd hoped we could be more than a fuck in an elevator, but if this is how you want it. You got it."

He disappears down the hall without a backward glance.

I slam the door behind him.

Knowing that despite how much I hate him...

I *want* him.

When he comes around again, and something tells me he will...

I'll need to cling to this feeling of hate like a lifeline.

Chapter Fourteen

Two Months Later

Clover Callahan is infuriating.

I abhor a martyr.

I'm still not sure why I bothered trying to apologize. I should have left it well enough alone. A chance night in an elevator. World-class fuck. End of story.

Yet, I'm still thinking about her. Obsessing about her. I've made a million plans to run into her. Then I get pissed again and make other plans.

It's not like I know where she is. I stopped having Zed tail her the day she kicked me out of her dressing room.

She's still living rent-free in my brain, though, that's for goddamn sure.

Doesn't help that she's all over the fucking news.

Ronni Miller has found herself in the middle of a shitstorm related to that asshole Don Kircher. Consequently, Netflix and Kris Blakely have Clover making the media rounds on her own in an attempt to keep heat off Ronni and the show.

From all accounts—and I've made it my business to know—the buzz on *The Boyfriend Experiment* is incredible. Everyone knows, just like everything else in Hollywood, the project will be shelved without a second thought if there's any ongoing controversy.

However, the way Clover is charming her way through the press circuit and turning things around? A big, fat bonus should be forthcoming.

I turn on the wall of monitors at the far end of my office. Clover is making another appearance this morning. As if she's taunting me, her beautiful, sunny face appears on every screen. She's being interviewed by Hoda Kotb on the third hour of *The Today Show*. I turn up the volume because I'm a fucking glutton for punishment.

God, she's radiant in a tight, black pencil skirt that hugs her luscious ass and a bright-pink blouse cut low but tasteful. Her black hair is slicked back into a sleek, low ponytail revealing dramatically large silver hoop earrings. Her eyes are rimmed with black, making them appear even more like a tropical sea.

Holy hell, she's wearing those pink stiletto pumps from the elevator.

I'm instantly hard.

Goddammit.

"Tell me about this experiment you're doing, Clover." Hoda's eyes sparkle enthusiastically.

Clover dips her chin and looks up coquettishly. "Whatever do you mean?"

"Well, you dropped out of sight for a few years, got divorced, and suddenly got a starring role on a new show produced by the dream team of Ronni Miller and Kris Blakely. Talk about a comeback!" Hoda nods encouragingly. "Word on the street is your life is imitating fiction"

Clover laughs. "You could say that. My character, Jenna Lewis, in *The Boyfriend Experiment* goes through a breakup and decides her taste in men is terrible. To avoid making another mistake, she dedicates a year of her life to dating guys she'd never have considered in the past."

"Go on…" Hoda waggles her eyebrows.

"I decided it was an excellent idea for myself." Clover clasps her hands enthusiastically. "I gave up my thriving career because a powerful man asked me to. When it all fell apart, I was left scared and alone. Luckily, I insisted on a prenup which meant all of the property I owned before I got married—including my house—remained mine."

Hoda looks skeptical. "You had nothing to do with your husband's business dealings? Wasn't he your business manager?"

"None." I shake my head. "In answer to your question, Harrison Finklestein was my business manager when I was actively working. When I quit the entertainment business, I didn't have any business to manage."

Hoda looks down at her notecards and goes in for the kill. "Clover, you have to be aware that many people are speculating the money you received in your divorce settlement is money your ex stole from his clients. Are you refuting that?"

"Yes. Unequivocally. Everything I kept in our divorce was mine to begin with. I had no idea what he was up to. None." Clover's bottom lip quivers. "The truth is, I was completely blindsided. I'm mortified that all of this happened."

Hoda pauses. "Does having a new show give you the strength to move past this?"

"It was a blessing in disguise. It gave me renewed purpose. *Hope*. I'm just discovering who I am. What I like. The next time I get married, it's going to be different. I'll be with someone who'll love me for who I am, not for who they want me to be. Or, for what I can do for them."

"For all of the independence women are supposed to have today, there seems to be a backlash against standing up for yourself. Did you experience any of that in your divorce?" Hoda digs her journalistic hooks in.

Clover pauses. "You know, for me, it is nuanced. As young women, Ronni and I met on a set of a horrifically misogynistic show. The *LA Times* did a great job—an accurate job, I might add—of exposing what went down." She takes a drink of water. "We were in a constant state of being praised and cut down. It kept us in line. My marriage, in retrospect, mirrored that dynamic. When I found out about the infidelity, I was able to break the pattern."

"Are you saying you were groomed?" Hoda's mouth is wide open with shock.

What the fuck?

I'm up in a flash. I stand right in front of the monitors.

Clover is gorgeous. She's serene, but I know the truth before she speaks.

"I've learned through therapy that yes, I was groomed. As a cast member on *Hawaiian High*, I was the cute, chubby kid. Kircher and the other producers isolated us from our family. We were told what to eat. Who to hang out with. Who to please. I was lucky, if you could call it that. None of those men were attracted to the fat girl." Clover bites her bottom lip. "What no one realizes is my parents sent me there on my own because of Kircher. He convinced them I'd be fine. We needed the money. The next thing I know, I'm on that island with no support and no parental supervision. I *had* to keep the job, I was supporting my whole family. I didn't know it wasn't normal to be constantly criticized. Controlled."

She takes a deep breath and lets it out. "And then the show ended. I was barely seventeen. Lost. Alone. I had to emancipate myself from my parents. The next thing I know, I'm involved with a music producer who promised to make me a pop star." Clover winces. "God. I thought I was in love without even realizing he was using me. Luckily, I had a few hits, so I made some money, but it was the same tragic Hollywood story. I wasn't his only conquest, there were many. When I finally clued in, I was back to square one."

"I had no idea." Hoda shakes her head sadly.

"No one did." Clover shrugs. "Then I met Harrison Finklestein at an industry party. He love-bombed me when I was twenty-one. I was estranged from my family—heartbroken, alone and desperate for any type of connection. He was rich, successful and rising quickly within the Hollywood ranks. My knight in shining armor, or so he made it seem."

Clover takes a deep breath to control her emotions, she's on the verge of tears. When she recovers, her voice is strong. Determined. "I married him, thinking it was my ticket to a normal life where I could be a wife and mother. Last year I discovered that he was the worst of them all." She takes a deep breath. "Through my own bad decisions, I lost another decade to manipulation and lies. I'm older and wiser now, and it won't happen to me again. I promise you that."

"You've been through a lot, Clover." Hoda takes her hand and squeezes.

Clover's eyes now fill with tears. "Omygosh. You're making me cry, Hoda!" She sniffs and composes herself again. "I'm not a victim. I'm a survivor. Something changed deep inside me when I caught my ex cheating with my best friend. I realized I'm never going to be some wind-up doll who will allow a powerful man to take over my life again. I'm strong. I know my value. My worth. Hopefully one day I'll be in love again. When I'm ready. With the right man."

"So...is that what led to this dating experiment?" Hoda deftly changes the mood into something lighter.

"Yes, and it's so much fun. After we wrapped filming, I figured why shouldn't life imitate fiction? Why not become my character, Jenna?" Clover winks.

Hoda smirks. "So it's *not* some PR stunt? You're dating a new guy each month?"

"It's no PR stunt. I'm approaching dating differently." Clover claps her hands. "I'm sticking to guys I wouldn't ordinarily be attracted to. I want to get myself out there. Do you know anyone, Hoda?"

"You're gorgeous, you won't need my help..." Hoda makes googly eyes at the camera.

Clover pretends to be serious. "Oh, but I do. My first dip in the water was a disaster. I nearly started heading down the same worn path..." She purses her lips and flicks her eyes from side to side.

Hoda leans in. "Oooh I sense a story."

"Yeah, and no one knows about this so don't tell..." Clover looks at the camera and back at Hoda. "The first guy I was with after my ex was actually a wolf in sheep's clothing. I'd seen him a couple of times and he was handsome as hell. And—you can't write this stuff—we literally got trapped in an elevator."

"Noooooo." Hoda shrieks. "What happened?"

I'm losing my shit. I cannot believe she's telling our story on national television. Is she going to say my name?

"You should know I'm *extremely* claustrophobic. He seemed so sweet and kind. He distracted me. Yada Yada Yada, eight hours went by, we were rescued and he left town the next day." She raises her eyebrows. "Unfortunately, a couple weeks later, I found out he wasn't who he said he was. The day we wrapped production, he showed up on set to give me a half-assed apology. Which I rejected, thank you very much. The jerk was seriously *angry* at me for not accepting him at face value."

Fuckity-Fuck. Is that how she sees me?

My stomach plummets to the ground. Of course it is. I wasn't thinking of her feelings, I was thinking of mine. And my ego.

Fascinated by her perspective, I hang on every one of her words.

"I don't have a good picker. So, whatever my instinct is, I'm doing the opposite." Clover laughs. "He was hot though, extraordinarily hot." She fans herself.

"Well, I don't see how we can top that story. Good luck with the experiment, Clover." Hoda smiles to the camera. "Coming up next..."

I click off the monitors.

Huh.

Is that how I came across? Is her version of what happened between us accurate?

Yes. You know it is.

Christ. I've been doing everything completely wrong.

Most of what she disclosed in the interview just now is stuff I learned from my investigation materials but hearing it from her lips is devastating. What she went through...

I think back to my early twenties when I first moved to New York for business school. My scholarships only covered tuition, so I was flat broke. With no choice but to support myself, I started my first company where I created themed meme websites and drove high-volume traffic to them using all sorts of techniques. When traffic reached a peak, I allowed companies to run ads on the sites, which I got paid a fortune for.

It was my first goldmine. In three years, I banked two million dollars. Sold the company for eight million dollars a week before graduation.

I've never looked back.

Year after year, I've meticulously reinvested my money into bigger and bigger media properties—each one more successful than the last. Today, I'm one of the wealthiest and most powerful men in the world—my life is filled with expensive cars, bespoke custom clothes, real estate and private jets.

Not to mention, I can fuck practically any woman I want.

Except...ever since that night with Clover, I'm just not interested.

At first it confounded me, but I've given it a lot of thought.

The first time I had sex was a few months after I launched my business. I'd just pocketed my first hundred grand and was feeling on top of the world. I told a few people in my business school program about my good fortune and the next day, Elise Giraldi informed me I was taking her out. She was pretty and assertive, so I agreed.

By the end of the night, I'd paid for dinner and lost my virginity. Our relationship lasted a few months and consisted largely of me buying her designer shit in exchange for sex. Eventually, she dumped me for someone richer and I decided relationships weren't for me. Too distracting.

Looking back, it's virtually impossible for me to ascertain if any woman I've been with in the past twenty five years has wanted *me* or was more interested in my bank account. Considering I've treated these relationships like business transactions anyway, I'm partially, if not wholly, at fault. The realization of which...*sucks*.

And then there's Clover.

I can see now that my bias toward her in the beginning was also my fault. I projected characteristics of the women I've been involved with onto her, which is blatantly unfair. Even worse, I made assumptions about her life and marriage that were shaped by how much I hate Harrison Finklestein.

Clover was *never* the money-hungry monster I'd made her out to be in my head.

When she and I were stuck in the elevator and she knew me only as "JJ," Clover was genuinely attracted to me. Not to Joar, the rich guy. She liked JJ, the guy who listened to her. Focused on her pleasure. Talked about pop culture, food, music and places we've travelled. That night, she got to know the real me—not just the man who fought and clawed his way through obstacles to better himself.

That's what made our sex out of this world.

We had a genuine *connection*.

Something fundamental shifts inside me. I want a future with Clover Callahan. A future where she can soar and be everything she wants to be. Where we can fill in each other's gaps. Make one another whole.

Maybe have a family. Or, explore the world together hand in hand.

Somehow I know that with Clover, anything and everything will be possible.

Even if I don't deserve her.

Chapter Fifteen

One Month Later

Dear Lord,

Please put me out of my misery.

Love, Clover

A fake smile is pasted on my face.

I nod at the appropriate time. Feign interest. Murmur "mm-hmms" and "wow" every now and then.

The truth? I have no fucking clue what this guy is even talking about. He yammers on and on and on. I'm lulled into a trance, listening to his droney voice.

"Clover?" He raps his knuckles on the table.

I'm jolted alert. "Yes, I'm listening."

"Were you asleep?" He leans back, offended.

"No. No." I shake my head. Smile. "I was just resting my eyes. I was out late last night."

A little white lie.

He studies me. Nods. "Yeah, I get it."

Sighing, I look across the table at Frank, a perfectly friendly man. Nice-enough looking. Checks all the "average-guy" boxes. Medium height. Short brown hair. Brown eyes. White dress shirt. Blue jeans. Navy blazer. Brown shoes.

He's just so freakin' *boring.*

I had such high hopes too.

We met in line at Starbucks in West Hollywood. He bought my coffee and asked me to dinner. It was the first time anyone asked me out like that. In my effort to do the opposite of what I'd usually do, I said yes.

Still, he's a stranger. I knew it wouldn't be good for him to pick me up at my house. I live alone, after all. My brilliant idea was to meet him here at BOA Steakhouse on Sunset. I thought: high traffic location, valet parking, good food. What could go wrong?

Well, I'm out of practice. I didn't remember BOA is a celebrity seen-and-be-seen spot. Paparazzi camp out around the building an hour before it opens until closing.

Six months ago, I wouldn't have cared. No one would have looked in my direction.

They do now.

Marketing and PR for the show have been on overdrive. I'm on national entertainment shows. My face is plastered on several billboards around Hollywood. Even my social media is exploding.

All of this exposure means I'm recognizable again, which brings its own set of challenges. It never occurred to me I'd need security. By the time I fought my way in through the barrage of flashes, the host took mercy on me and showed me to a back corner table. Where I waited. And waited.

This guy was friggin' thirty minutes late!

One of my *biggest* pet peeves.

God. I should have freakin' *left*.

Because as if being late wasn't annoying enough, from the second he sat down, this guy hasn't stopped talking about himself. He owns a high-end plumbing fixture store frequented by, apparently, *very* wealthy clients.

My God, the name dropping. Stories that go on too long. Laughing at his own jokes.

I'm so over this date.

"Frank, if you don't mind, I'm going to skip dessert tonight." I give him my best smile. "It's been such a long week."

He looks disappointed. "Oh, I was hoping we could go grab a drink at SUR."

"The *Vanderpump Rules* bar?" I'm surprised. He doesn't seem like the target audience.

"Yeah. You're the first famous person I've ever dated. Wouldn't it be fun to have the paparazzi follow us? Maybe run into Lala? Or Scheana?" He practically claps his hands with glee.

When I'm able to pick my jaw off the ground, I'm not in the mood to be nice anymore. "Nope. Not tonight."

Look, I watch *VPR* as much as the next person, but no. Just no.

"It's got to be so cool to see yourself on billboards. In all the blogs," he powers on. Completely clueless. Lost in his fanboy ways.

Argh. I've got to wrap this up. This is a friggin' *nightmare*.

It doesn't stop. "How 'bout I come over and we can take a selfie together?" His face is hopeful. Like a dopey golden retriever waiting for a treat.

"Uh, no thank you." I scoot my chair out a bit. Desperately wave the server over.

Frank pouts. "You're not as much fun as I thought you'd be."

The server hands me the check. I shove my credit card at him. Frank makes a feeble attempt to hand over his own card. "We can split it."

I. Just. Can't.

"I've got it." I'm terse. The transaction is completed in under two minutes.

I stand and walk toward the door without saying another word, keeping a pleasant smile on my face. The last thing I want is for visible annoyance to be posted to socials.

"Man, I can't believe I had a date with Clover Callahan and she paid." Frank trails behind me, talking way too loudly.

My new hope is that pictures of me and Frank aren't sent to every major news magazine so they can make up some bullshit about us being engaged. Or me being pregnant. Or whatever story they'll concoct.

If it weren't for the fact phones have been trained on me since the second we got here, I'd give the guy a piece of my mind. Instead, I have to remain calm, walk out to get my car and hope that whatever pictures get posted to social media don't make me look three hundred pounds.

Standing at the valet, I count down the seconds until I can jump into my Mercedes and get home. Snuggly pajamas. A fire. Some ice cream. A YouTube deep dive on *Sister Wives*.

Heaven.

My car pulls up to the stand. As I walk toward the kid to tip him, a black Bentley squeals in behind us, sending me spinning into Frank.

"Are you okay?" He uses the opportunity to run his hands down my back.

When they creep lower toward my ass, I push him away, angrily. "Manners, Frank."

Behind me I feel an energy force. The same thing happens on every single date I've been on this month. Goosebumps erupt all over my body. My nipples tighten. My pussy clenches. I squeeze my eyes shut, when the woodsy, leathery scent of Joar-fucking-Jacoby fills my nostrils. I will myself not to look.

It's too dangerous.

"Get. The. *Fuck*. Away. From. Her." His low, throaty, commandeering voice is directed at my date. "It's time for you to go."

I take several cleansing breaths to no avail, my nostrils are filled with his delicious manliness. It's important to keep up appearances with this crowd though, so I turn and put on my sweetest voice. "I'm fine, thank you."

"Clover?" Frank's pathetic hang-dog look makes me cringe.

I shoo him, trying to be as kind as possible. "It's best if you head out."

"I'll call you," he says over his shoulder as he scampers away.

My skin prickles when Joar comes up behind me. Leans down and whispers in my ear, "Hi, Clover."

God, I'm so sick of this. He somehow shows up to every single date I've been on. I whirl around to face the man I hate with every ounce of my being, who just happens to be the man I want to fuck with every ounce of my being too.

It's so *confusing*.

"*JJ*," I sneer. Flick my gaze quickly away.

His driver gets out and stands to the side. Joar acknowledges him with a wave as he returns his attention to me, smirking, "You look scrumptious. Your date couldn't handle you?"

"That is *none* of your business." I toss my head. Flounce toward my car.

That's when I make a big mistake. I look back at him. To find his violet eyes regarding me like he's about to toss me on the hood of the car, yank my panties down and fuck me raw in front of this entire crowd of people.

Oh God. Why does that make me even hotter?

Nevertheless, the reality of the situation is: I'm being cornered by curious photographers. All around me bright flashes of light close in. Dozens of people yell, "*Clover.*"

My claustrophobia kicks in. I freeze.

In a flash, Joar's strong arm winds around my waist and he whisks me to the driver's side of my car. "You're safe now," he assures.

I stiffen when I realize he's touching me. No matter how much he wants to change my mind, I don't trust this guy. I hate what he did to me. Hate that he's still having me followed. It's not cool.

He may have given me the best sex of my life, but I can't allow myself to weaken and find myself naked and writhing under him.

It would be all over then.

"I'm fine, thanks," I say through gritted teeth, extricating myself from his grasp and sliding into the driver's seat.

With one hand on the hood and the other on the outside handle, Joar leans down, concerned. "Be careful. Don't let the paps tail you."

"I'll be fine." I keep my eyes straight ahead, but my adrenaline begins to spike.

He doesn't move for a beat. "Should I have my guy escort you home?"

"No!" I pound the steering wheel a little too emphatically. Hell. Considering how aggressive the paparazzi are, it wouldn't be the worst idea. Plus he already knows where I live...

No. Stay strong.

Joar moves a half step away, still peering at me. I can feel it, though I refuse to look up at him. "Would you ever consider having a real conversation with me?"

Instantaneously, I cave in and gaze deep into his gorgeous eyes, which up close are swirls of so many blues—I guess that's what makes them appear purple. "I can't do it, JJ. I don't trust you. Following me and showing up everywhere is stalkerish. Creepy. Just the fact that you'll go to these lengths to get your way means you still don't understand why what you did is unforgivable. You're not the kind of man I want in my life."

"Ah." His jaw sets. Hurt flickers and then floats away into steely reserve. It's like JJ transforms into Joar right before my eyes. "You see things a little differently than me, sweetness. I am not the kind of man who begs. The offer stands if you change your mind, but you'll have to come to me."

He shuts the door.

I whisper, "Fat chance" to no one in particular.

Hopefully this Joar chapter is over now.

Except, why do I feel so defeated?

Chapter Sixteen

A Few Days Later

Watching Clover go on dates with these stupid men has been fucking excruciating.

Considering the losers she's been "finding herself" with, I'm fighting the urge to feel insulted that she won't give me a second chance. In the past month, she's been out with a musician friend of Ronni's husband, a firefighter, an Olympic gold medalist in snowboarding, and the shithead from the other night.

So far, she hasn't fucked any of them. I know this because I've followed her.

I'm not particularly proud of my stalkerish ways, but I am who I am. Let's get real. I may not beg, but when I want something, I pull out all the stops. Laser focus on the puzzle I'm trying to solve. Find a way to make it happen.

In Clover's case, it's also not particularly wise. The woman has deep-seated trust issues for good reason, as I've come to learn in the weeks after the greatest sex of my life. If I'd done a better job on my research *before* charging up to Vancouver BC like a bull in a china shop, I might not be in this predicament.

Such a rookie mistake on my part.

Of course, I'd also let my anger at Finklestein get the best of me, which tainted my perspective even further. I'm kicking myself now. Had I been smarter, she and I'd be in a much different place.

Of course, maybe we'd be no place at all. If I'd known about her past, odds are I wouldn't have even bothered to make the trip to Canada. I'd have moved on to the next deal and never met her.

Which means, I'd never have witnessed her come apart just by listening to my dirty talk. Or known what it was like to be buried balls deep inside her velvet heat. Or realized what a talented, strong, feisty goddess she is for having endured such unthinkable treatment. For emerging from a shitty situation with her integrity intact.

I guess things are playing out the way they're supposed to.

Other than she hates me and I'm losing my goddamn mind because of it.

I've never gone without sex for this long. Fucking my hand while visualizing Clover sucking me off is *not* cutting it. I'm not about to fuck anyone else. Not that I could. I'm ruined. I can't get it up for anyone but Clover.

Which is mind-blowing.

Despite how much I once hated her and how much she now hates me, Clover Callahan is it for me.

The *one*.

Eventually, she's going to be *my* woman.

An affirmation that continuously taunts me. Punches me in the gut. Hits me over the head with an anvil.

Because in reality, I may never have her.

Probably won't.

Unless tonight I'm able to turn things around.

I'm back in LA. Victor pulls my Bentley through the arched hedges of the driveway to the London Hotel valet. I get out. Nod to the doorman. Push through the front doors. Stride past the teal velvet couches in the lobby and make my way to the bar where Seth is waiting.

"Joar." He lifts his martini glass.

I sit on the barstool next to him, facing the entryway. "Seth." I nod. Order a Jamison 18 neat.

"Did you read the reports?" He sips his drink. "Profits on the latest acquisitions are through the roof."

I lean back, casually glance at a couple walking in, then return my attention to my best friend. "Yeah. I'm pleased."

"There are several portfolios I emailed as well. Have you decided on the next target?" Seth turns toward me. "It's a great time to make a move."

Over the past two decades, I've accumulated all the top production facilities and business, management, and booking agencies throughout the world. I have no plans to slow down on that front. "Yeah, the next phase is performance venues. Big theaters first. Stadiums down the line." I take a sip of my whiskey. "But, that's not why I asked you to meet me. Tonight, you're my wingman. I have my eye on one very special prize."

Oh, who is it?" Seth is intrigued.

I don't answer right away because a vision appears in the entryway and I can't help but take a moment to appreciate. Clover floats in wearing a knee-length, light-blue dress and silver sandals. Her long, black hair curtains her back in soft waves. "She just walked in."

Seth turns to see who I'm looking at. "Clover Callahan? I thought that was over before it ever started."

"Not by a long shot." I finish my drink and throw a hundred dollar bill on the table. "If I close this particular deal, it will make me a happy man."

I slide off my stool and walk toward her. She looks around the room until her gaze fixes on me. Her face scrunches up in annoyance, but I also see a flash of desire. "You're still following me?"

"No, you arranged to meet me here." I lean over and kiss her cheek. "You look beautiful."

"JJ—*Joar.*" She huffs out a breath. Shakes her head. "You've got to stop this madness. I did not arrange *any* such thing."

I take out my phone and pull up the Raya dating app. "*We* did. See?"

"Huh?" She peers at my phone. Studies it. Looks up at me solemnly. "God*dammit.* You tricked me. *Again.* Do I need to get a restraining order? I'm being serious. This isn't okay."

I cock my head, annoyed. "Clover, something about this profile called to you. You're the one who reached out to me." I point to the phone.

The Hate Date

Handsome, fit, 40-something, well-off confirmed bachelor seeks a cool, sexy woman to spend time with. Only one problem. I do not date.

In fact, I hate dating.

So why am I on a dating app, you ask?

For me, meeting people is easy. Trusting someone is hard. Finding both connection and attraction with someone you trust is impossible.

This is why the dating ritual is time-consuming. Disappointing. Stupid.

It's why people get involved with the wrong partners.

I'm on this app to put it all out there and see if someone picks up what I'm selling.

Here is my proposition:

If you're receiving access to my profile, then one thing is out of the way. I find you attractive, and you find me attractive.

How do we go about figuring out connection and the trust?

I propose we meet and do an activity I hate. You pick.

If we survive the night, we'll have a connection and hopefully you'll trust me too and we'll do something you hate together.

Who knows, maybe we can learn to love the things we hate. Together.

Are you in?

For our "Hate Date," here is a list of eight activities I hate for you to choose from:

Dancing

Fast Food

Commercial Flights

Reality TV

Shopping

Charity Galas

Amusement Parks

Elevators

Clover squeezes her eyes shut, like she needs to take a moment. "I didn't have any way to know this was you. The profile photo wasn't your picture. Besides, what kind of hypocrite goes on and on about connection and trust...and then *lies* about their identity?"

"For fuck's sake." I'm annoyed. "I set this profile up specifically for *you* to find and respond to. I posted Seth, my attorney's picture, because I knew if you saw it was me you'd instantly scroll past." I point to him sitting at the bar. He waves. "I wanted you to reach out to me and I made sure you did."

"God." She pinches her nose with her fingers. "What is wrong with you? You shouldn't have bothered. My mind hasn't changed. Everything you do is a fucking *game*." Clover turns to leave. Spins back around. Spits out, "It's like you can't even *help* it."

I take a chance and grasp her face. Pull her in and just go for it. My lips smash against hers. I hold her to me while my tongue works its way inside so I can pillage and plunge. Devour her. It feels like home. I've missed it so bad. She whimpers. Sags against me.

Her hands grip my wrists. I brace for her to shove me away.

Except *no*.

She holds me in place. Deepens our kiss. Now it's me who's groaning.

Hoping this is a breakthrough.

"JJ," Clover whispers against my mouth as she breaks the kiss. "Why? Why do you do this to me?"

I stroke her hair, pleased that she's used my nickname. "Pick."

"Pick what?" Her face is pained. Confused. She's warring with herself.

"Your hate date." I continue petting her. Soothing her.

She bobs her head up and down, just slightly. As if she's thinking to the rhythm of a song only she can hear. My heart seizes when a tear rolls down her cheek. I wipe it away with my thumb, wondering if I've gone too far. If my selfishness of wanting her is genuinely hurting her in a way I can't understand.

"Let's start at the top," she murmurs.

I'm stunned. Elated.

I wrap my arms around her. "You had that preselected, didn't you? You're dressed up for dancing."

"I love to dance. So, yeah. It's what piqued my interest in responding. I felt like if I could get someone who didn't like dancing to enjoy it, there could be a chance." She manages a smile.

I take her hand. "Let's go. I'm assuming you have somewhere you'd like to get your groove on?"

"Yeah. I booked a private dance lesson." She doesn't let go of my hand but won't look me in the eye either.

"Victor will drive us, if that's okay," I say as we push through the front door. "I don't want to be distracted now that you're letting me spend time with you."

"It's fine." She seems resigned to a fate worse than death. She's definitely not as excited as I am.

I open the back door of the car for her. She slides in and immediately takes out her phone. I scoot in beside her. "Victor, this is Clover. She'll give you the address to where we're going."

"Here." She hands her phone to Victor. "Don't show him, though. I want it to be a surprise."

He takes it, taps it into his own phone GPS and hands it back. I catch his eye in the rear view mirror, and it's safe to say I'm worried. His smile splits his face and he shakes his head at me as if to say, "You have no idea what you're in for."

Clover stares out the window, fully turned away from me.

I got her here, which was half the battle.

Now, I have to find a way to keep her.

Chapter Seventeen

The Same Night

I should have known he'd find a way to wear me down.

Let's be honest, I always knew I was no match for Joar Jacoby.

The man's a brilliant businessman. Ruthless negotiator. Devilishly handsome. World-class lover. He can have anything and anyone he wants. Somehow he's decided it's me.

What I haven't figured out is *why* he wants me.

I mean, sex. Sure. We're combustible together. He's my fantasy in the dark of the night when I'm alone with my vibrator. Which, by the way, doesn't come remotely close to the real thing.

Once you've had Joar's attention focused on making you come, nothing else compares.

Don't get me started on his cock.

"We're here," Joar's driver, Victor, announces as he pulls up to a little studio on the ground floor of an apartment building on a quiet street in North Hollywood.

Joar peers out the window. "Pole dancing?"

"Yep. I've always wanted to try it." I don't bother waiting for Victor, I get out of the car and walk up to the door.

A slight woman in a unitard is waiting. "Hi. I'm Regan. You must be Clover. I'm such a fan."

"Thank you, Regan. It's lovely to meet you." I'm tempted to follow her in, but I can't help but look back to see if Joar's behind me.

I nearly burst out laughing. The man in a bespoke suit is clearly terrified. Yet, trying to look enthusiastic. Failing miserably. This is totally why I wanted to go on a date with the guy I thought wrote that profile. It's my test.

Now it's JJ—Joar's.

He jogs to catch up with me. "Well, this is not what I expected."

"Wow, I surprised the great Joar Jacoby." I flutter my eyelashes. "Meet Regan, our private pole dancing instructor."

Regan assesses us. "Let's get you changed. I have the clothes you ordered here." She picks up a shopping bag, reaches in and hands me a bodysuit. "This is for you, Clover." She rummages around and hands Joar a pair of board shorts. "You can make do with this today."

There are two dressing rooms separated by a curtain. Joar holds the first one open for me. Once he's situated in the room beside me, he finds his voice. "I'm gonna *love* seeing you twirl around that pole."

"I'm going to laugh my ass off when you're up there." I neatly fold my dress and pull on my black bodysuit. Wow. It leaves nothing to the imagination. My nipples poke out like they're trying to break free.

Joar steps out wearing nothing but the board shorts. Holy fucking hell. He's even more ripped than the last time I saw him. Every muscle on his exposed skin is carved in marble. I can't help but stare. He notices me ogling him and grins, so I roll my eyes and walk away.

He follows me into the studio, which is stark white but surrounded by mirrored walls. Ten poles are scattered evenly around the room, screwed into the ceiling and floor.

Regan gestures for us to sit. "Tonight is going to be challenging but exciting. Take it from me, hitting a move for the first time is the best feeling in the world."

She stands and gracefully jumps up on the pole. Launches into a series of twirls and spins. Climbs up to the top, hooks her legs around the pole and plummets all the way down where she catches herself just before she hits the bottom.

I can't help but jump up and cheer. "Omigod. Yes. I want to do that."

"All I can think about is how much that's going to hurt my junk." Joar cups himself. "Should I have some protection on the goods?"

Regan laughs heartily. "We'll start off slow, you'll be fine."

For the next twenty minutes, we hang upside down, propped up on our shoulders, forearms and heads as Regan shows us simple moves. When we master the basics on the floor, we both learn how to invert straddle, shoulder mount, and how to do a basic climb on the pole. In all my years of dance classes, I've never moved my body this way. It's tough but liberating.

"I thought I was fit, but this is fucking hard." Joar wipes sweat off his brow. We're taking five before we move into the next phase of the lesson.

He's so competitive. Mostly with himself, I realize. "You're being a good sport, Joar. Thank you."

"I'm having so much fun." He looks almost boyish the way he smiles at my praise.

I have to admit, my heart softens. Just a smidge.

Regan joins us and directs a question at Joar. "Would you like to learn how to spot Clover?"

"No, that's okay," I find myself blurting out. If Joar touches me, I know where it's going to lead. I'm willing to play this "hate date" out tonight, but that's it. Finito. If I let him have any physical contact...

I'll lose all resolve.

To his credit, Joar doesn't bulldoze the situation and insist. He hangs back as Regan leaps up on the pole in an inversion move and slides down the pole, stopping just shy of the floor. "Are you sure you don't want to try this?"

I do. So badly.

"I'm happy to spot you, sweetness. It doesn't have to mean anything. This is all about you." Joar takes a step toward me. All rippled muscles and heat.

"Let's try it," Regan encourages, guiding me to the pole.

She helps me get into the inversion straddle position and shows Joar how to hold on to my waist to support me as I get my bearings. Using half my own strength and half of Joar's support, I'm able to walk my hands up the pole a few feet up. I'm not remotely as graceful as Regan, but the sense of accomplishment is addictive.

Joar's support of me is effortless, like I weigh nothing, which is definitely not true. I'm a lot heavier than most actresses, at the low end of what some would call plus-size. Our faces are close together, concentrating on our task at hand.

"Joar, now take most of Clover's weight and let her slide down a few inches so she can get the feel of it." Regan is close to the two of us, ready to step in as necessary.

I say nothing but, for the first time tonight, I look directly into Joar's violet eyes. What I see in those depths takes my breath away.

Utter. Total. Adoration.

What is happening?

"Yes. Good. Eye contact is key to trust." Regan claps. "On the count of three, Joar, you keep hold of Clover.

Clover, you trust your partner and slide down a few inches then stop yourself."

Our eyes lock. I realize how utterly sensual—no sexual—this exercise is. Despite my misgivings, I feel connected to him on every level. I hear Regan count us down and I let myself go. Joar is right there with me, and I'm able to slide down the pole and catch myself with his assistance.

Exhilarating.

When the lesson is over, I see Joar slip Regan a few hundred bucks. We quietly make our way to the dressing rooms. I'm sweating like a fiend, but haven't felt this happy in, well, forever.

"You thanked me earlier, but I should be thanking you." Joar touches my elbow.

I tilt my head in surprise. "For what?"

"For expanding my horizons. This was the most fun I've had since that night in the elevator." He's serious.

Sincere.

I shrug. "You're welcome."

"Clover..." He's about to say something but stops himself.

Instead of asking what he was about to say, I slide open the curtain to my dressing room. "I'm going to get changed."

"Yeah...me too." He promptly ducks inside his own room.

A few minutes later we emerge fully dressed. A lot of the adrenaline from the pole lesson has dissipated, replaced with a bit of anxiety. I'm shy and unsure of what comes next. What I *want* to come next. My heart is beating erratically from the nerves.

Joar watches me tentatively. "Would you be up for a late dinner? I'm starving."

"Okay." I hear myself say. "Nothing fancy though."

He nods. Places his hand at the small of my back as we exit the building. Victor is waiting for us. Joar stops to speak to him while I slide into the back seat of his Bentley. He gets in beside me. "We're going to the perfect place."

A few minutes later, Victor pulls into the drive-thru at In-N-Out Burger. "What do you both want?"

I can't help but giggle. This is so unexpected. He's knocked two hate dates off the list in one night. "Double double animal style, no onions. Fries. Chocolate shake."

"Same." Joar looks over at me and slides his hand across the seat. I take it. He threads his fingers with mine.

In this moment, I decide to let go of my past. Take a leap of faith like I did on the pole.

Give in to what I want.

Because even if he's been going about his pursuit of me all wrong...

Right now, all I want is Joar.

Chapter Eighteen

The Same Night

Clover and I are parked at the Griffith Observatory, looking down on the lights of downtown Los Angeles.

I called an Uber for Victor at In-N-Out so we could spend some time alone. If you had asked me six months ago if I thought watching a beautiful woman devour a fast-food hamburger would be the biggest turn-on of my life, I'd have said a most definitive, "no."

Tonight? I'm so aroused just being in the vicinity of Clover Callahan, I'd go through every drive-thru in the area if it meant the night wouldn't have to end.

"Do you seriously hate fast food?" Clover is sprawled out next to me in the passenger seat. "I once postponed a flight to get In-N-Out."

I pat my flat stomach. "I don't indulge that often. Though, it was surprisingly delicious. I can see missing a flight for it."

"Yeah. Nothing like a double-double food baby." She cups a small swell of her belly and sighs contentedly.

She's relaxed. Gorgeous. Happy.

I have so much I want to say. Things I want to ask her. Apologies I'd like to make. History I'd love to share with her. I learned so much about her that night in the elevator. When we were naked. Isolated. Free.

A big part of me regrets not telling her the truth that night. Or opening up more. Maybe we could have talked it out. Gone deeper. Perhaps we wouldn't have wasted these past few months.

I push these thoughts away.

The past cannot be changed. It's my number-one rule of business and I need to apply that logic here. Tonight, thanks to the "hate date," I have a chance to get us back on track. Which is hilarious because the concept was born out of desperation. An emotion I haven't felt in nearly thirty years.

The idea came about when Clover posted a poll on one of her Instagram stories about whether she should join celebrity dating app, Raya. When the results were overwhelmingly "do it" I had to take charge, and fast. I pulled in a connection to fast track my own profile—using Seth's photo—and tailored it to pique her interest.

The activities I purported to hate are things I'm fairly indifferent to but are most definitely activities I learned Clover loves from either her Instagram posts or from our conversations in the elevator.

Three days went by with a fuck-ton of women trying to connect, but no Clover. On the verge of deleting it, I checked one more time to find she'd swiped "yes." I was *fucking* pumped, but disciplined. I waited a few days before I accepted the match—to build anticipation, and all that.

It worked.

What can I say? I shot my shot and scored a direct hit.

A few DMs later and she agreed to meet "me" at The London. I figured once she saw it was the real me, there was a miniscule chance I'd convince her to go on my so-called "hate date."

But, she did. The idea of pole dancing might have thrown me for a minute there, but we had a blast.

I swear I've won the lottery.

She's here. With me. Tonight.

Only one problem: now that I've got her here, I'm not sure what to do. Take control or let her lead? On the one hand, I'm dying to throw her over my shoulder caveman style and fuck her on the hood of my car. Shit. The memory of her tight, hot pussy... I've been semi-hard most of the night. On the other hand, maybe I should just follow her lead.

I'm a decisive man in every respect of the world. Why is this such a dilemma?

Because you're in love with her.

No. You're in *lust* with her. Get it straight.

You sure about that?

"You've gone quiet on me, Joar." Clover pats my hand, which is resting on the console between us, like I'm her old chum.

I shift in my seat to face her. "I talk too much some-times. I'm enjoying being present in this moment with you."

Her entire demeanor softens altogether. I'm trying hard to be vulnerable. To break down enough barriers tonight so she'll at least consider spending time together.

"I've been hard on you." She hooks her index finger with mine. "For good reason. I'm hurt. Angry. I felt such a connection with you that night, it crushed me when

I learned you weren't who you said you were. When I found out you manipulated me so deftly. It brought up all sorts of bad shit."

I feel a shift between us. A bit of trust restored. A tentative truce. I don't want to fuck this up.

So, I take this opportunity to come clean. "Let me start at the beginning so you can understand my perspective at the time."

She bites her lip. "Okay." Nods for me to go ahead.

"Your ex-husband was my college roommate. We have a bad history, which I'll get to in a bit." I wiggle our locked fingers. "Jacoby International, my company, has been acquiring media-related companies for many years, including agencies like Eminence. I've had my eye on his operations for years and waited for the perfect time to take over. The Kircher poker situation gave me the opportunity to not only take his company but to ruin him. That's the truth. He was stealing from his clients and it infuriated me."

Clover's brows knit as she thinks about what I said. From her expression, it seems fairly clear she had no idea of why I'd been involved. "God..."

"I admit it—I jumped to the wrong conclusions about you. Figured you were in on it with him. Maybe even introduced him to Kircher, considering your past connection," I confess sheepishly. "Now, of course, I know the truth. I didn't do enough homework then. Let some of my old biases creep in. For that, I'm deeply sorry."

She winces. Shakes her head sadly as my words sink in further. "You need to tell me more about this history with Harrison." She turns in her seat to face me.

I look out over the city, recollecting the worst and scariest time of my life. In great detail, I tell her about my time at Yale with Harrison. How he nearly cost me my entire future without remorse. How that incident gave me the drive to create my empire from nothing.

"Joar, I didn't know any of that. I wish you'd said something. If we had this conversation that night in the elevator..." She looks sad as she repeats my earlier thought. "...It would have saved me—both of us—a lot of..."

"We were caught up in the moment. It didn't even occur to me. I was so lost in your beautiful body," I remind her. "I was in a different headspace."

"Yeah. You thought I was a monster and you fucked me anyway." Clover closes her eyes. Processes.

She looks serene.

So, *so* beautiful.

I lean over and whisper, "I'm sorry. For the record, I realized how wrong I was about you within the first hour. Everything we shared in there meant the world to me. *Everything.*"

A tear trickles down her face. She wipes it away. Shuts her eyes. "Harrison swept me off my feet at a vulnerable time in my life. We had an uneventful marriage, but I always thought love would conquer all. I was so naïve. Essentially, I supported his career by giving up mine and he betrayed me with my best friend. I hate what he did to me. Everything I'd sacrificed as a young woman to find success was in vain. Ten wasted years." She looks up at me. "But, to hear the extent of the hurt he inflicted on others? It's beyond devastating."

"He's a selfish prick," I can't help but state the obvious. "He always was."

Her eyes blink open. "Yes. Unfortunately, selfish pricks are what I'm used to. Harrison felt familiar, so I gravitated toward him. The things I endured on the set of *Hawaiian High*—the barbs about my weight, my castmate committing suicide, being alone with no protection from my family. I grew up too fast. He was my safety net, or so I thought. Do you see why I can't ever go back to that place?"

Clover's fingers thread with mine. I lean over and press my lips to hers. Our kiss is sweet. Restorative. I pull away because we have more to talk about before things go further. "I can't change who I am, Clover. I'm the CEO of the second-biggest media company in the world. I started it from scratch. I've seen your interviews. I know you're afraid of powerful men—for good reason..."

"And you're the most powerful man of them all." She shakes her head. "You scare me."

I rest my forehead against hers. "I know, but I won't hurt you again."

"Don't make any promises, Joar." Clover's breath hitches. "This attraction between us is...powerful. Intoxicating. I have the feeling if I get too lost in you I'll drown."

I pepper her lips with tiny kisses of encouragement. Hope. "I won't let you. I'm not those men. Not by a long shot."

"I need to feel your cock inside me again," Clover murmurs against the corner of my mouth, shocking me to the core. "I want another round of what happened in the elevator."

I turn on the engine and back out of the parking space. "So do I. Let's go. Your place or mine?"

"Yours." She slides her hand to my thigh.

By the time I fire up the engine, Clover is fondling my junk. Squeezing gently. Rubs me just right so I'm harder than steel. I try to put all my focus on the road but I'm losing the battle. We're on the main drag when she unzips my pants. "Holy Christ," I gulp.

"Eyes on the road, Joar." She pulls my cock fully free. Leans over and engulfs me into her hot, wet mouth, fisting me at the base.

Just like I've dreamed about.

Throughout the twenty-minute drive to my penthouse on Wilshire, I'm lost in the tantalizing torture at the hands—and mouth—of Clover Callahan. She laves my balls, pumps me, licks me like a lollipop, takes me deep down her throat and swallows my tip. Leaves me just on the precipice of shooting off like a rocket before pulling back and starting the entire process again.

I'm shaking like a drug addict by the time we arrive at my place. "C-C-Clover. We're here. Almost at the valet."

"Okay." She sits up and tucks me back into my pants. Wipes the edges of her lips with her thumb and forefinger. "We'll finish up later."

Those perfect lips, swollen from sucking on my cock, mesmerize me.

"I'm going to fuck the ever-loving' hell out of you—hard and dirty—all night long." I lean in and kiss her like she's mine.

By tomorrow, if I'm lucky, she will be.

Chapter Nineteen

The Same Night

I feel like I'm living in slow motion.

The valet opens my door and helps me out. Joar's at my side. He takes my hand and leads me inside the building, through the lobby into the elevator. The second the doors close his lips crush mine. We're gasping. Biting. Clawing at each other. Mouths fused together.

He reaches under my dress and plunges his fingers inside me.

Utter detonation.

I scream his name when I come, not caring who hears us.

This man sets me on fire. I'm giving in to wherever the night takes us.

I might get badly burned, but it will be worth it just to feel him inside me again.

The elevator opens directly into his penthouse, which is pitch black except for the sparkly lights of the buildings all around us.

He takes my hand, leads me through the bleary darkness. "Soft light. Fire," he speaks into the air and like magic the room is bathed in a buttery glow and the fireplace is set ablaze.

We make it a few more steps before Joar grips my face with both hands and pulls me to him. He leans down and our desperate kisses begin again. One of his hands slides around my neck and unzips my dress. I pull away from our frenzied passion and skate my fingertips over his swollen lips. Awed.

Unsure if any of this is real, I reach down and unbuckle his belt. He unzips his pants and kicks them off while I rip open his shirt. Buttons fly everywhere. I reach down and take his thick cock in my hand. Run my hand up and down his length as he slides my dress off my shoulders. It falls away from my body, pooling around my feet.

"Get this underwear off," he growls. Rips off my thong while I unclasp my bra. I cry out with unabashed pleasure when his lips seal around my nipple. I thread my fingers through his wavy hair to hold him in place. He alternates sucking and pinching my tight buds, which shoots zaps of pleasure all the way to my pussy.

Holy shit, my entire core shakes and trembles. Pressure builds. I cry out in ecstasy when I come.

Nothing has ever felt this way.

So right. So perfect.

But, I'm entering into in a dangerous fantasy world where he and I can genuinely mean something to each other. When I know I can't—*won't*—allow myself to ever play second fiddle to a powerful man again.

I've lost too much time. Given up too much of myself.

As long as this is just sex, I won't let my heart get crushed into powder. "I need you inside me, Joar."

"Yes. Yes. You are so fucking beautiful, sweetness." Joar presses himself against the length of my body. He runs his hands up and down my back, grips my ass and lifts me effortlessly. My legs wrap around his waist and my arms wind around his neck as his cock lines up with my core.

The underside of his shaft is nestled between my slick pussy lips. So, so close to being inside me. I can't help but undulate, desperate for this man. "I'm on the pill," I cry out. "I'm clean."

"I am too," Joar pants as he rocks me up and down against him. "I'd kill to be inside you bare."

"Then do it. Fuck me, Joar. Fuck me all night long. Fill me with your come," I scream, not recognizing the woman who spews out the words of a porn star. I can't help it. It's what I want.

What I *need*.

And I'm not afraid to ask for it with him.

Strength ripples from his sinewy muscles as he carries me down the hall to his bedroom. Our mouths are melded together. The sounds we make border on animalistic. I squirm against him until finally the tip of his cock finds its way inside my pussy. I lock my ankles around his lower back and relax completely, allowing him to push all the way in.

"Holy. Jesus," Joar keens as we burst into the bedroom, connected at last. He turns and presses my back against the wall with his entire body, supporting my legs under his arms. I'm impaled by his thick length as he thrusts, circles his hips and roots his way deeper than I ever thought possible. At this angle, his crown slams against my cervix and hits the sensitive bundle of nerves just above my G-spot.

He does it over and over until I'm mad with desire.

The next orgasm hits me like a freight train. The sheer force of it nearly knocks me out. "*Joar*," I hear myself cry repeatedly, but he doesn't let up. He pounds into me like a jackhammer. I'm riding wave after wave until I seize around him again, this time clenching so tight that he has no choice but to spill inside me.

He grunts and shouts through his own release, continuing to rock into me as we recover from the most monumental sex of my life. Our bodies are almost on autopilot, moving together in tandem. His cock remains inside me, pulsing and twitching, like it's meant to live there and doesn't ever want to leave.

Like we're two pieces that fit together perfectly.

Because we do.

Joar kisses my entire face as he carefully eases my legs down one by one. I nearly fall because my body feels like jelly. "I've got you, sweetness." He helps me across the room to his masculine, wood-planked custom bed adorned with platinum and cream-colored bedding. It must be a double king.

He pulls back the soft cloud of a comforter and settles me against the pillows, turns and walks toward a door and disappears inside. I'm not sure whether to snuggle under the softest sheets I've ever felt or ogle him when he returns. I opt for both and pull the silky cloth to my nose so I can peek out and watch for him.

From behind the door, I can hear a faucet running for a moment. Joar reappears in the doorway, a silhouette against the bright light of the bathroom. He's a muscled god, easily the best-looking man I've ever seen. A man who's laser focused on me as he saunters toward me confidently, his cock still partially hard, bobbing against his belly.

Joar sits next to me on the side of the bed, peers down and tugs the sheet away from my body. "Are you trying to hide from me?" he teases. "Let me clean you up."

"I can do it." I reach for the warm washcloth.

His palm splays along the side of my face. "Please. Let me take care of you. I have a lot to make up for..." His voice cracks then recovers. "How is what just happened between us possible? Did you feel it?"

He watches me intensely. Seeking confirmation.

Approval.

"It was perfect," I whisper and hold the comforter down and away from my body so he can wipe the remnants of our release from my belly, thighs, and pussy. He's gentle. Loving. The intimacy of the act nearly makes me cry.

No one has made me feel this way, ever. I bite my bottom lip, trying to keep it from quivering. Trying to process what we just shared. It was magical. Extraordinary.

Don't get used to it.

Joar climbs in next to me so we're face-to-face. Wraps his arm around me to tuck me firmly against his chest. He kisses my nose. "I'm so happy you're here with me."

"You're an incredible lover, Joar." My heart beats wildly. The air is charged with something more than the passion we just shared, but it scares me. I have to keep perspective.

Joar chuckles, seemingly oblivious to my urge to diminish making love into a hook-up. "I know I have a lot to prove, Clover, and I plan on it. Tonight, I'm giving you exactly what you asked for. I'm going to fuck you all night long. Are you still on board?"

"Oh..." I'm silenced by Joar's mouth as he devours me. The man can *kiss*. He sucks on my tongue and I melt into him like butter. Our hands roam everywhere as we work each other up in our cozy little cocoon.

He pulls my leg across his torso and urges me to straddle him. "Ride me, baby," he coos when I oblige. He guides his cock inside me. "I've been dreaming about watching your luscious tits bounce like this for months."

"God, Joar." I rise up on my knees and sink back down, making sure my boobs jiggle. "You feel incredible."

Joar suddenly grips my ass to hold me in place. "Stay put. Let me drive or this will be over before it starts." He rocks me back and forth. Thrusts up into me. "It might surprise you, but I've never had sex bare before. I'm losing my mind with how fucking miraculous your pussy feels right now."

"How about now?" I cup my breasts. Circle my hips in a figure eight, ignoring his directive.

Joar's eyes track my fingers, which are now pinching my nipples. Then lifts his shoulders to watch where we are joined. "Fuck, baby. You do it for me. I don't even think you realize how much."

"Yeah. Yeah. How about you rub my clit?" I close my eyes to try to ignore his sentiment, which I can't handle. It's too much. I'd rather get lost in our sexual connection. I'm overflowing with Joar. He circles my nub with his thumb. My nipples tingle. Pressure builds. This orgasm isn't an explosion, it's a rolling, full-body tremor. My back arches. I feel it in every nerve ending from the tips of my toes to my scalp.

I'm moaning. Sobbing. Wailing. I bite my lip to stop the tears, but I can't.

So much for not giving in to sentiment.

"Shhh. Clover. Baby," Joar whispers. "You're breathtaking when you come. Please... I want to get you there again." He spreads my pussy lips with his thumbs. "Give me your hand. I want you to feel my cock stretching you."

"Oh, I feel it." I practically giggle through my tears but allow him to place my fingers at the root as he pumps up into me. "God, you're so thick. I'm still not sure how you fit in there."

His breath is more labored now, I can feel him straining. Waiting for me.

"I'm so close, so close," I cry, throwing my arms over my head so my breasts jut out.

He pinches my nipples hard. My eyes squeeze shut. It's not enough. I'm frantic. Gyrating. Chasing. It's right there. I need something...

When I look down at him in desperation, I find him studying me. "Let me." He skims his hands around my body. Flattens his hands against my lower back. Presses me down against him. Rocks me back and forth. "Just relax, sweetness. We have all night."

Our eyes lock. "Okay. I trust you."

"Clover." Emotion floods him and he stills inside me for a moment before gently shifting me on his cock in increments. Expertly reading my reaction because he knows precisely when my clit hits his pubic bone just right. "Yes. That's it."

Joar moves me back and forth. The stimulation is so overwhelming, so thorough, I have to brace myself with my arms on either side of his head. My breasts sway above his lips, allowing him to suck on my nipples as our bodies slap together.

"Omigod, Joar. What is happening?" I start losing my grip on reality again. The pleasure is so all-consuming.

How can it get so much better every time we fuck?

How?

Joar can't control himself anymore. His hips are all over the place, bucking and thrusting. His head thrashes from side to side as he rocks me faster and faster. I bear down, clenching my teeth because I can't help it. My body is trying to suck Joar inside of me entirely.

Suddenly, it's like dynamite blows up. We both erupt until I'm overflowing with our combined release, which pools and trickles between us.

Many minutes later when I'm barely semiconscious, I flop to Joar's side, exhausted.

He rolls toward me and envelopes me with his big body. "In the interest of transparency, I want to go all caveman on you right now. Tell you I'll never let you leave. Tie you to this bed. But, I'm not going to pressure you. Or make demands. Or steamroll." He kisses the side of my head. "I'm letting you take the lead. You giving me your trust means something. I trust you too, Clover. We have something of value here. I hope we've turned a corner and you want to see where this can go."

"I'm happy, Joar. For now, can we leave it at that?" I'm so comfortable right now, I have no plans to bolt.

I also have no plans to stay.

I must live in the moment. Do what feels right to me in real-time. As much as I want this to be something, Joar has more to prove. Tonight's a first step, but I'm not going to jump in blindly.

Impulsiveness leads to bad decisions. Like marrying a powerful man who wants you as arm candy. And a cock vessel.

He squeezes me to him. "I'm happy too."

I nestle back against him. Close my eyes. Let myself relax.

Let myself believe this is real for a few minutes.

Chapter Twenty

The Next Morning

When I wake up she's not in bed with me.

Which is more disappointing than I could ever imagine.

I almost don't want to get up to discover she's gone home. I should just stay here where my sheets still smell like her. Mentally replay our night of marathon sex like a movie reel.

Except...the smell of bacon wafts into the room. Is that...coffee?

I'm up like a shot and don't even bother to put my clothes on. I pad down the hall into the vast open-plan living space and cross over to the kitchen. Clover is fussing with something on the stove, wearing nothing but one of my T-shirts, which hits her mid-thigh. The cotton stretches tight across her juicy ass. My dick takes notice, hardening against my belly.

"Don't sneak up behind me and try to stick your cock where it doesn't belong. I take breakfast seriously, even if I hate cooking," she admonishes without turning around.

I chuckle just loud enough for her to hear. "You're giving *me* a hate date."

She bursts out in laughter. "Don't get ahead of yourself, Joar. I just figured if I'm ever going to cook, it might as well be in this dream of a kitchen." She peers back over her shoulder. Her hair is tied up in a messy knot. Her face is freshly washed, no makeup. When she smiles, she lights up the entire room, which is already filled with sunshine.

"In all seriousness, you don't have to cook for me." I ignore her warning about my cock and stand behind her. Grind against her ass as she stirs a pan filled with some sort of egg mixture. "How 'bout I fuck you from behind while you scramble the eggs?"

Her entire body shivers. "I'll pass. But...how about I ride your big, fat cock and feed you these eggs?"

She's my dream woman. Holy fuck.

"That works." I kiss her neck. Suck it a bit. My hands run along her sides and I slip one under the T-shirt to find her pussy bare and wet. "For the record, it's JJ to you, Clover. *Only* you."

She slaps my hand away to no avail. "Fine. My God, you're relentless. Stop it. You're distracting me."

"Admit it's a *good* distraction." I nip her earlobe and flutter my finger on her clit. Bring my free hand up to her luscious breast and pinch her nipple through my T-shirt. Her head lolls back against my chest.

"Joar..." She's breathless as I keep up the pace. "I don't want this to burn."

I pump my dick against her ass. "*JJ*," I correct. "Take it off the heat. I'll make you come within a minute. Two tops. Then you can finish and I'll take you up on that fucking-me-while-feeding offer."

"Ohhhhhh...kayyyy," Clover moans low and sexy.

She's dripping all over my fingers. I apply more pressure to her little nub and rub her in tight circles. Pinch her nipple hard. She explodes, bucking against my hand. I lighten my touch until it's scarcely a feather on her clit. She shudders through an aftershock. Two. Clenches her thighs together, trapping my hand.

"That's it, baby." I withdraw my hand when she finishes. Suck and lick my fingers clean. "Delicious appetizer."

She's flustered, but manages to shake it off. "You're insatiable, *JJ*. Go. *Get away*." She shoos me. "Sit down and take that abomination of a cock away from my ass. I want to finish making you breakfast."

"This abomination is here for one purpose. To live inside that sweet, wet pussy of yours. Or, maybe your hot, smoldering ass." I smirk, yet do as she asks. Kind of. I pull the chair directly into her line of sight. Sit and stroke myself as I watch her cook.

Her eyes flick to my hand expertly working my shaft as she shuffles a few pans. "You're going to be the death of me."

"Just keeping him awake." I lean back a bit. "Not that he needs any help with you around, sweetness."

Clover dramatically holds up a hand in front of her eyes to shield her vision. I can't help but laugh. She remains focused, and it's clear she's adept in the kitchen, despite proclaiming that she hates to cook. Within minutes, she hovers over a plate, sprinkling things. Arranging. Wiping the edges with a paper towel. "I'm done. Are you hungry?"

"I am. And excited for the fucking and the feeding as you can plainly see." I stroke faster, rub a bit of pre-come around the head of my dick.

Clover turns and stops for a second to watch me fist myself. Grabs the hem of my T-shirt and pulls it up and over her head. Her nipples are tight and puckered. She licks her lips. Picks up the plate loaded with eggs in one hand, a fork in the other. Strides toward me in her naked, curvy glory. The sun catches her blue eyes and they appear to sparkle when she reaches me. "*Yes*, Mr. Demanding. Your *wish* is my command."

I grasp her hips with both hands and guide her to straddle my lap. She balances the plate while I position my crown against her opening. She bends her knees and takes all of me in one motion.

"Oh, *fuck*." I didn't expect her to be so bold.

She shifts from side to side slightly until she sighs with contentment when her body adjusts to accommodate my size. Plants her feet on the floor. Scoops up a forkful of her concoction and hovers it close to my lips. "Taste."

Clover feeds me a bite of the most flavorful eggs I've ever had. Creamy, almost like a more decadent potato puree. Spicy. Buttery. Crunchy with tiny bits of bacon and slices of green onion. "Delicious." I lick my lips.

Clover clenches and releases my cock in her pussy while she forks eggs into my mouth, taking a bite herself every now and then. Her taut nipples brush my chest. When the plate is empty, she sets it down on the table next to us. Threads her fingers through my hair and starts moving. Rolling her hips. Squeezing her thighs. "Not a bad way to enjoy breakfast, huh, JJ?"

"God, I like when you call me JJ." I jerk my hips up to emphasize the point.

She presses the side of her head against the top of mine. My fingers dig into her hips as I guide her to stand. I turn her so she's facing away from me and pull her back down on my cock, reverse-cowgirl style. This position allows me to have freedom to stroke her body. Her sides. Her thighs. Her waist. Her arms. Clover's back is pressed to my stomach. Her head lolls back on my shoulder. I cup a breast. Roll her chocolate nipple between my thumb and forefinger. Splay my other hand along her belly and press her against me so hard I can feel my cock pumping up inside her.

Clover flings her arms above her head and loops them back around my neck. In that moment I know she's giving me her trust to take over, and it means everything. "I've got you, baby."

"How do you know my body so well?" she purrs as I change my angle to hit the spot that makes her go off like a rocket. "You know how to make your cock hit me in the exact right place. Every. Single. Time."

Because this is fate.

I almost say it out loud but decide against it. Her walls are still firmly up and I'll need to work hard to knock them down.

For now, we have this—fucking. Our bodies were made for it.

My finger dips down to circle her clit. "We fit. Your body is so beautiful. *Everything* about you is *so* beautiful."

"Omigod, Joar." She comes apart. I follow, shooting my seed deep inside her.

I tighten my arms around her to keep her upright and impaled. "I may need a nap," I say as I kiss her cheek.

Her hand sneaks down to where we're connected. She rubs the base of my cock with her finger. "Sure, as long as naps mean more of this."

We kiss and stroke each other for a while until I soften enough to slip out. Clover climbs off me and walks toward the bedroom, gesturing for me to follow her into the master bathroom.

"What do you have planned now?" I tip her chin up and kiss her fully on the lips when we end up in the master bathroom.

She steps into the custom triple-sized walk-in white-marble shower. Turns on all of the jets. When the temperature is to her liking she motions for me to join her. "I'm drenched in come. Will you clean me up?"

"Fuck, yeah." I pick her up and step into the shower. Set her back down so I can grab some of my pine-scented body wash and squirt it all over her. Taking my sweet time, I massage the gel into her arms, breasts, stomach. I rinse her thoroughly. Shampoo her hair. When she returns the favor, I realize I've never showered with a woman I'm falling for. It's so intimate. *Sexy*.

Clover sits on the wide tile bench. "Come here, JJ. I want to suck your cock until you're hard. Then, I'll bend over this bench so you can eat me out from behind. It's your choice if you want to fuck me against the wall or if you'd prefer to jack off all over my tits and face. I'm good with either."

I can't even speak. My dick fills instantaneously.

The nasty dirty talk is, quite possibly, the most arousing foreplay I've ever had. I love that she asks for what she wants. I can picture it. Want to make it happen. All of it.

"You're the perfect fucking woman, Clover Callahan." I press my dick against her lips and she engulfs me with her mouth. I thread my fingers through her wet hair and watch her lips stretch around my cock. Each time she blows me, I can't believe how much better it is than I ever imagined. "I don't want to choose. Let's do all of it. Every single thing."

An hour later, Clover lies against my chest. Softly snoring. Naked, except for the towel wrapped around her hair. I trace my finger lightly along her shoulder, imagining what it would be like if she were with me all the time. Living together. Making a life together.

Phenomenal.

That's what it would be like.

Now, I just need to convince her.

Chapter Twenty-One

Six Days Later

I burst through the garage into my house like a bat out of hell.

Jog up the stairs to my office. Grab my iPad. It's dead. I plug it in and wait. While it's charging, I change into sweats. Make a pot of tea.

Catch my breath.

I'm running on adrenaline, not quite sure what compelled me to flee JJ's this afternoon like I was being held captive. Other than things got too intense.

When he was on a business call, I bailed.

Without saying a word.

Not my finest moment, to say the least. I guess I've still got a lot of emotions to unpack.

Returning to the den, I take a minute to regroup. Admire the workmanship in my favorite room. Over the past few months, I've completely renovated the house to get rid of all of the bad Harrison juju. My final project was this old, stodgy office, which is now painted white and features wall-to-wall bookshelves filled with colorful romance novels. An electric kettle with a ton of mugs for tea. Two overstuffed, double-sized chairs. A pile of cozy blankets.

My own little BookTok slice of heaven.

From the time I was on my own in Hawaii, there's not much I've loved more than getting lost in a romance novel.

I've read the sexiest, most erotic books with the most creative backdrops and scenarios. Motorcycle clubs, hockey players, firefighters, small towns, rockstars, vampires, reverse harems, tattoo parlors, restaurants, bars, snowboarders...you name it, there's a romance novel about it.

I'm obsessed.

Though I have a new personal favorite trope now. *Billionaires.*

Talk about relating. I couldn't believe it when I stumbled on a treasure trove of authors who write about insanely wealthy men. Up until my sexathon with JJ, I'd been voraciously reading for the past three weeks. At first, I told myself it was to prove that my aversion to men with money was justified. After all, in my experience, billionaires are arrogant assholes. Selfish pricks. Womanizers. Cheaters.

Just like my ex.

The fictional billionaires all have reasons for their arrogance. Are secret philanthropists. Workaholics. Loyal. Excellent lovers.

Just like JJ?

Yes and *no*. Just like *Joar*.

Omigod. I had to get away from him. Take a sex break. I've spent almost a week in his stunning penthouse apartment. Mostly naked. Generally fucking. Or sucking. Or cuddling. Sometimes sleeping. I've never had so much sex in a six-day time span. Or a month time span. Maybe even a six-month time span.

I'm sex drugged.

Scared shitless.

Catching too many feelings. Too fast. Too intense.

Tonight, I needed to be alone. To curl up with a book. Give my tender pussy a rest. Get some perspective. Because I've been sucked right into Joar's vortex just like I was afraid of.

I feel out of control, like I'm hurtling into my next great heartbreak.

At some point, he'll get tired of me and move on to the next conquest. Or, he'll leave for a month to work on some mysterious acquisition in London.

Either way...

My phone buzzes. I glance at the screen. It's Joar. I let it go to voicemail. Then, shut it off. Place it away from me on the desk and return to my book.

For a few hours, I manage to get lost in the tragic tale of a beautiful woman who is evicted from her apartment, then rescued from homelessness by three mysterious but handsome billionaire best friends, who happen to be searching for a female they can share.

My first reverse harem book is eye-opening. It never even occurred to me that one woman could have two cocks in her pussy and one in her ass. Although, Joar is so hung he's the size of two average-sized cocks, so I'm able to more than imagine it.

Annnnndddd. I'm horny.

So, so horny.

Why did I leave his apartment again?

Right. To take a sex break. Get some perspective.

I retrieve my phone and see I've missed at least ten calls from Joar. I also have multiple unanswered texts.

4:45: Clover, where are you?

4:50: Did you leave?

4:51: Your purse and phone are gone. WTF?

5:10: Sweetness, I'm worried, did something happen?

6:22: Please call me.

6:25: Jesus fuck. I'm going out of my mind. Please fucking call me.

6:48: Did I do something to piss you off? Talk to me.

7:18: Goddammit Clover. I'm losing my fucking mind.

7:19: This is so frustrating. I don't know whether to be scared or pissed.

7:30: Pissed

7:47: Fuck this. I'm coming over. I'm going to find out if you're okay.

7:50: Leaving. Be there in 20

Oh no. He's furious. What was I thinking by just leaving without saying a word?

I know the answer. The truth is, I panicked. I knew he was going to talk me out of it. I needed to catch my breath.

I'm a grown-up though. After the beautiful week we spent together, I should have let him at least know I was leaving. Expressed what I needed. *Maturely.*

Would he have let you leave, though?

I glance at the time. He should be here any minute. I decide not to look in the mirror. There's no time to do anything about how I look anyway.

He's seen it all at this point. I haven't worn makeup in days. Or clothes, for that matter.

I hear the buzzer to my gate. Taking a deep breath, I answer. "Hello?"

"*Let. Me. In.*" Joar's raspy voice is seething.

With a heavy sigh, I unlock the gate using my remote. I'm not frightened. Not for my safety, that is. Mostly, I'm scared about my emotional well-being. If I get too attached, this guy has the power to devastate me. I feel things with Joar that I've never...

Shit. Despite every red flag, I let it happen.

We need to have a conversation. He's here. Might as well get it over with.

Not like I have any choice.

From where I'm waiting in the foyer, I hear the door to Joar's car slam. Heavy footsteps approach. The doorbell rings.

"Hi, Joar." I make sure to look him in the eye when I open the door. Use his full name deliberately.

"What. The. *Fuck?*" He steps inside and slams the door behind him. "Why would you leave like that?"

I have no excuse. Nothing to say. All of my reasons—excuses—seem petty and immature right now. Because they are.

"Words, Clover. Please use them." He stands before me, palms extended.

"I panicked. I'm sorry I worried you. Or pissed you off." I pinch my nose with my fingers. "I needed some space and now I've made everything weird. Would you like to come in and have some tea with me? I owe you an adult conversation."

His anger dissipates slightly. "If something had happened to you, sweetness..." His voice hitches.

"Physically I'm fine. Mentally, not so much. Come with me." I hold out my hand.

He hesitates but places his hand in mine. I lead him through the foyer into my reading oasis. Pour him a cup of tea and gesture for him to take the chair opposite mine. He looks around the room, confused. Awed. "Wow, this is something."

"It's my sanctuary. I come here to get lost in my books. For years, I hid them from Harrison. Now, I'm embracing the things I love." I gesture around the room.

He stands and looks around. Pulls out a book. Studies it. Puts it back. Repeats. "Are these all romance books?"

"Yes." I sip my tea and watch him.

He sees the book on my chair. "What are you reading now?"

"It's reverse harem." I hold it up. "Three men. One woman."

His face says it all. He's shocked senseless. "Is that your *fantasy?*"

"Yes. Yes it is," I say with a straight face.

His eyes hold mine, but he doesn't say anything. It's like he's searching for *what* to say.

"Good thing my lover has a cock so big it's like having three at once." I smile sweetly, exaggerating just a little.

Joar shakes his head. "*Clover.*"

"I'm sorry. Really." I tilt my head. "I got in my own head. Felt a little trapped."

He winces. "*Oh.*"

I let the silence sit there between us. I'm not compelled to overexplain like I used to when Harrison would get mad about stupid little things. I own my shit. But, I don't need to apologize for my feelings. Only my actions. "I should have said something. It was disrespectful and immature of me to grab an Uber when you took that business call."

"I thought we were having a great time. I've never, in my adult life, blown off work for nearly five days. I certainly haven't ever wanted to spend time with someone more than I wanted to work." He buries his face in his hands, then looks up at me with those probing violet eyes of his. "Did I read this wrong?"

I pull my knees up to my chin and wrap my arms around my legs. Classic protective stance. "I don't know."

"What?" He looks stricken.

"You're making me feel things, Joar. Things I'm afraid of. I heard you talking about leaving for London and realized that we were living in a fantasy sex bubble." I press my face into my knees.

He moves from his chair to the edge of mine. "Fantasy sex bubble? What the fuck is that?"

"The thing that happens when you have mind-blowing sex. Probably the best of your life. All you want is to do it again and again and again. Days go by. You don't see anyone or anything but him. Everything else ceases to exist. You catch feelings that aren't real because the fantasy sex bubble isn't reality." I gesture wildly, trying to make my point.

Joar catches my arms. One by one. Threads his fingers with mine. "The feelings are real, baby. I have them too."

"But we *can't*, Joar." I try to pull away, but he holds fast. "You and I won't work. I'm sorry if I led you on. I just can't do it. Go down this path again with a man like you. I can't lose myself. It's taken too much of my emotional energy to rebuild after the divorce. I won't survive it."

He's confused, that much is clear. "I don't understand what you'd lose about yourself. Please talk to me."

"Have you ever had a long-term relationship? You've never mentioned one." I manage to pull free. Touching him messes with me. I want to jump into his lap. Kiss him. Drag him to my bedroom and pull out my vibe so we can recreate my reverse harem book.

"No. you already know this. I've never been married or engaged. But, I've certainly dated many women over the years. All you have to do is fucking Google me." Joar's slightly offended. "For fuck's sake, Clover. I'm nearly forty-eight years old. I've been a little busy building my company."

"Yeah. You're also a confirmed bachelor. I'm almost thirty-three and was married for a decade. Don't you see? We're in different places in our lives." I shake my head.

He's stricken. "Why does any of that matter?"

"Because you'll want everything I have to give." My true fears spill out unwittingly. "And I'll give it. That's who I am. But, you won't. I'm not an idiot. Your wealth and influence rivals Jeff Bezos... Or the Murdochs. I'm just another deal to close. What happens when you succeed?"

"Wow. Okay. Good to know. Glad you have such a high opinion of me." He stands. Jaw set. Glares at me.

I know I've gone too far. At the same time, the man has essentially had a tail on me since we met—no, even beforehand. When he still thought I was involved in Harrison's shady business dealings. He showed up at every location I had a date. Then he tricked me into going on a date with *him*.

This man's been pursuing me in one way or another for almost six months. We've fucked. A million times at this point. But what does he want now? Marriage? Babies?

No. I'm sure that's not remotely on his mind.

"This morning I overheard you on your call. You're leaving for a month. You should go. Acquire your media whatever." I shake my head sadly.

Because whatever this is, it's over.

It has to be.

I'm not going down this same, sorry road again.

Chapter Twenty-Two

The Same Night

I stare at her in disbelief.

So far, I've held my anger at bay.

Mostly.

When I got off my call this morning after finalizing my London schedule, I'd been looking forward to spending the entire day with Clover. I didn't realize she overheard my travel plans before I had the chance to tell her myself tonight.

Shit. I understand why she's confused by my intentions.

Of *course* I want her to know she's more to me than just sex. Of *course* I want us to take our relationship to the next level.

A committed, secure, officially exclusive level.

I'm perceptive enough to know that if I say it now, it will seem disingenuous. We need more time together so I can gain her trust and show her who I really am. Clover needs to realize I'm not even remotely like her ex.

So *no*, this is not ending. She doesn't get to run away because she's scared.

"You're not pushing me out of your life," I state simply.

She curls into herself. "I think I should, though."

"No. We're just getting started. This isn't ending. Not until we see where it takes us." I take a step toward her.

"Joar. Listen to yourself. I don't want to be in the kind of relationship where it's you controlling me. Telling me how it is." Clover starts to cry. "This year was supposed to be about figuring out who I am. How to survive on my own. Instead I'm getting caught up in this...whatever it is with you. If I don't set up boundaries—like the other day with Isis..."

For fuck's sake. Isis Management and Talent Agency is one the many companies in my portfolio. I casually mentioned it to Clover as a potential option when she mentioned she wants to change her agent. "Seriously? That's why you bolted? Because I suggested you sign with my agency?"

She squinches her nose. "No, not entirely, but you have to admit it was a little, uh...*patriarchal?*"

Ugh. Direct hit. "So, because I'm older than you. Own a company that's the best in the industry and want you to have access to it, that's being patriarchal? *Huh.*"

"Don't '*huh*' me." She raises her voice, startling me.

I throw my hands up. "*What did I say?* I'm genuinely confused."

"God, you're so *intense.*" She sits on one of her over-sized chairs. "You have to admit, the circumstances surrounding us are strange. You've had me investigated, hid your identity, and pursued me relentlessly. This past week we've been more than intimate. You've been inside my body for what seems like hours every day, which heightens the extreme nature of what's going on between us. I'm honestly not sure whether to be scared. Or flattered. Or whether I like you or love you or hate you. I don't know what any of this all means—"

"*Fuck me.* I don't know how *not* to be intense. It's my M.O," I interrupt, realizing the irony of my reaction a half second too late. My voice softens. "Look, Clover. It's how I've accomplished everything in my life. When I set my mind on something, I go into hyperfocus."

She watches me. Tears trickle down her face anew. Fuck. I've made her cry again. I want to wipe them away, but I'm afraid to touch her right now. Afraid she'll end this and I'll lose her.

Being out of control is *not* a good feeling.

Is that what she's trying to tell me?

Is that how I make her feel?

"Why me?" she whispers so softly I'm not sure she realizes I can hear her.

I crouch beside her. Tentatively place my hand on her knee. "You're the most interesting and intelligent person I know. You make me feel things I've never felt. I want you with me. I want to know everything about you. I want to make you proud to be with me." I spew out a bunch of platitudes because I truly don't know how to express what I'm feeling without scaring her.

She doesn't say anything. Just stares at me with water-filled eyes.

"Why *not* me?" I squeeze her knee.

"I can't lose control of my life. It already feels like I am." She places her hand over mine.

I shake my head sadly. "Ah. We're both in the same boat, then."

"You see? This won't work." She attempts to pull her hand away but I hold it fast with mine.

"It can, if we want it to." I rise to my knees. Cup her cheek with my free hand. "Shouldn't we at least try?"

Clover presses her forehead to mine. "Great sex isn't a relationship, Joar."

"I know that." I decide not to press any further. She's tapped out. "It's still early. Could we table this conversation and hang out tonight? No sex. We can do whatever you want. Even pole dance." I'm willing to do whatever it takes to get us to the next step.

Huh. This compromise thing is such an unfamiliar feeling.

She looks surprised. "Really?"

"Yes. I can learn from my mistakes." I lean in and kiss her softly. Chastely.

Clover scoots toward me. "You'd watch a marathon of *Vanderpump Rules* with me?"

"Sure?" Inwardly I cringe, though I'm certain I'm not able to hide my reaction.

"It was on the Hate Date list." She narrows her eyes.

She paid attention.

I change my expression to one of exaggerated joy. "Sure! I can't wait!"

Clover lets out a breath. "Thank you for listening to me."

"Always." I stand and hold my hand out.

"I'm starving. Should we order food?" She allows me to assist her, then moves toward the door and looks back. "Indian? Chinese?"

I'm not falling into any decision traps tonight. "What's your favorite?"

"I'm craving fried rice. Pork dumplings. Almond Chicken." She taps her finger to her lip. "But samosas, naan, and Tikka Masala sounds good too."

I shrug. "Why choose?"

"Why choose?" She looks at me in wonder.

I step toward her and tuck her hair behind her ear. "We can have it all."

"*Joar*..." Her face softens.

"*JJ*." I kiss her cheek. "I *always* want to be your JJ. I think you like him better than Joar."

⸻

Three hours later, we're curled together on her giant sofa watching a blond firecracker named Lala calling out some DJ kid on his shit. I didn't think I'd be into this show, but I'm enjoying it for what it is.

Not that anyone but Clover needs to know it.

She filled me in on the backstory of the show. Apparently, we're catching up on a couple of seasons she missed.

"God, he sucks." Clover jabs her finger at the screen. "Shut. The. Fuck. Up."

"What did I miss?" I rub my hand up and down her arm.

She cranes her head up. "You're not into this at all, are you?"

"Actually, I'm finding it entertaining. Disturbing, but entertaining. I just spaced out for a minute." I squeeze her to me.

"He told Lala that she needs to 'be real.'" She rolls her eyes all the way back into her head.

I kiss her temple. "He's a world-class asshole. I can't believe he's so sanctimonious in his righteousness."

"Ooooh. Big fancy words." She laughs heartily. Pats me on my stomach. "I'd have said, 'what a fucking douche canoe.'"

We look at each other with affection. Genuine, pure adoration. It's instinctive when our mouths collide with insatiable hunger, tongues intertwined in passionate, feverish kisses.

It's animalistic when she rips off my shirt and I shove her pants down to her knees. The rest of our clothes fly everywhere. We're rapturous. Groping. Clutching. Rubbing. Crushing our lips together with impassioned kisses.

I'm breathless when Clover pulls out my cock, which is hard as steel. She bends down and takes me deep inside her mouth. Swirls her tongue along my shaft. Digs the tip into my crown. Strokes my perineum and cups my balls. Soon, my hands grip her cheeks and I'm shallow-fucking her face, making her gag. Careful not to go too far, even though I know she can take it.

She gives the best goddamn head I've ever had.

I'm able to stave off my orgasm, just barely. My fingers pump inside her as my thumb rubs her clit furiously. I twist her body up and to my side so I'm spooning her. Guide my cock into her from behind. Band my arm around her stomach to keep her locked to me as my lips fasten to her sweet spot in the hollow of her neck.

"God, Joar," she moans.

I pinch her nipple and give it a twist. "*JJ.*"

"Ahhhh. Fuck me, JJ," she cries. "*Make* me come. I want to come with your cock buried inside me."

I didn't plan on sex tonight. I really, really didn't. It's futile to resist, though. We're meant to be doing this. "I'm going to fuck your hot little cunt until you cream all over me. Do it, baby. Come on my cock right now."

I piston my hips like a wild man. Press my entire palm against her pussy and massage while my thumb furiously rubs her clit. She spasms so hard, I can feel every one of her clenches against my cock. When she thoroughly lets go, her entire body convulses like she's been electrocuted. Her high-pitched keening cries fill the room as she soaks me. The wet sounds of my thrusts send me over the edge and I empty everything I have inside her with my own banshee cries.

Our bodies move together for a while afterward.

I hold her tightly against me.

It becomes even more clear in this moment why I've never settled down before.

Why no other woman has ever held my interest.

A transcendent connection like ours is once in a lifetime. Sex like ours isn't possible without it.

Does Clover realize this?

Is she going to give us a chance long enough to find out?

Chapter Twenty-Three

Three Mornings Later

It's four in the morning.

We've been back at Joar's house for the past two days. He's sound asleep, softly snoring. Breathing out little puffs of air with his arm is flung over his head. He looks so innocent. *Peaceful.*

When he's *anything* but.

The things he does to my body.

And he's so insanely handsome. I've never been so attracted to a man in my life.

He makes me feel things I never thought were possible. In the sweet moments when we're cuddled up watching TV and feeding each other ice cream, I'm fully convinced Joar wants a real relationship me.

Even though he was pissed at first when I bolted a few days ago, he was also patient, kind, and understanding when I explained why I freaked out.

Our connection is so intense.

Too intense.

It can't be real.

We've slipped right back into the fantasy sex bubble. Haven't worn clothes in three days. Joar takes me to heights I never knew were possible. I think I do the same for him—there's no denying we're magic sexual beings together.

JJ's my unicorn lover. The man who invented Hate Dates. Cuddles like it's his job. Fucks me just the right way.

JJ makes me feel satiated. Fulfilled. Exhausted.

Loved.

Joar's domineering and opinionated. The man who wants to possess me.

Joar makes me feel anxious. Uncertain. Insecure.

Scared.

I turn away from him. Shut my eyes, knowing it's useless. Sleep eludes me because I'm so far out of my comfort zone, I don't know what to do or how to act.

I'm in over my head with no safety net.

Tomorrow, he's leaving on that business trip for an entire month.

I don't know what it means for us. Or if there *is* an us.

My mind whirls with confusion. What is the status of our relationship? Will he fuck someone else in London? Do I have the right to ask?

I'm walking on eggshells. A baby deer navigating the dating world after being married for ten years. I have no idea how to be in a new relationship with a powerful, commanding, enigmatic, bossy man without comparing him to my ex. I swore I'd never be with a man like Joar.

Yet, here I am. Sucked back in.

"Can't you sleep?" Joar's voice startles me. I didn't even notice he woke up.

I don't turn around, afraid to look at him. "No. I'm in that stupid vortex where I'm beyond tired and I'm putting so much pressure on myself to get to sleep, the anxiety of it all is keeping me awake."

"Should I make you come?" He rolls me toward him and kisses my temple. "Would that help relax you?"

I sigh. "Sex isn't always the answer, JJ."

"Disagree completely." He yawns. Looks at me with sleepy eyes. "What's going on in that beautiful head of yours?"

"Do you realize we never resolved anything?" I sit up and turn to face him. "I know it's crazy early in the morning, but..."

He scrutinizes me, probably wondering what the hell is going on with me.

"We need to talk." I crawl over him to roll off the giant bed. Pick up my sundress. Slip it over my head. "This is a clothing-mandatory conversation."

"Okay." Joar squeezes his eyes shut for a second before reluctantly swinging his feet to the ground. He locates his joggers and T-shirt and dresses quickly. "Let's go talk."

He follows me out to the kitchen, where I put on a pot of coffee. "I'm sorry..."

"Don't." He holds his hand up.

"Don't what?" I cross my arms over my chest.

"Start any conversation with 'I'm sorry.'" Joar takes a seat at the counter. His hair sticks up everywhere and his eyes are puffy. He's JJ right now. Vulnerable. Nothing like the powerful man in a suit. "Now all I'm thinking is that you're about to end this."

Crap. Am I?

I decide to be brutally honest. "I don't know."

"Are you fucking serious?" He reels like he's been slapped.

The coffee's done. I stay calm. Take a minute to pour us each a cup. He shoves it away when I place it on the counter. Stares at me with blatant disgust.

I try again to find my words. "Well... Yes, I'm serious. Because I left, you brought me back and once again, we haven't stopped fucking in three days."

"Oh, *hell* no. We're not just *fucking*, Clover." He smacks his hand on the counter. "We've been in perfect sync for over a week except for one day when you got scared. Making love to you is all I can think about. Isn't this a normal part of a new relationship? I'm not going to apologize for wanting to have as much sex with you as humanly possible." He sits perfectly still, his expression can only be described as exasperated.

"What relationship?" My voice quivers.

He stares at me, aghast.

"I'm serious, JJ."

He blinks rapidly. "What do you mean?"

"I'm a mess. I want to know what happens when you go to London. On a trip you never told me about." I wrap my arms around myself. "And—before you say it—I know I don't have the right to ask."

"*What?* Of course you have the right to ask. Who do you think I am?" He shakes his head. Winces as if what he's about to say is going to hurt. "I'm treading lightly, Clover. *Very* fucking lightly. After you bolted that day, I don't want to do or say anything to spook you."

I move toward him. Place my hand over his. "No, JJ. You can't think that way. It means you're not being authentic. Don't manage me. Be *honest*. Otherwise, it feels like you're still trying to close a deal. But, I have no idea what the terms are."

"You. You're the deal I want to close, sweetness. I want to be with you. No terms." His voice is sweet. Caring. He turns his hands and twines his fingers with mine. "I'm sorry I raised my voice. I guess I thought it was obvious. I want us to be together. A couple. Committed. All of it."

Now that he's said the words which linger in the air between us, I'm sad.

I *want* the same thing.

I also know I can't jump into this relationship. Not like this. My gut told me to run a few days ago. Take a break and process.

Because I'm fucking terrified.

God, how do I find the words to tell him? I can't help but furrow my brow.

From his expression of resignation, Joar somehow already understands where my head is at. He lets go of my hand. "*Ah*." He leans back on his chair. "Go ahead. Just say it."

"Fine. When you're in London, I think we should take a pause. I'm going to Seattle to visit Ronni. I'm meeting with CAA. I need a couple of good, solid reading days. This entire thing with you is happening too fast. My head is spinning." I take a sip of coffee. Bite my lip. Brace myself for a volatile reaction.

But no. Joar merely stands and moves toward the window overlooking Wilshire. "What does a 'pause' mean?"

"Focus on your deal in London. I'll have some breathing room to figure some stuff out. I was married for ten years. You're the first man I've..." I catch my breath and redirect. "JJ, here's where I'm coming from. Since before I met you, there hasn't been a time where you haven't pursued me. At first because you hated me. Then because you wanted to fuck me. Now because you want a relationship? It's a lot. I need a small break. A reset." As the words come out, I know they're honest.

True.

I'm taking a huge risk. Asking for time. Honoring what I need.

Because we are not on level playing fields right now. Not even close.

"Got it." He doesn't move from the window. Doesn't look at me.

"Do you?" I throw my hands in the air.

He whirls around. "What do you want me to say?"

"Say you understand." I shake my head. Toe the floor with my bare foot.

He approaches me, his violet eyes narrowed in hurt. "*No.* I will not lie to you. I do *not* understand. Not even a little bit. It's ridiculous. If this means you want to go back to stupid fucking online dates, I can't comprehend what you're saying. At *all.* Not when you're the only woman I want."

"JJ." I take his hands in mine. Look him in the eye. Will him to see my point of view. "Of *course* I don't want to date anyone else. Our physical relationship is unlike anything I ever imagined. It's intoxicating. My desire for you is out of this world." I shake my head slightly. "I just don't trust myself in a new relationship. That's the honest truth. Maybe if our circumstances were different, I'd be able to let go and fall into this whirlwind romance." I squeeze his fingers. "Our history might be short, but it's complicated. I'm so flattered you want us to be together. Can't you let me have a little space to catch up to you?"

He rips his hands from mine. "*Fuck* this. I pour my heart out and you essentially say, 'It's not you, it's me'" He storms across the living room. Turns and disappears into the bedroom.

I knew he'd be mad. Now my stomach's in my throat. I can't keep him. Not like this. I also don't want to hurt him.

It's not like we're in love.

Right?

Tentatively, I tiptoe into the master suite. He's in his walk-in closet packing. He glances up when I appear in the doorway but doesn't stop what he's doing. "You know that wasn't what I meant."

"Whatever." His voice is dismissive. "I just texted Victor. The plane is being fueled early. I might as well get this show on the road." He doesn't look at me. Just holds up a couple of ties like he's deciding on which one to bring.

"This isn't how I wanted this conversation to go." I lean against the door. "This isn't the end..."

"Just stop." He tosses a folded-up piece of paper at me, which falls at my feet.

I pick it up and unfold a printout of two first-class tickets to London on Virgin Atlantic with a post-it note stuck to the front that says,

10 a.m.

My living room

Don't be Late.

A hate date—commercial flight.

"For the record, I planned on surprising you. I'd hoped you'd come with me for a week before our work commitments kicked in. Thought we could explore London. Hang out. Fuck. Make some memories. Be a *couple*." He slams his suitcase shut. "But, *c'est la vie*. You want space, you'll get your space. I'm going to take a quick shower, then I'm getting the fuck out of here before I lose my shit completely."

Holy crap. Did I read the situation all wrong?

Maybe. Maybe not.

The fact remains, I'm the one with residual mental baggage.

I'm the problem. It's *me*.

Before Harrison, this sort of gesture from a man would've been a dream come true. I learned that—at least in my marriage—these kinds of trips have nothing to do with romance. There are always galas or business dinners that I'm expected to attend where I'm supposed to smile. Shut up. Play the perfect wife—er, girlfriend.

Why would this be any different? Joar is a million times more important than Harrison ever was. Who's he kidding? There'd be no hanging out in London doing couple stuff, I'd go and essentially be on my own all day.

At night, I'd be his personal fuck bunny.

So, while I appreciate the *thought* he could shoehorn some romance into his business trip, this gesture cements the fact we are *not* in the same place.

Because I've heard it *all* before.

It's not what I want.

"I should go," I state simply.

"That's best." He's like a stone statue. Devoid of emotion. "No need to prolong the inevitable."

I take a long look at him. He stares back.

"Okay. Have a great trip. Good luck on the transaction thingy." I wave, grab my things and call an Uber to go home for the second time in a week.

Confident I'm doing the right thing.

I was fine before Joar.

I'll be fine after.

Chapter Twenty-Four

Two Weeks Later

When it rains it fucking pours.

Especially in London.

In July. Typical.

I'm trying to pay attention to Basil, the Site Manager, who is rambling on about why construction on the new studio is behind schedule, which means I'm running late for my next meeting. This puts the rest of the afternoon into a spiral. This trip is turning out to be a shit show.

I hold up my hand. "Look. I'm done with excuses. You have one week to get this back on track. Stop nickeling and diming on stupid shit." I kick the ground. "We have hundreds of millions of dollars of productions in the balance, Basil. If you don't turn it around, I'll find someone who will. Count on it."

With that proclamation, I storm back to my waiting car. Seth is hot on my heels. "Joar, hold up."

"I don't want to hear it." I keep moving without turning around.

He catches me right before I slide into the back seat. "There's trouble brewing, I just need you to slow down for a goddamn minute."

"What the fuck else?" I whirl around.

"Finklestein is trying to make a deal with the feds. He wants to turn on Kircher and the rest of them to get less time. Claims he has some damning evidence." Seth squints. "Also claims he has surveillance footage of you and his ex-wife."

"Get in," I growl.

He scoots into the seat next to me. "Do you think she set you up?"

"No." I shake my head. I've avoided all things Clover for two miserable weeks. No calls. No texts. Nothing.

I may not know much when it comes to her, but I do know she's not involved in Finklestein's bullshit.

We sit in silence for a good ten minutes as the driver maneuvers through London traffic to get me to the next meeting. I think about what Seth said. Fuck. It's time to stop pining for a woman who'll never be mine and use logic and reason. From the second I sunk my dick into Clover when we were trapped in the elevator, I haven't been myself.

No, that's a lie. It was the second I saw a photo of the woman who'd been married to Finklestein.

I've been totally obsessed with her.

Ignoring my responsibilities for what? To essentially stalk her? First in Vancouver B.C. Then in LA when she was going on those stupid fucking dates?

And WTF with the personal ad? A fucking hate date? The stupidest goddamn idea I've ever had.

Who the fuck have I become?

I'm *not* this man. No wonder Clover wanted space.

I'd better get a grip on myself.

It's time to put this "you can't trust Clover" shit to bed with my best friend. Once and for all. Even if the only reason is for Seth to have peace of mind.

Maybe then he'll shut the fuck up about her.

"Fine. Put Zed back on the job." I glance up at Seth. Then pull out my phone and scroll through email.

Ignore the bile in my gut for the rest of the drive.

Seven hours later and I'm ecstatic to be back in my suite at the Savoy. I haven't had much time to think about my conversation with Seth about Finklestein. It's been a solid fucked-up day of putting out fires. Keeping things on track. Juggling all the balls.

Now I'm *finally*, blissfully alone. I glance around at ornate but tasteful furnishings in my empty room. This is *not* the life I pictured. Not even close. I never thought I'd be pushing fifty and have no one in my life but staff and business acquaintances.

No parents. No siblings.

No real friends to hang out with other than Seth.

Until Clover.

Who doesn't want me because, as she rightfully pointed out, I have no idea how to separate the best sex of my life from having a relationship. I've never bothered to figure out the difference, I guess. It was never a priority.

I miss her so goddamn much. She makes me want to do better.

It's been fourteen days since I've been inside her. Kissed her. Held her in my arms.

Without her near me, I can't sleep or eat. Every bone in my body aches. I have no idea how to cope.

On my flight here, I was so distraught. I drank myself into a stupor to drown out the demon voices in my head.

It was a miracle Seth managed to sober me up in time for our first meeting.

Stop!

Moping doesn't help. I'm not a fucking *moper*.

I've got a big day tomorrow. Sleep is mandatory tonight. I change into soft cotton shorts. Flip on the TV. Shut it off in disgust. Consider ordering an expensive bottle of fine whiskey to dull the pain and knock me out. Decide against it. The plane bender was a one and done. I've never used alcohol to cope. I'm not starting now.

Flopping down on the bed, I shut off the light and try every trick I know. I stare at the ceiling to count sheep. Instead, I picture myself relaxing in an overstuffed chair in that ridiculous office filled with books. Clover's leaning up against my chest reading some smutty scene to me out loud. I'm caressing her rounded belly filled with our child.

Shaking my head vigorously, I will the image away. It just makes me so fucking *sad*.

I swallow the lump in my throat. I'm trying so hard to honor her. Not stalk her. Give her space.

I'm so lonely, though. Not able to resist another minute, I fire up Instagram to see her face. Pull up Clover's profile. Scroll through her feed to a post of her in Seattle at some restaurant. She's with Ronni Miller and some women who look familiar but I can't place. The caption reads, *So lucky to be at the (soon to be) first Michelin star restaurant in Seattle!*

Fuck, she's stunning. Her long, black hair shines like glass. Full, red lips. Aqua eyes lined in black. Low-cut black sleeveless dress. Strappy high black sandals. Wide smile, like she doesn't have a care in the world.

I guess she doesn't. Clearly, she's enjoying herself.

Enjoying her freedom.

To her, I'm just a blip on her radar.

What if Seth is right and she's playing you?

No. I don't believe it. I *should* leave well enough alone.

Except, that's not in my nature.

And now Zed is back on the job.

You still have time to call it off.

Ignoring my inner voice—for now—I open up my texts. Nothing new. Open up her contact to find her...

Blocked???

What the fuck?

Wracking my brain, I try to figure out when I blocked her. I have no fucking clue.

I tap "Unblock" and hit confirm.

Minutes go by. I don't know what I expected. Maybe a slew of text messages that were sent but never made it? For Clover to magically realize I've unblocked her?

God, this day couldn't be more frustrating.

Except...

Before I can stop myself, I'm doing it. I'm dialing her number.

She picks up on the third ring. "*Joar?*" She's hesitant.

"*JJ.*" My nickname rolls off my hoarse, strained voice.

The silence is thick. Muddy. Oppressive.

Clover breaks the silence. "Are you okay?"

"Uh..." I have to think about it. "No. Not really."

I hear a bit of rustling. "Hang on, I'll go somewhere private."

"I'm bothering you. If this isn't a good time..."

"It's fine. I was just finishing a meeting with my new agent." I hear her call out "goodbyes" to a few people. "Okay. I'm here."

"I'm not sure why I called you," I confess, though I know it's a masochistic need to hear her voice.

She hesitates. "Yeah, the last time you called it didn't go well. You broke my heart if I'm honest."

"What?" I'm stunned. "When?"

"Um. On the plane?" Clover sighs. "You were irate. Told me to fuck off. That you never wanted to see me again."

I pace around the room. Ashamed. Panicked. "I don't remember."

"Well, you sounded very, very drunk so I'm not surprised." There isn't judgment in her statement, for which I'm grateful. There *is* resignation. As if she's used to being treated this way.

Harrison.

Fuck.

I'm mortified. "I can't stop fucking everything up with you..."

"Joar, *stop*..." She doesn't finish her sentence, but I notice she's dropped the "JJ."

I laugh bitterly. Get ready to end the call. "I'm sorry to bother you. I know, I know. You're just not that into me. I heard you loud and clear."

"Um...hold on. Did you listen to *anything* I said that morning?" Clover's voice goes up a pitch. "Because I said no such thing, JJ. I poured my heart out. Confessed my deepest fears about getting lost in a relationship with a powerful man like you before I gave myself time to process what nine straight days of fucking meant."

"That's *not* what I took from our conversation." I'm petulant and, apparently, altogether obtuse. "You said you wanted space."

Clover's voice is tentative. "Yes, I did—do—need that space. To make sure the feelings I have for you are real. That you and I are not living in some sex-hazed fantasy."

"My feelings *are* real. I fucking miss you so goddamn much." I grip my chest over my heart.

She sucks in a breath. "The truth is, I left something unsaid that day. I regret it—but please know I couldn't find the words because I'm petrified..."

The silence between us lingers. My heart thunders in my chest.

"*Please*, sweetness. Say it," I all but beg her. "I'm going out of my mind. I can't function properly. I'm a wreck."

"I miss you so much." She's so quiet, I can scarcely hear her.

"Hold on for one second." I check my settings and connect to Wi-Fi. "Let me see you. I'm FaceTiming."

Seconds later, Clover connects and her face fills my screen. Her mouth opens to speak, but I'm too quick. "Clover you have to know you *are* something to me—so much. I want to give you what you need..."

She holds up her hand to shush me.

I realize I've steamrolled her again by interrupting. I mimic zipping my lips and look at her through the screen. Waiting for her cue.

"I've realized I don't want to be your *something*." Her aqua eyes remind me of a tropical sea in the bright sunshine.

My heart stills. For a minute, I had a modicum of hope she and I had a chance. Now...

She turns her face to the sky, as if she can't face me when she says, "I don't want to be your *something*, Joar. Not when I could be your *everything*."

God, doesn't she know?

She already is.

Chapter Twenty-Five

One Week Later

I just got off the phone with my new agent, Thad Bellamy from CAA. So much good news.

My show just scored a prime Thanksgiving weekend release date. It shows the Netflix executives have tremendous faith in Kris and Ronni. There's no doubt the jury's out on me as a lead, but hopefully I'll change their minds. According to the trades, the series is poised to sit at the top of the charts throughout the holiday weekend.

Thad thinks the second season will be greenlit too. No official word—yet. Hopefully in the next few days.

Most everything that's happening in my career is already in motion. I'm hoping Thad can take things up a notch. He's presented me with a few projects, which

I'm supposed to consider. So far, nothing makes me overly excited. I'd rather wait until the series drops. Why commit to something now when I'll have better opportunities to choose from later?

If Thad's worth his salt that is. He'll be able to negotiate more favorable terms when I'm in demand.

Even though I was technically retired from show business for a decade, I'm a lot savvier now than I used to be.

The doorbell rings. I'm not expecting anyone yet. All I can see through the peephole are flowers. Bright, colorful, exotic flowers. When I set them on the table in the foyer, I open the card.

Be there soon. XO JJ

It's been a week since we laid things out on the table. It released a pressure valve for me. We've FaceTimed for hours before he goes to sleep. Kept things as low-key as possible. The time together—even though we're two thousand miles apart—helped me relax my fears a bit.

Now that I'm paying closer attention, I've been surprised at how naturally lighthearted and fun we are together. Oh, and still sexy. Very, *very* sexy.

At the same time, it occurs to me that not much has *actually* changed. This is how we've always been together.

In the elevator. On the hate date. In our sex bubble.

It's our default.

The difference is, I'm not in my own head second-guessing everything. I'm not going to put that kind of pressure on myself again. I just want to see him. Kiss him.

Fuck him.

It won't be long now, Joar's jet lands any minute.

As if he's reading my mind, my phone buzzes from where it's plugged in beside me. "Hi."

"I'm on the ground. Should be there in a half hour." He sounds out of breath.

Hearing his gravelly voice when I know he's in the same city makes me feel a certain kind of way. "Okay."

"You know I'd have been there a week ago if I had my way," he grumbles. "Now, I know there are conversations to be had. But, it's been nearly four weeks since I've been inside you. I will not be able to wait. Get ready, because I'm not going to be gentle."

My pussy contracts at the thought. I hiss, "*Joar*... If I wasn't horny enough, I sure am now."

"*JJ*..." he guts out.

"I'll text you the gate code. The key's under the mat. Come find me in my room. I'll be waiting." I giggle, determined to keep things playful.

At least for tonight.

He groans. "Naked?"

"Do you want me to be?" I tease.

"Oh, I want more than that." His voice grows even more serious. "Put on those pink pumps from the elevator. Only wear the shoes and your pink bra. While you're waiting for me to arrive, take out that dildo you used on yourself when we *finally* had video sex last night. Get yourself stretched. Ready for me."

Now it's my turn to moan. I made him wait all week, and why exactly? God, he turns me on so easily, it's insane. "*JJ*...."

"Do *not* allow yourself come," he demands.

"But—" I'm in my closet searching for the requested shoes.

He cuts me off. "Do. Not. Come. I'm hanging up. Be there in about ten minutes."

Crap. That doesn't give me much time. I find the pumps and rummage through my lingerie drawer. The pink corset I wore when we were stuck in the elevator was from wardrobe. I didn't take it home with me. The closest thing I have is a pale-pink push-up bra. It will have to do. When I finish putting it on, I step into the heels and lie back on the bed. From my nightstand, I take out my dildo. Lube it up. Insert it. Pump it a few times.

I bend my knees. Gasp when I locate my G-spot. I'm so wet, every time I pump the plastic shaft into myself, the sound and smell of my arousal fills the room. Vaguely, in the distance, I hear the front door open and shut. I'm in the zone, though. Bucking against vibrations. Trying desperately not to come.

"Look at that pretty little pussy all filled up," Joar snarls as he tears his shirt off. "I'm going to fuck you so hard right now, sweetness. Say it's okay."

I beg him, "Hurry, JJ. Hurry."

Joar's naked in seconds. Crawling up the bed in between my legs. The stubble on his face is thick, nearly a beard. His shaft is like a missile, homing in on my body. "Give me that." He pulls the dildo out of me and throws it to the floor. "Now that I'm home, *my* cock's the only thing I want inside you." He pushes my legs up with his palms and slams inside me to the hilt with one thrust.

"Omigod." The pleasure is nearly unbearable. I'm so utterly full. My entire core contracts. I'm not going to come this easily, am I? "JJ...I can't..."

"Yeah. That's it. Come all over me, baby." He hovers above me, hammering his hips like a piston.

And I do. I come so hard, I'm flailing in exquisite anguish.

He's relentless, though. "I'm not letting up on you. Not tonight." He widens his knees and spreads me apart. His hands skate around to grip my hips. In one motion, he pulls me into his lap. I hold on to his shoulders for dear life as he rocks me back and forth on his shaft. I wrap my legs around his waist and hook my feet together. Let him take me. However he wants me.

And he wants me hard. Deep. Pounding. Drilling. Rutting. Whatever the word, it's weeks of his pent-up desire.

For me.

Only me.

I know it without any shadow of a doubt.

"Fuck, *sweetness*. Fuck," he cries out. His face goes slack when he comes. Fills me. Marks me. Buries his head in my neck, still pulsing.

We're intertwined and sweaty, but not nearly satiated.

He's still hard. Ready. His stamina is unbelievable.

I squeeze my thighs around him and lean back slightly so I can see his face. Violet eyes blink hazily. Little silver hairs dot his beard.

"*Hi.*" I stroke the soft hairs on his chin.

"*Hi.*" He frames my face with both hands. Bends so our foreheads are touching. Sips from my lips. Pushes his tongue into my mouth. Moves my head where he wants me as he explores every inch of my mouth. Feathers kisses along my jaw. Sucks the skin close to my ear. All while our bodies move together as one.

Joar raises up on his knees and gently places me on my back. Never losing contact. He covers my body with his, caging my face with his arms. Strokes my hair. Pumps his hips lazily as he drinks me in with his eyes. "You're so incredible. Making love to you. It's all I ever want to do from now on. How do we make that happen?"

"Easy. Don't ever leave me again." I skim my fingers up and down his back and kiss his bearded chin.

He squeezes his eyes shut. Gathers me to him. "I want that, Clover..."

"It's okay, JJ." I touch my lips against his. "Try your best. That's all I ask."

I'm breaking—no smashing—my suit rule. Joar is controlling. Busy. Demanding. Everything I didn't think I'd want in a man.

And yet, now I know for sure.

He's the only one for me.

"You're mine," Joar whispers, breaking me out of my brief trance. "Tell me again that you're mine. That we're together now."

I kiss him deeply. "I'm yours, but you're mine too. We're together. We're going to do this."

"Oh, *baby*." He traces his finger down my collarbone. Cups my breast. Bends his neck to take my nipple in his mouth.

Our bodies sync effortlessly. We're one. Exploring each other with wonder. We've leveled up, somehow.

Nothing's defined, but so what?

This feels so *right*.

We pick up the pace, seeking another high. He's watching me intently. Lovingly. Making sure I'm close. "What do you need?"

"Nothing. I'm almost there," I say dreamily.

He slips a hand between us and rubs my clit. "No almosts. We're a couple now. I want you with me."

I want it too. His touch sends me over. "Now, JJ. Now." I clench around his cock and he lets go when I do.

We're laughing. Panting. Possibly weeping a little at the intensity.

Moments later, he cradles me to his body in what has become my favorite position. "I swear, being with you is my dream come true."

"Me too." I circle his flat, brown nipple with my finger. "I want this so much."

"You're not spooked?" He kisses the top of my head.

I crane my head up. "Surprisingly, no."

"You'll tell me, though? Talk to me if this scared-rabbit thing happens again, right?" He looks worried.

I lean up and capture his lips. "What would I get spooked about?"

"Nothing." He returns my kiss. "I'm just making sure."

Despite my doubts, the time apart made me realize being with Joar doesn't have to be so all-encompassing.

We're officially together now.

That's good enough.

Chapter Twenty-Six

A Couple Days Later

Clover's a nervous mess.

The Netflix executives are due to meet and make a decision about her series today. It's entirely possible they'll drop it altogether. Ronni Miller managed to get herself embroiled in yet another scandal that affects the entire show.

Chaos abounds.

She's on the phone with her lawyer in my office. Knowing how stressful this has been, I gave my house staff the night off so we could be alone. I'm filling the oversized tub in the master bath with bubble bath. Candles are lit. Rosé is poured. I have the newest episode of *Vanderpump Rules* ready for her to watch on the iPad.

I love taking care of my girl.

Love it.

I place a Post-it note on the door.

Bathroom. Ten minutes. Don't be late.

Exactly ten minutes later I hear, "JJ?" Clover strides into the bathroom and sees the bath. "Omigod. Did you do this for me? It's a repeat hate date!"

I gather her to my chest. "Who else is in the house with us? I don't drink rosé."

"Thank you." She tilts her face up to mine. I crush my lips against hers. Savor her. Cherish her.

I help her out of her clothes. She's stunning. All creamy skin and curves. My dick hardens as per usual, but I resist the urge to start things up. Instead, I make sure the water is the perfect temperature as she settles in the tub. Hand her a glass of wine.

"You're all set." I turn to leave and let her relax. I know I'm a lot, so I make sure to give her space from time to time.

"Don't leave." Her aqua eyes plead. "Stay with me."

I spin on my heel. "I'd love to. Give me a minute to change out of my suit. I'll turn on *VPR* in the meantime." I hit play on the iPad.

As I'm entering my walk-in closet, my phone buzzes. It's Seth.

"What's up?" I put it on speaker while I undress.

"Zed turned up some insanely incredible shit." Seth is beyond excited.

Fuck. Fuck. *Fuck*.

I hastily grab the phone and turn off the speaker. "Not right now."

"Yes, right now." Seth is stern. "We should get on top of it. I think it involves Clover."

I pinch the bridge of my nose. "*Clover?*"

"Nothing yet, but we're getting closer," he assures me.

I pace back and forth in my closet, phone in hand. "I thought I told you to stop the surveillance on Clover."

"Joar..." Seth warns.

"Do it," I demand. "This is not up for discussion. She's my girlfriend, Seth. She's not involved."

"I say this with the utmost of respect, my friend, but you're one of the most powerful men in the world and you're getting in too deep without finishing this investigation. Be smart. If there's even a miniscule chance she's working with her so-called ex, you could put yourself and your business in complete jeopardy." He tsks.

"JJ?" I hear Clover call from the master bath.

Fuck.

"If you don't call him, I'll do it myself," I growl. "Do not second-guess me on this."

I hang up and slam my phone on the watch cabinet. Throw my dress shirt in the dry cleaning hamper. Grab some joggers and a T-shirt and head back to my sweet girl. I pull up her vanity chair next to the tub. "Sorry, Seth called."

"Everything okay?" She looks up at me. Bubbles float around her neck and shoulders. My heart fills every time I see her.

There's no way she's in cahoots with Finklestein. She hates him. Hasn't talked to him in over a year, from what she's told me.

I believe her.

"Yeah." I point at the screen. "What's Lala up to now?"

Clover takes a sip of rosé and gives me a play-by-play of the show. I listen to her enthusiastic recap. I'm so happy to see that her worries have been cast aside for a bit. That's all I wanted for her tonight.

"Do you want to wash my hair?" Clover takes out her hair tie when the show ends. Her long, black tresses cascade across her shoulders and float around her gorgeous tits. Her brown, puckered nipples are visible above the bubbles. She's my erotic mermaid.

I scoot closer. "Of course I do." I grin. Take the shampoo from her and squeeze it into my palm. Clover hands me the wand. I wet her hair, massage her scalp and gently rinse the soap out. I drag out the whole process on purpose.

Vowing that this ritual will become our new thing.

"I feel so much better. Thank you." Clover swirls her hands around the water, her mood a lot more relaxed than it was earlier.

The water's lukewarm now. Most of the bubbles have dissipated, so her delectable naked body is fully visible. My cock is hard as steel, but I remind myself tonight's not about sex. It's about caring. Snuggling. Chaste stuff.

"You're welcome." I take the bath sheet off the warmer. "Let's get you dried off."

"As long as you get me wet again." She winks as she steps into the warmed cloth I'm holding out for her.

So, maybe sex isn't off the table then.

I wrap her up and tug her to me. "Count on it."

An hour later, we're cuddled together. Sex drunk.

Gently, tenderly, Clover presses her lips against my chest. "I've never experienced such profound happiness, JJ," she murmurs, her voice filled with sincerity. "For the first time in my life, I don't feel alone. You make everything better."

"I feel the same way, sweetness. Being with you brightens my darkest days." I thread my fingers with hers. "I'm glad all of the bullshit is behind us."

Please. Please. Please.

"For the record, take it from me. Everything's going to be fine with the show. They'll air it." I pepper kisses along her forehead.

She turns in my arms so I'm spooning her. "Maybe, but as I'm navigating this situation, I have some misgivings about Thad."

"Oh?" This is music to my ears. I want Clover to have it all and Thad isn't an A+ agent, he's a wannabe poser at best. From what Clover's shared about her so-called opportunities, he's a lazy phone-it-in fuck-tard.

"I'm not greedy. I know Ronni gave me a break I never expected. It's just now that I'm playing a lead, it's a little disheartening for him to talk me into playing supporting characters in low-budget films." She sighs. "I'd rather stay home and read. Of course, I can't say anything while we wait for Netflix to make a decision."

"You don't have to act if you don't want to, baby. I know your folks pushed you into it, but you should do the things you love." Clover and I have slowly, over the past few weeks, made an effort to get to know more about our pasts. One area she's not super forthcoming about is her family.

She stiffens for just a second. "I mean, I have fun with it. I continued to work after I was emancipated at sixteen."

"You were so young." It genuinely pisses me off. What kind of parents were they? I mean, I was at least abandoned as a baby. I've never known anything different.

Her voice is soft. "I had no choice. They spent all my money."

"What the fuck?" I can't help my outburst. What she's gone through is so wrong.

"Yeah. I had to sue them. Got most of it back, thank God. Then I cut them out." She's eerily cold about this.

I hold her tighter so she knows she can trust me. I want to learn about every part of her. "Brothers or sisters?"

Clover sits up suddenly. Faces me. "A brother, but I haven't talked to him in nearly twenty years. Solange was the first person I met in LA. She was like my sister. We did everything together. She was with me when I met Harrison. I'd never have believed..."

"Yeah..." I draw little circles on her knee with my finger. "It's fucked up what she did. What he did."

"I never saw the signs. None. When she sent me that video..." She looks up to the ceiling, then down at me. "Honestly, I was more upset about her betrayal than Harrison's. I swear to God, my stupid BOA Steakhouse date might have had it right. Maybe I should make friends with the chicks on *VPR*. We could get drunk on wine and trade stories and become besties."

"That Sandoval guy is such a douche canoe," I tease. "So...may I ask you about Harrison or would it be weird?" I prop my head up on my hand.

She shrugs. "Only if you don't ask about our sex life. Which, by the way, was pretty much nonexistent the last couple years of our marriage. Made it kind of hard for me to get pregnant and have the family we planned."

The idea of her pregnant by another man makes me want to punch the wall.

"Well, I'm glad you didn't have kids with him." My tone is rougher than I intend.

She smiles wistfully. "I'm glad too. I do want to have children, though. Have you ever thought about it?"

"Not until you. Should I get you pregnant tonight?" I boop her nose.

Clover looks down at her belly. Caresses it. She's beautiful in the dim, silvery-blue light of buildings in the city. Without saying anything, I know she's picturing herself with my baby inside her.

She's not freaking out.

My finger moves up Clover's thigh. She watches me inch closer to her pussy. I decide it's not the right time to talk about her ex. Not while we're in bed together. I decide to ease out of the topic. "Have you heard from Solange? Is she still with Harrison?"

"I have no idea. I haven't heard anything and I don't care. I blocked her. I'm looking forward, not behind." Clover reclines back against the pillow. Flings one of her legs over my hip, opening herself wide.

I lean over and nuzzle her inner thigh. "I think you got the better end of the deal."

"I did. I got you." She moans when my finger sinks inside her.

My lips graze the hollow of where her thigh meets her torso. "Oh, you've got me."

"God!" she cries out when I suck her folds between my lips. Plunge my tongue deep inside her and savor her essence.

There's nowhere I want to be except here, in my bed, making love to the woman I would do anything for. I'm never going to let anyone hurt her. *Ever*. No matter what.

Including myself.

My vendetta against Harrison has gone on long enough. I'm tapping out. No matter what Seth finds, because even though I've told him to stop—I know he won't. He's trying to have my back. I'm going to be relieved when it's all behind us.

As for me, there are more important things in life than what happened to me in foster care. Or, back in college. Clover doesn't dwell on her past. It's an amazing quality. She embraces life to the fullest by living in the moment. Right now, the life she's building is with me.

It's time for me to make some changes.

She's my number-one priority from now on.

Above everything—and everyone—else.

Chapter Twenty-Seven

A Few Days Later

Content.

It's the only way to describe how I feel with JJ. Every fear. Every doubt. *Gone.*

He's my one. While circumstances were not ideal when we met, I think back to the day I saw him at The Cactus Club and our eyes met... Instant connection. He felt it too. We talk about it all the time.

Though our road to getting here has been rocky, for sure, we're where we need to be. By this time next year, who knows?

As long as we're together, I don't care.

This morning Joar left for Sydney for a ten-day business trip. The timing's perfect. I'm on deck to do a ton of prerelease press for *The Boyfriend Experiment* all this month. Not only is the show finally going to air after the delay due to Ronni's troubles, but it also drops next year on friggin' Valentine's Day. And...we've been picked up for another season.

Life is so amazing right now. Better than it's ever been. I'm even happy to be home for a few days after essentially living at Joar's condo for the past month. We've spent a few nights here in WeHo, but considering his office is so close to his place, it saves so much time just to stay there.

Flipping through the mail as I push through my front door, I immediately notice how warm it is. No, it's unbearably hot. I fling the pile of mostly junk on the counter and check the temperature. Sure enough, the air-conditioning isn't turned on. It's friggin ninety degrees in here. When I flip the switch, there's a weird buzzing sound, but the cool air promptly makes a dent in the stuffy heat.

Ahhh.

Tomorrow I'll call a technician to check it out.

Right now I have no time. I've got to change for lunch with Kris Blakely at the Polo Lounge. Settling on a dark-pink Chanel sleeveless shirt dress, nude pumps and a multicolored scarf tied in my hair, I manage to get there a minute before she does.

"You're gorgeous." Kris is one to talk. She's always effortlessly chic. Today she wears a simple black pantsuit with a yellow tank top.

I hug her tightly. "I'm so happy to see you."

We're seated in a prime booth location on the patio. Hollywood movers and shakers are scattered at tables all around us. God, I haven't been here in years. I find myself distracted by all of the celebrities.

"This series is going to catapult you to a new level. Are you ready?" Kris puts on reading glasses and scans the menu.

She expressed this to me throughout filming, so it's not a new sentiment. Sitting here with so many industry people, though, it hits home. "I don't know."

"We should get you into media training. You'll need a stylist. PR." Kris sets the menu down. "Has Thad talked to you about all of this?"

Thad. I can admit it, he fucking sucks. "No."

After we order, Kris subtly points out a man and woman a few tables away. "Sandy Hoffman and Ira Malik."

"I know who they are. They're with Isis Management." I glance at a distinguished man with long, gray hair and a sophisticated woman with a crimson bob who is slightly younger.

"Yes. Why aren't you represented by them? They're the best." She gestures with her fork.

I puff out a breath of air. "Because I was being stubborn."

"Don't be so stubborn that you shoot yourself in the foot. I guess I should ask how it's going with Joar?" Kris looks me directly in the eye. "He's—a lot."

I like Kris, but I don't know her well. Ronni's best friend and business partner has stuck by her throughout her issues, so I know she's trustworthy. She's not my person, though. I go for simplicity. "We're together."

"Oh." She raises her eyebrows. A look of confusion flashes across her face. Just for an instant.

Instantly my hackles are up. She's about Joar's age, did they...?

No.

Please, no.

"Is there something you need to tell me?" My tone is probably more angsty than I'd have liked. That being said, as much as I've grown to trust JJ, I can't ignore who he is.

What he's done in his past.

Kris rests her cheek on her palm. "Oh, God. Clover, it isn't like *that*." She shakes her head. "I've known Joar a long time. He's always been on the right side of things ethically, as far as I'm concerned. A little intense, as you probably know. I'll say this. He's married to his company. Not someone I'd have pictured you with after Harrison."

"Yeah..." I'm relieved, of course and interested in what she has to say, but I'm certainly not going to reveal my private business.

"You know he's had a private investigator following both you and Harrison for the past year, right? Has he told you that?" Kris stabs a piece of lettuce like she's pissed.

Acid pools in my belly. "It was a while ago."

Kris clenches her jaw. Then her face softens. "*Clover...*"

No.

I drop my fork on my plate.

Fuck.

"It's none of my business." Kris takes my hand. "I don't know Joar well enough to judge. I just thought you should know he's having you followed. Probably has to do with your ex."

I nod. Push my plate away because I'm not hungry anymore. Not in the least. "Thank you for letting me know. I'll talk to him."

Kris finishes her salad. I rip a roll apart.

"Have you considered moving over to Isis?" Kris leans back in the booth, deftly changing the subject. "In my opinion, you should get rid of Thad. They'll take good care of you. It's the fastest-growing agency because they do the best work."

I shake my head. "I don't want to mix business with pleasure."

"Bullshit. Pardon my language, but I'm not good at sugar-coating things." Kris takes out a compact and reapplies her lipstick. "I'm going to always tell it to you straight when you're under my wing."

This shocks me. "I'm under your *wing*?"

"Yes." She nods. "I've got your back."

I believe her.

Nothing is resolved when we leave. I'm left feeling confused. Hurt. A little betrayed. I'm trying hard to compartmentalize because I won't speak to Joar until he lands in a few hours.

Retail therapy is the one thing that's going to make me feel better right now.

For the next few hours, I wander Rodeo Drive. Mindlessly shopping in boutiques. Jewelry stores. Lingerie. I spend a small fortune on new designer stuff. On the way home, I stop by Target and buy loads of junk food. Cozy new loungewear. A bikini. A bunch of trinkets. Throw pillows. Candles.

Joar should be landing soon so I head back to WeHo. I turn my Mercedes up the winding Hollywood Hills road. I'm forced to pull over when three firetrucks and several police cars whiz past me. Up the way, I see smoke billowing.

Yikes. Someone's house must be on fire.

I'm about to resume my drive when I notice my dashboard light up.

Joar.

As rattled as I feel, communication is key. I'm not going to play games. "Hey."

"God, how can it be I miss you already?" His gravelly voice nearly breaks my heart.

I'm quiet as I decide what to say.

"Clover? Is something wrong?" He's instantly serious.

"I had lunch with Kris Blakely today." I pull back on the road and head toward home. It will be better to do this where I'm comfortable.

"Oh no, did something happen with the show?" He's genuinely concerned. "Maybe I can do something."

I pull around the corner and head up the steep hill. "No, the show's good. She wants me to sign with Isis."

"Aha! I knew I liked her." He chuckles.

"She also told me you were still having me followed." I make the final turn down the driveway. Omigod no! All the firetrucks and emergency responders are scattered around *my* house, which is thoroughly engulfed in flames. "Omigod JJ!" I scream. "My house is on fire."

I park behind the emergency vehicles and instinctively run toward the front door. I have valuables. Collectibles. Photos.

A firefighter grabs me from behind. "Ma'am, you cannot go any closer. It's too dangerous."

Frantically, I whirl around and notice the hoses trained on my roof. Dozens of emergency workers are attempting to put out the inferno.

"Is anyone in there?" The firefighter who is restraining me asks. "Pets?"

I shake my head. "No."

"Go back to your car. Someone will be right with you to take a report. Do not, I repeat, do not come any closer." He points me back to the car and gets on the radio.

When I slide back into the front seat, Joar is screaming my name. "Clover. Clover. Sweetness. Don't do this. Answer me. Please let me know you're okay."

"Joar?" My voice is emotionless, I feel like I'm floating and watching this scene from above.

I can hear his sigh of relief through the phone. "Thank God. Baby, what is happening?"

"I'm watching my house burn to the ground." Weirdly, I feel entirely detached from the situation. "Looks like I'm homeless."

"One second, baby." Joar's muffled voice is barking orders in the background. "I'm on my way back. We're refueling and I'll be in LA as soon as I can get there."

"Okay," I hear myself say as I watch the flames shoot out my bedroom window.

"I'm not having you followed. Don't believe that." Joar's voice seems so distant. "I love you. I love you so much. I'm never leaving you again. Not for anything. Do you hear me?"

"Okay." I'm suddenly so *tired*. "Oh look. The roof is falling in."

My ears are blown out by a screaming wail as loud as I've ever heard that goes on and on and on.

A guttural cry coming from the depths of my soul.

Chapter Twenty-Eight

Minutes Later

"Clover?"

"Clover?"

"CLOVER???"

Ohmyfuckingjesusgod.

It sounds like Clover is being murdered, her screams are so tortured.

It *kill*s something inside of me.

When the woman you love is suffering and you're not there…

No fucking words.

It won't happen again.

Not on my watch.

I've never felt panic like this.

And there's not a goddamn thing I can do.

Fuck!

By the time Seth and my assistant arrived at Clover's house, the EMTs on the scene had sedated and sent her to Cedars Sinai. The trauma of watching her house burn to the ground sent Clover into shock. Then uncontrollable hysterics. My team made sure she was placed in a private room under an assumed name. The last thing she needs are reporters and paparazzi nosing around.

I've logged nearly sixteen thousand steps on this flight. Pacing the aisle back and forth, waiting for updates. Of which there were precious few.

Her house is a total loss. I'm not able to get any information about the cause of the fire.

The landing gear clicks into place. Thank Christ we're *finally* back in LA.

My blood pressure is through the roof. Never, and I mean *never*, have I been so stressed.

Pure agony is the only way to describe waiting the forty-five minutes until my jet refueled. Unbearable is the only way to describe a fourteen-hour flight when my woman is sedated in a hospital.

As we coast to the gate at the private landing strip, I spot the helicopter waiting on the tarmac. The jet comes to a stop. The crew has been privy to my shit attitude this entire trip so they give me a wide berth when I push past them and bound down the stairs. The pilot waves me over. Hurriedly, I jog to the door at the side and take my seat. Buckle in. We're already confirmed for special clearance on the hospital helipad.

A few hospital personnel are waiting when we land. The second I disembark, I'm whisked downstairs to Clover's room. I peer in the door where she's sleeping peacefully.

"Mr. Jacoby?" A nurse tugs at my suit jacket. "Show me your ID please, then I'm cleared to let you in."

I reach for my wallet to find my pocket empty. *Fuck.*

Frantically, I pat and press all my pockets. Empty. *Fuck!*

"I left my wallet on the plane," I plead with the nurse. "What do you need for me to prove who I say I am?"

A doctor walks up beside her. "Problem?"

"I'm Joar Jacoby. My girlfriend is in that room. I just flew fourteen hours to get here. Can I go in?" I'm about to get on my hands and knees if it will help me get to her.

He grimaces. "I'm sorry, Mr. Jacoby. It goes against hospital policy."

I'm on the brink of losing my shit when I realize my energy in this atmosphere will exacerbate the situation.

"I'll find my ID. In the meantime, how is she?" I keep my voice calmer than I feel inside.

He looks at his clipboard, then back at me. "You're not her family so I'm not authorized to discuss her medical care with you."

Fuck.

Now I'm getting frustrated.

"Clover doesn't have any family. I need to be by my girlfriend's side, so I'm a little stressed." I make sure to appear cool and collected. "Thank you in advance if there's anything more you can do. Or make an exception. In the meantime, where should I wait?"

He points off to an area in the back, where I take a seat on a disgusting plastic couch. Check my phone. Twenty-four missed calls and texts.

I fire off a text to Seth to get my ID from the plane, then I turn my attention back to the task at hand.

Fifteen are work-related calls, mostly because I blew off the meeting in Australia to get here.

A few are from Ronni. As I scroll through them, I'm equally touched, annoyed, and angry by her demands to come back to LA to be there for Clover. Touched because my girl has a real friend looking out for her. Annoyed because her friend has the impression I wouldn't drop everything for the love of my life. Angry because Kris Blakely told Clover about the surveillance. Which is what we were talking about when Clover realized her house was on fire.

I decide to text her while I'm waiting.

Joar: Do you have a problem with me?

Kris: Hi Joar

Joar: My girlfriend is in the hospital.

Joar: You had lunch with her.

Joar: I know what you said.

Joar: Don't fucking play games with me.

Kris: You put a tail on her. I asked why.

Joar: WTF?

Kris: Didn't you?

I don't even bother answering. She's such a fucking know-it-all.

Instead, I text Seth for the millionth time today: *If you haven't already*, get the goddamn tail off Clover.

"Mr. Jacoby. Clover is awake. She's agreed to see you." The nurse from earlier taps her toe impatiently.

I'm up like a shot. I follow her to the room and burst through the door as various technicians are checking her vitals. Her aqua-blue eyes dart to me right away.

She bursts into tears. "JJ. You came back."

"*Sweetness*." I can't help it. I run to her and sink to my knees by her side.

Thankfully, no one makes me leave. They finish up whatever it is they're doing and slip out.

I lean over and press my lips to hers. Engulf her in my arms. She clings to me, sobbing. Her hands clutch me like I'm her lifeline. I want to be that for her. Make sure she has the best care. Pamper her. Do anything and everything in my power to make her feel loved and protected.

And I have a *lot* of power.

When she's all cried out—for the moment, I fear—she pulls away. Blows her nose.

I pull up a chair close to her. "I've been out of my mind trying to get back to LA. I can't stand that I wasn't here for you." I brush the hair out of her eyes.

She sits up. "I feel fine physically. Before you came in, the doctor said they're going to release me soon. I'm sure I collapsed from the shock of it all. I saw my house cave in, JJ." She buries her face in her hands. "I lost everything."

"Baby. *Baby*." I pet her head. There's nothing to say. "I *love* you. We'll figure it out. Have they told you what happened?"

Clover winces. "The air conditioner malfunctioned. Electrical fire. When I stopped home before my lunch meeting with Kris, I realized I'd left the AC off when I was staying with you. I turned it on to cool things down and noticed it made a weird buzzing noise, but I didn't think anything of it. Well, maybe a passing thought to call someone out to look at it. You know how it goes. It was hot. I was late. All I could think about was getting to lunch on time and making sure the house was nice and cool when I got back."

"My God." I pull a chair up close.

Even in a hospital gown, face drenched in sorrow, Clover is the most beautiful woman in the world. I want to climb into bed with her. Comfort her. I'm about ready to do it when her doctor comes in.

"Clover, good news. We're releasing you. I've prescribed some anti-anxiety medicine for you to take as needed." He gives her an empathetic smile and hands me a soft packet. "Your clothes and also a set of scrubs and some slippers to go home in, if you'd like to stay comfortable."

Clover nods. "I appreciate all you've done."

When the doctor leaves, she grips my hand. Bursts into tears again. "What am I going to do? All I have are the clothes I wore to lunch yesterday and a few things I bought yesterday."

"We're just going to my house. Don't forget, you have clothes and toiletries there already, and you can always wear one of my T-shirts. Tomorrow we can get whatever you need." I take out the paper-thin blue shirt and pants. "This will be fine for the ride."

She swings her feet over the side of the bed. I help her up and wrap her in my arms. We sway together for a while. Every part of our bodies presses together. It's the first time I can ever remember being this close to a woman I'm involved with where it isn't about sex.

It's about a deep, all-encompassing love.

The overwhelming need to protect her from all of life's difficulties.

To shield her from danger.

Clover Callahan is my everything. My reason for existing.

Our mouths join. Her fingers rake through my unruly hair. "JJ, I can't believe you flew all the way back."

"Get used to it, baby. This is who we are." My arms wind around her shoulders. Cage her against my chest.

The timeline on our relationship is about to get sped up if I have anything to say about it.

Tomorrow, I'm calling a real estate agent. We're going to find our perfect forever home.

I'll pull in all my connections to find the perfect engagement ring.

I love her.

I'm marrying her.

Who knows, maybe she'll be Mrs. Jacoby sooner rather than later.

Chapter Twenty-Nine

Three Days Later

Trauma.

Such a weird word.

When I left the hospital, a staff psychologist provided me with some booklets about surviving a residential fire. Essentially, what it says is: I've been through a traumatic event and it's going to take a while to process it all.

Isn't life about surviving the shit that's thrown at you?

Lecherous, abusive workplaces.

Philandering, thieving husbands.

Electrical fires.

I toss the booklet aside. I don't need anyone to tell me to shower and get dressed. Or to sleep, eat, or fuck. I've got all of that covered.

I've never found any of the psychology mumbo-jumbo particularly useful.

Pick up the pieces. Move on.

It's what I do.

Nothing is insurmountable. Even getting the insurance adjuster a list of what was lost in the fire—arguably my biggest task—is going to be a breeze. Harrison and I already painstakingly documented our property and assets in the divorce. Other than my renovations and buying a ton of paperbacks to fill my library, I'm essentially already done.

Grabbing my iPad, I tuck my feet under myself and open my Kindle app to start the latest Lauren Rowe novel.

"There you are." Joar strides into the living room a few minutes after noon, looking delectable in a dress shirt and slacks. His assistant, Sahid waves as he leaves. They've been working on the Australia deal since four this morning. "I'm starving. Are you hungry?"

"I could eat." I set the iPad next to me.

Joar moves closer. His hair is getting longer on top. I flick my eyes up his body. "What would you like?"

"My insurance adjuster is coming over in an hour. Maybe something quick." I unfurl my legs. Bite my lip.

His violet eyes are hypnotic. Hard. Intense. After hours of working, he's turned his attention fully on me and I'm a grateful hostage. When he looks at me like this, his gaze holds my body captive as if he's physically restraining me.

Joar's voice is low, shredded. "*Clover...*"

So many thoughts run through my head as he prowls toward me.

Ever since Joar and I started—whatever our relationship is—I've resisted being pulled in by this man who seems—at times—dangerous to my own sanity. Yet, we're like magnets. Together, we revive something deep inside ourselves.

Faith, maybe?

I'm feeling so Zen. He and I have some things to work out, but who doesn't?

He flew twenty-eight hours round trip to get to me. That tells me everything I need to know.

He says he loves me. Though I haven't acknowledged it yet.

Or said it back.

Do I love him?

Yes. I do.

Will I tell him? Sure. When I'm ready.

The fire changed me. Overnight. I have a different perspective. I don't feel the same constraints as before. Don't feel the need to rush what we have. Life can change in a blink of an eye. I'm living proof.

For good. For bad. Doesn't matter. Change is change.

What Joar and I have is good. Life is short. I like being with him. I like fucking him. Cuddling. Making breakfast. Going on his Hate Dates. Spending time when we can.

I'm not ashamed to admit I've been going about this thing with him all wrong. Confusing the dynamic of my marriage with what Joar and I have is like apples to oranges.

I've felt more in sync with Joar in the past couple months than I ever did with my ex. Thinking back to before London, when I called everything off, I was in a tailspin of self-doubt. Confused. Misdirected.

Joar and JJ are one and the same man. If I love part of him, I love all of him.

He lets me be myself. My strong self. Neurotic self. Sexy self. Scared self.

It's time for me to embrace a new perspective.

What I've decided is this: if I don't want to be controlled, then I won't let Joar control me. If I want to work, then I'll work. If I want to spend ten days reading, I'll spend ten days reading.

I *want* to be with Joar. So, I'm going to be with him.

Despite what Kris told me.

He swore it wasn't true—he's not having me followed anymore.

I want to believe him, so I do.

Right now, I want something very, very badly.

I think he'll like it too.

"I want to suck your cock." I grab his belt and yank him to me when he's within reach. I can feel nothing but the heat radiating between us as I make short work of his slacks and briefs. I've never loved giving head as much as I do to Joar.

"God, yessss..." His voice cracks.

When his clothes pool around his ankles, Joar kicks them off, leaving him wearing nothing but his shirt and socks. He wedges a knee between my legs. Plants his hands on the back of the couch above my head. Cages me in. His shaft bobs against my lips. "Suck me a little first then I'm dying to fuck your face, sweetness. I'm gonna push my cock all the way down your throat."

"Mmmmm." I dart my tongue out. Lick his crown. Suck it between my lips. Grip him with one hand and take as much of his shaft in my mouth as possible. My free hand skims along his hip around to his ass, where I grab a handful of his taut muscle and pull him closer.

"Fuck, yeah." Joar pumps his hips into me. We keep eye contact. Soulful, reverential contact. Energy sizzles between us. Urgent. Frenetic.

I feel him gather my hair at the nape. He winds it around his wrist until it pulls at my scalp. Uses the leverage to hold me in place as he thrusts deeper, touching the back of my throat. I gag. Saliva pools and drips down his shaft. He watches me take him. "Good girl, Clover. I love what you're doing, it feels so amazing."

His encouragement gives me confidence. I allow myself to relax as he pushes past my gag reflex. I manage to stay calm and breathe through my nose when his cock slips into my throat. Joar's face is awash in the type of pleasure that makes me feel invincible.

Still, he's watching me. Making sure I'm okay. I am, it's a lot, but I blink a couple of times to let him know it's okay to keep going.

"Baby, holy fucking Jesus." He slides back and forth deliberately, surely. Allows me to get used to this strange sensation. My mouth is stretched so wide it's becoming painful. Inadvertently, I swallow against him, causing his eyes to roll all the way back in his head. He jerks, shooting his hot, creamy release down my throat.

Seconds later, Joar gently cups my cheeks and pulls out slow and steady. He sits next to me on the couch and gathers me against his chest. Massages my jaw with his thumbs. "Are you okay? That was intense."

I nod, unable to speak, but happy I was able to give him that.

"Your turn, sweetness." He works his hand down the front of my joggers. Slips his fingers past my panties and strokes through my folds. "You're soaking. I think you liked deep throating me."

"Mmm." I work my jaw and wriggle against his hand.

Joar presses me back against the couch. Pulls off my bottoms in one movement. Slides his palms up the back of my thighs, spreads me wide and buries his face in my pussy. Plunges the fingers of one hand inside me and flicks against my bundle of nerves deep within my walls.

"Bear down," he commands before sucking my clit between my lips. His fingers press and circle the deep spot when I lean up on my elbows and push. My entire core shakes and quivers and my orgasm rushes through me, erupting like an unleashed dam, soaking both of us.

Joar rips off his shirt and wipes us off. "You squirted. I made you squirt."

"I guess it's quite the oral sex kind of day," I mumble. Use my joggers to soak up what I can get to. "Your couch is ruined, though."

"Worth it." Joar throws the shirt on the ground. Kisses me deeply. I savor our combined releases because it's us. We taste perfect.

I cling to his waist and pull him on top of me. Joar rips my tank over my head, flings it to the ground and engulfs my breast with his mouth. His cock hardens to steel against my thigh.

"Fuck me, baby." I thread my fingers through his hair. "Fuck me like you love me."

He stills, and arches up to look at me. "I do love you, Clover. I love you more than anything in this world. I told you that in the hospital. When you didn't say it back…"

"I heard you. I just wanted you to be sure." I run my hand along his scalp. "Not because of the fire."

Joar tugs my hips up. Lines his cock to my opening and consumes me with one dominating thrust. "I've loved you for so long, you don't even know."

"JJ…" A flush explodes across my chest and spreads to my face. My entire body is overwhelmed with a feeling that is heavy and light. Warm and fluttery. There has never been a moment for me where everything has been so incredibly right. "I love you, too." I pull his face to mine. "I love you so much."

Joar looks at me in wonder, as if I'm a fantasy. As if I'm something he could never deserve.

Something he could never keep.

Yet, he owns every part of me. Mind, body, and soul.

We are electricity. A current of emotion and need and desire that obliterates everything I thought I knew.

Everything I'll ever know.

Except for one thing.

I belong to this man.

Forever.

Chapter Thirty

One Month Later

I've missed New York City.

Nothing compares to the vibe here. Dynamic energy pulsates on every street and in every person. Ambition permeates every building. Creativity wafts through the air. When I moved here after college to get my business degree at NYU, I felt at home. Like I could vocalize what I wanted and the city would provide it to me. I knew I'd be successful. And I am. I've built the fastest-growing media empire in the world. I'm fucking omnipotent.

Indestructible.

No complaints. I've realized having Clover in my life is worth more than any amount of success, power or money.

But, I like having all four.

The car drops me off at my building. Everyone from the security guards to the baristas react with astonishment when I stroll through the lobby. It's been five months, I realize. No wonder they look like they're seeing a ghost.

A whistling, grinning ghost.

Hopefully, I'm not walking funny. On the flight over, I initiated Clover into the mile-high club. Three times.

Seth is waiting in the conference room along with the heads of every department. For the next five days, it's an all-hands-on-deck strategic planning session for next year. Rather than wait until December, I've always felt that the best time to plan for the future is in the fall. Less distractions. No holiday-related excuses.

The day is tough, but productive.

We have a two-hour break to catch up on emails and work, then my upper management is meeting for a working dinner at Jean-Georges.

I'm about to catch the elevator to my office on the top floor when Seth stops me. "I'm coming with you."

"Sure." I gesture for him to join me.

When we're alone, Seth turns to me. "I know you said to take surveillance off her, but I didn't."

"*Godfucking dammit.*" I pound the side of the wall. What a way to ruin my day. He should know better, Seth has been my best friend for thirty years. I've never been so mad in all my life.

At least he has the decency to look somewhat contrite. Neither of us speak until we reach the top floor. When the doors open, I storm past several support staff, including my longtime New York-based assistant, Shandelle, push through the glass doors to my office and throw my briefcase across the room. Not giving two shits that everyone can see my wrath.

Seth calmly follows me. Takes a seat on a white leather couch in the seating area. I press a button on the wall and the glass panels turn opaque and soundproof.

Only then do I bellow, "What the *actual* fuck."

"You're going to thank me in a minute. Let me know when your temper tantrum is over." He crosses his leg. Reclines back. Waits.

Something in his expression terrifies me. The weight of what he's about to tell me feels like cement sacks on my shoulders. I want to draw out this moment of not knowing. I want to keep living in a world where Seth hasn't uncovered information that could potentially shatter everything I've built with Clover.

Out of some sense of self-preservation, I turn my back on him. Stand at the window.

My office overlooks Central Park, a breathtaking sight that never fails to captivate me. The floor-to-ceiling windows bathe the room in natural light and provide an unobstructed view of the greenery and meandering pathways of the park.

Ultimately, I'm not a loser who buries his head in the sand. I turn to face my best friend. "Spit it out. What did you find?" My voice is filled with curiosity. Apprehension.

He takes a deep breath before speaking, carefully choosing his words. "There's no easy way to say this." He clears his throat. "I've come into possession of several voicemail recordings regarding the fire at Clover's house..."

"What?" My heart sinks to the bottom floor of this building. I'm enraged. "Just tell me. Fucking *tell* me."

Seth remains the calm in my storm. "*Joar*. Clover and Harrison are splitting the insurance money. It was part of a secret deal they made in the divorce."

"Not a fucking chance." I don't believe this. Not for one goddamn minute. The house is in Clover's name. Something's fishy.

Seth pulls out his phone as I take a seat opposite where he's sitting. "Let me play the recordings for you. They're from Harrison's mobile."

He taps his phone. Clover's sweet, sing-songy voice comes through the speaker.

"Harrison. I'll be gone for the next few days. You can go to the house when I'm not there."

I look at him quizzically. "So?"

"Joar, these are messages Clover left for Harrison the day before the fire." He glances down at his phone. "Let me play the rest of them before you interrupt again."

He taps his phone.

I got your message. Just make sure you don't leave anything behind. I'm serious. I'll call you when I leave the house.

Hi. Okay. I'll make sure I'm gone between eleven and four.

Hi. I checked the policy. This will work.

Hi there. Yes. Untraceable.

Hi again. Yes you'll get your share after the check clears.

Hi. It's happening.

A tidal wave of emotions crashes over me. Anger. Disbelief. Confusion.

To think Clover, the woman I've fallen in love with, may have actually been involved in something this sinister—I have no words.

It's what my gut told me in the beginning. Before I met her. Knew her. Loved her.

Am I the fool who took one look at her gorgeous face and spectacular tits and let my dick interfere with logic and reason?

"You know the phone records, financial transactions, and even witness statements during our investigation all point in this direction." Seth's voice is filled with caution.

It's inconceivable I misjudged the situation with her. My instinct is impeccable.

Isn't it?

"Could there be an alternate explanation?" I search for a glimmer of hope.

I long for it.

Seth's somber gaze meets mine. "I wish I was giving you better news. The tech team pulled these off surveillance. They've thoroughly reviewed these recordings. The facts seem to point towards a collaboration between Harrison and Clover. It's something we need to address because this could be a huge fucking problem if word gets out. I need you to tell me what you want to do."

The two of us go over every possible scenario. Attack it from all angles. With the mountains of evidence we have about Harrison's misdeeds, this fits right into his M.O.

Fuck.

I wish I could just ignore this.

But I can't. I'm still embroiled in the last vestiges of the Eminence acquisition—all related to Harrison's legal troubles. I'm in love with his ex-wife—who's working with him. This is sinister. I don't want it to be true, but I heard it with my own ears.

"Yeah. Okay." I'm stunned stupid. "You can head out. It's going to take me a minute to figure out how to approach this. We'll talk after the dinner." I remain composed until he shuts the door behind him.

Once he's gone, anguish overtakes my body. I'm torn between loyalty to the woman I love—thought I trusted—and the need to protect my empire and reputation. If Harrison and Clover have been conspiring all this time and...committed *arson?*

I can't be with her. No fucking way.

It sickens me. My world feels like it's been smashed to smithereens.

Why would she help him though? Why would she burn down her own house? I was on the phone with her. She was hospitalized, for fuck's sake.

My blood turns to ice.

Could it be she's an amazing actress and... *Fuck me.* If Harrison's legal troubles continue to drive down the valuation of Eminence, he might be gathering funds to do a reverse merger. I wouldn't put it past him. The guy might be an idiot, but he's definitely book smart. And devious. I wouldn't put it past him to try to pull one over on me.

Through Clover, though?

Could she be that demented?

Holy motherfuck. I need time to process this information. Determine the best course of action.

Time I don't have.

As if she's psychic, my phone buzzes. I pick up. "Hi, Clover."

"Not sweetness?" She laughs. "Wait until you see the dress I'm wearing for dinner tonight. It's pretty darn sweet. Should I come up?"

I pause for a split second. If all of this is true, I can't bring her to dinner with me. I don't play that way. I'd better confront her now. Sever the limb. It's going to be painful no matter what, why fucking wait?

"Yeah. I'm in my office. Sixty-eighth floor." I don't bother saying goodbye. The mere sound of her voice when I just heard the voicemails feels like a million knives in my belly.

Five minutes later, I hear a tap on the door. I press the control panel and buzz her in. I'm now sitting behind my executive desk.

I need the barrier.

Clover swooshes into my office with her beguiling grace. My heart literally aches. She's breathtaking.

Mine.

A soft-pink dress effortlessly floats and skims her body, ending mid-thigh. It's classy, subtly accentuating her curves except for the plunging v-neckline which reveals a darker-pink bustier.

The one she wore in the elevator.

Oblivious to my turmoil, she twirls around on silver platform sandals. The skirt of her dress rises almost to her waist, a delicate gust of air teasingly reveals a glimpse of her lacy thong. The fabric dances around her, fluttering and caressing her skin. Her every movement is delicate choreography. An enchanting ballet that thoroughly captivates my attention and momentarily clouds all judgment and reason.

My body reacts. As furious and confused as I feel, I love this woman. I don't believe she's capable of such a heinous crime.

I need to bury myself in her body. Be as close to her as humanly possible.

My cock's straining against my zipper already.

Clover Callahan is mine, and I'm going to have her.

Right here. Right now.

Even if it's the last time.

Chapter Thirty-One

The Same Day

I glide into Joar's office on top of the world, a surge of confidence pulses through my veins.

I'm going to knock Joar's socks off.

Fuck him senseless.

Maybe let him put his socks back on before dinner.

Ha!

One of the "glass is half full" parts of losing all your clothes in a fire is shopping.

When you're able to shop in New York City, the glass is full and overflowing.

This morning, knowing he'd be in meetings until the dinner we're attending, Joar handed me his black AMEX and encouraged me to replace the charred remnants of my six-hundred-square-foot walk-in closet. With the help of a stylist Ronni recommended, I spent the day browsing designer shops on 5th Avenue. Having someone solely focused on making me look good was a welcome respite from the drudgery of paperwork and insurance investigations I've faced for the past two weeks.

Now, I have a new wardrobe which declares, "I'm rebuilding my life with style, grace, and a touch of extravagance." It's been a whirlwind day that's left me feeling a sense of empowerment and endless possibility.

And yes, I've spent a fortune.

Tonight I'm wearing an exquisite soft-pink dress that I carefully selected for this special occasion—my Jacoby International debut with Joar. It exudes elegance, femininity, and allure. The ethereal fabric gracefully drapes over my curves, falling just above my knees. Its neckline plunges provocatively to reveal a hint of the surprise I bought for my man—the identical bustier to the one I wore in the elevator when we first, uh, got together.

"What do you think?" I twirl around on my silver platform sandals, deliberately shooting him a mischievous smile. I've fully embraced the effect I have on Joar. I intend on seducing him before dinner, despite how weirdly formal he was when I called him from the lobby.

I'm nervous about this dinner. I need the connection with him.

Tonight's a big deal. He's presenting me as his romantic partner during an important company meeting. I want to make him proud, but I also want to be relaxed.

Orgasms relax me.

As if he's reading my mind, Joar's gaze, intense and fiery, finds me. I can't help but feel a surge of exhilaration.

Hunger in his eyes.

Desire that echoes my own.

He rises from behind his desk, a predator in pursuit of prey. The way he stalks toward me sends shivers down my spine. Ignites a sense of greater anticipation, if that's even possible.

"You're fucking *perfect*." His hand, firm and rough, finds its place on my waist, halting my twirl. A soft gasp escapes my lips as his free hand yanks up my dress and he shoves his fingers deep inside me. His touch sends an electric jolt through my entire being.

"Joar," I breathe, my voice dripping with desire. "I need your cock inside me."

In response, he pumps his fingers in and out of me with an intensity that leaves me breathless.

"*Clover*..." His primal growl, agonized and barely restrained, rumbles from deep within his soul. He roughly grabs my chin with his fingers and sucks the side of my neck. His aggression triggers something primal within me, heightening the air of tension between us.

Suddenly, his lips crash against mine, our kiss fueled by an insatiable hunger. The world around us fades into oblivion as his passion envelops me, igniting a fire that blazes through my veins. Our bodies meld together, moving in perfect sync. Our tongues dance in a fierce embrace. The taste of him is intoxicating, I'm drunk.

Drunk with desire for JJ.

Only JJ.

His thumb flicks my sensitive clit. I'm already so aroused, I can't speak. My keening moans combined with my body's reaction to his touch are the only things I'm capable of using to express my desire for him.

Stars explode behind my eyes when I come. My knees buckle, but Joar holds me up. Our mouths part. My eyes lock with Joar's again.

Heavily panting, Joar's expression is anguished. Longing. "I fucking *ache* for you," he whispers, his voice laced with both desperation and devotion. "You've burrowed your way into my *soul*."

I lean in, my breath hot against his ear, my voice laced with a seductive, playful whisper. The sunshine to his surliness. "Then fuck me." I turn and bend over his desk. Lean on my forearms and look back. "Bury your big cock inside me. Give me everything you've got."

In an instant, the world falls away. Joar's behind me. My dress thrown up and over my waist. Underwear ripped off.

He thrusts his cock, thick and engorged, all the way to the hilt into my soaked pussy. Over and over, he rams himself into me. Cages my shoulders with his arms. Grips my hips so hard, I know I'll have visible bruises.

In these moments, I'm filled with the man who has given me everything. I wholly surrender to my all-consuming love for him. A love that knows no bounds.

I'm all in.

Balanced on my high heels, my calves burn with every pump of his hips as I become lost in a maelstrom of passion. "Come again. Show me you love me, one last time," he growls into my ear.

Before I can process what he just said, Joar reaches around and rubs my clit, setting me off again. "JJ....ah hhhhh." My walls tighten around him, milking him until he spills everything he's got and more.

When he pulls out, I sense a subtle shift in Joar's demeanor. He makes sure to secure the hem of my dress against the desk so it doesn't get messy. "Stay still," he demands, then disappears behind a door to the side of his desk.

Returning with a towel, tension ripples beneath Joar's composed exterior. As he wipes our combined release from my pussy and thighs, I can't help but wonder if his strange mood is somehow connected to me.

A flicker of uncertainty tugs at my heart. "JJ, is something wrong?"

"We need to talk." Joar's words are tinged with a mix of apprehension and concern as he finishes cleaning me up. Flips my dress back down.

I stand and turn to face him. My confidence wavers slightly, sensing the weight of the moment. My eyes search his for any indication of what is troubling him. "Just tell me."

Joar takes a deep breath. Struggles to find the right words. "I... I heard something today." His voice is heavy with unease. "Voice recordings of you. Seemingly confirming you've been involved in something illegal."

I feel the color drain from my face. My eyes widen in shock. If he believes this, did Joar really just *hate* fuck me?

My voice shakes when I respond. "I...I don't understand. What are you talking about? I would never do anything illegal. You *know* me."

Joar looks crestfallen. Conflicted.

My heart aches with betrayal. *Ultimate* betrayal.

"So, you *don't* know me then." I cross my arms protectively over my plunging dress. He doesn't deserve to see my assets for one more second. "Give me one good reason why I shouldn't walk out this door. I thought we were having a date night. I spent my entire day excited and proud to walk into that dinner on your arm. To have a little sexy time before we went. And you bring me up here to fuck me and dump me? Over some residual bullshit I thought was resolved a million years ago? No. Thank. You." I stride purposefully toward the door.

"I desperately want to believe you. To trust you're innocent. It's just...wait for a second." He walks over to his desk. "Let me play these for you so you know why I'm so upset."

Joar hits a button on his phone and my voice fills the room.

I got your message. Just make sure you don't leave anything behind. I'm serious. I'll call you when I leave the house.

Hi. Okay. I'll make sure I'm gone between eleven and four.

Hi. I checked the policy. This will work.

Hi there. Yes. Untraceable.

Hi again. Yes you'll get your share after the check clears.

Hi. It's happening.

"Clover, I need you to be honest with me," Joar implores, his voice filled with a mix of vulnerability and determination. "I can't ignore this, please help me understand."

Tears well up in my eyes and every ounce of optimism I had earlier is replaced by dread and fear.

It sounds precisely like me. But it's not. How is this happening? I'm shocked to the absolute core.

My voice trembles as I desperately plead, "Joar, I swear to you, I know what it sounds like but I never said those things. I have no idea where this came from. You have to believe me."

Joar's fists come up to his eyes. He's fighting an emotion I've never seen him feel. *Sorrow*. "I don't know what to believe."

Taking a deep breath, I settle in to the reality of the situation. If things were reversed, I'd feel the same way he does.

Doesn't make this hurt any less.

My faith in what we've built is eviscerated. "Can I ask you a question?"

"Of course." Joar scrubs his entire face with his hands.

"Why did you have such rough sex with me if you thought I was capable of this?" I'm crushed. "It makes me question your motives."

Joar looks at me like his world is collapsing. "No...it wasn't like that. *Fuck*. Baby..." He sinks down into a plush couch in his seating area. "I wouldn't do that to you.

When we're fucking, I just can't control myself some-times. I want you so much. I didn't even think..."

"Say I believe you. Say you believe me. Where exactly does all of this leave us?" I sit across from him.

His eyes are watery. "What is happening, Clover? Is someone trying to fuck with us? I look at you. Feel you. Am inside you. I *know* who we are. What we mean to each other."

"And yet, I feel sick to my stomach." I bend over, clutching my belly. I don't want to throw up, but I may not have a choice.

These ups and downs with Joar are exhausting.

Every time we seem to be on the right path, one of us throws up a road block.

Knocks us back to square one.

I'm beginning to think none of this is worth it.

Chapter Thirty-Two

A Few Minutes Later

I take a deep breath, try to steady my racing heart.

Trust doesn't come easy for me.

Witnessing Clover's shock and horror when I played the voicemails showed me everything I needed to see. Confirmed what I knew in my heart.

She's innocent.

Why couldn't I control my traitorous cock when she walked in the room? From her perspective, I understand why she's so upset. She came in here full of light and sunshine and flirtation.

Because she loves me.

I'm the asshole who manhandled her. Fucked her hard and dirty. Berated her. Then accused her of committing a crime.

Now she's curled into herself, devastated.

I don't deserve her. But, I can't lose her.

I'm awash in anger, confusion, and disgust. I can't make it right, but maybe I'll be able to take away some of the pain I've inflicted. "I believe you."

Before I can stop myself, I'm beside her, clutching her hand. Stroking her hair. When she finally looks up, her aqua eyes brim with agony. "It totally sounds like me. If I was you, I'd have run far, far away without looking back."

My brow furrows with regret. "Clover, I... I *know* who you are. I shouldn't have come at you like that." I hang my head in remorse. "I'm truly sorry. And, for the record, I just learned Seth disregarded my orders about having you investigated. He's my oldest and dearest friend. I know he thought he was doing the right thing. But, you should know, I'll choose you over him if it comes to that. I'm so very sorry, sweetness. About all of it."

The weight of my apology hangs in the air.

For long, agonizing minutes.

"I'm going to choose to take you at your word." Clover's voice trembles when she finally speaks.

Then it hits me at once. A jolt of realization. My jaw clenches with anger because it's so fucking obvious. "It was Harrison. I heard his deal with the feds fell through. He's going down and wanted you to go down with him."

Clover's eyes grow wide with awe. "Omigod. Now that you say that, Kris mentioned something about Kircher using deep fake videos to bring his 'enemies' down with him. If he used old voicemails from me to do this, I'm officially horrified. I bet the two of them thought they could get away with it." She laughs bitterly. "God, I sound like I'm in a *Scooby Doo* cartoon."

We smile at each other for a quick second. Then her expression turns cold and she looks away.

"You nailed it. That's exactly what happened. Stupid desperate assholes." Fire burns in my soul. "I wonder if he knows you and I are together."

She keeps her eyes averted. "I haven't been in communication for a really long time. It wouldn't surprise me, though..."

"Well, assuming he does, he probably was trying to get back at me too. Taking his business. Then his wife." I'm disgusted beyond belief at how low that man will go. "Let me talk to Seth. Find out where he got his intel. See what he can dig up."

"Do it. I want to press charges." Clover's voice is filled with determination. "I can't let him get away with this."

I squeeze her hand, which I'm still holding. Hope she finds it reassuring, though she still can't seem to look at me. "I won't stop until I destroy that motherfucker. He won't fucking get away with trying to hurt you this way."

She pulls her hand away. Gets up and stands at the window. The sun is setting, a brilliant watercolor sky of purples, oranges, and pinks, which reflect off her glassy black hair.

I can't see the pain in her eyes.

But I feel it.

I'm the one she loves. I'm also the one who's hurt her the most today. Not Harrison.

Me.

I move behind her. Gently rest my hands on her shoulders. "I don't know how to turn myself off." I'm filled with genuine regret. "I'm great at business. Shit at relationships."

Clover finally turns to face me. "It hurts when you don't listen, Joar. I hope you won't take it upon your-self to fix this on your own. I don't want that kind of relationship. We can get past what happened today, but you have to stop being an island. We're supposed to be in this together."

I take a deep breath, trying to figure out how to convey my deep remorse. "You're right. We're stronger together. I promise to do better."

She hesitates for a moment. "We can't change what happened but we can move forward. She glances out the window. "It's dark. You're extremely late for the dinner with your team. You should go."

Shit. This voicemail thing has derailed everything that's important to me. Harrison will pay.

Mark. My. Word.

Tonight's when my focus should be on my executive team and business. Instead, I've let my doubts about Clover affect both our relationship and my professional life. "*Fuck.*" This dinner is crucial. "But, it's not just me who needs to go. I want you by my side."

Clover is uncertain, that much is apparent. "I'll go because I said I would, Joar." She brushes past me and heads back to my private restroom. "Rebuilding trust will take time."

While she takes a second to freshen up, I pull myself together.

Until Clover turned my life upside down, I was determined to remain alone. I'd never let a woman derail my ambition. Have I let my ambition derail my own sense of self? Am I *really* fulfilled every time I acquire a new company? Or am I addicted to the rush. The power. The prestige.

My capabilities of being an adult in this relationship have proven to be less than ideal. I've steamrolled this sweet, sexy woman from the beginning. It's time for me to wise up and fast. A comment she made a while ago sticks with me.

I'm just another deal to close. What happens when you succeed?

It's time for me to be a real partner to Clover. To earn back my nickname. Then, just maybe, we can build something lasting.

Together.

She emerges looking fresh and pulled together. No one would ever guess what had transpired between us during the past two tumultuous hours. Quietly, we walk out the door, down the elevator, through the lobby into my waiting car. Clover turns away from me on the drive over but keeps her hand on my thigh.

I place my hand on top of hers. The road to healing won't be easy, but I'm committed to growing the fuck up where she's concerned. She's worth it.

We're worth it.

Ten minutes later, we walk hand in hand into the exquisite ambiance of Jean-Georges. The dimly lit space is adorned with modern decor, sleek lines, and tasteful artwork. An intoxicating aroma of culinary delights fills the room.

We follow the hostess to the private dining area where my team, who are engaged in lively conversation, are seated at a long table, beautifully set, bathed in soft candlelight. The panoramic view of the opposite side of Central Park stretches out before us, a breathtaking backdrop that adds a touch of magic to the atmosphere.

When we enter the room, everyone stops what they are doing and stares. In my twenty-five years of building this company, I've never brought a woman to a company event, so I'm sure they are shocked.

Seth catches my eye, horrified that Clover is with me. I shoot him a look that we've perfected over the years.

It's under control.

"Something came up, my apologies for being late." I tuck Clover's hand under my arm. "I'd like you all to meet my girlfriend, Clover Callahan. She'll be joining us tonight. Before we begin, please feel free to introduce yourself to her by describing your role and your number-one objective for next year. Seth, you go first, then I'll need a quick word."

I pull out Clover's chair and scoot her into the table while Seth complies with my request. When he's finished, the rest of the team meets Clover, and I take Seth aside. "It was voice AI. Harrison's behind it. Kircher's involved. I'll fill you in tomorrow."

He nods skeptically but takes his seat without questioning me further. We've known each other long enough for him to trust my judgment.

As the evening progresses, Clover is engaging and delightful, effortlessly connecting with each executive, charming them in the process. Even Seth is taken in by her anecdotes and stories about everything from pop culture to world leaders. It shouldn't surprise me, but she's a natural in this setting.

Conversation turns to Jacoby International business, where we toast to our goals of acquiring key properties in Dublin, Sao Paulo, and Seattle, and discuss how these expansions will elevate the company's presence in the global market.

Clover's mere presence and show of support fills me with a sense of calmness I've never had. All these years I avoided relationships because I thought they would distract me from my goals. Yet, being with Clover enhances them. Makes them more attainable. Worthwhile.

Who knows, maybe everything happens for a reason. Maybe I wasn't ready for her until now. Maybe that's why I've felt so drawn to her from the beginning, even though I didn't know her.

All I know is she makes my life better. In every way.

Three hours later, I emerge from the master bath. Clover is still dressed, sitting on the edge of the bed, exhaustion etched all over her beautiful face. I take a seat beside her. "Sweetness, I want you to know that I didn't mean to doubt you. It's just... The whole situation, the voicemails, it was overwhelming. I let my fear cloud my judgment, and I'm so sorry."

She turns to me, weary but determined. "I understand that it was a lot to process. Everything about today felt like a throwback to a time I never wanted to revisit. Living with a powerful man who manipulated me... It still haunts me. I need time to catch my breath, to figure out if this is the life I want."

Catching her breath...again. It's like a gut punch.

A well-deserved gut punch.

"I never wanted to make you feel that way. I *never* wanted to be a reminder of those painful times." I cup her hand with mine, my entire being aching with remorse. "You deserve so much more than that. You deserve to be with someone better than me. Please believe me when I say that I love you, and I will do everything in my power to make things right."

She sucks in a deep breath, like she's not sure what to say. "I love you too. So, I want to believe you, to trust that our love can overcome these obstacles. But I also need to prioritize my own well-being."

I nod, encouraging her to continue. To let it all out, no matter how much I won't like it.

She looks me in the eye, vulnerable yet strong. "Right now, I'm taking some time to myself. I want to process everything and figure out how to move forward. It doesn't mean I'm running away or giving up on us. It just means I've decided to take care of myself first. You're here for another couple of weeks. I'm going back to LA tomorrow to finalize the insurance claim. Meet with my lawyer. Stuff like that."

Resisting the urge to try to take over or convince her to stay, I keep my voice calm. "I get it, baby. I wanted us to spend this time together, but if you need to go, I won't try to stop you."

"Thank you." She stands and goes into the bathroom.

Unable to stay silent, I call after her, "Just know that I'm here for you, always. We'll talk things through when you're ready, and we'll find a way to navigate this together."

Sadness washes over me when she emerges from my closet dressed in loungewear, wheeling out one of my large suitcases. "Can I borrow this? I bought a few things today. I need a way to transport them..."

"You're not leaving your clothes here?" I blurt out.

"JJ..." She looks down at the floor. Then crosses the room and stands before me. Places her hands on my shoulders. "Today really sucked. But, I promise you, I just need a little time to find my strength again."

I pull her into my lap. Wrap my arms around her to hold her close. "I hate it. But I'm not going to fight it. I trust you know what is best for you," I whisper. "Please also trust that you're my everything. It kills me that you were all the way in, and I've given you reason to reconsider our relationship. I love you. So much."

Clover says nothing more. Presses her lips to mine. We crawl into bed. Kissing. Connecting.

When she takes off her shirt, reaches for my hand and covers her breast with it, I melt into her. Understanding that she doesn't want the last memory of us having sex to be what happened in my office earlier today.

I don't want this to be the end, but if it is, I want to give her everything I have.

More.

To show her, rather than tell her, how much I love her. Cherish her. Want a future with her.

We undress. I press soft kisses over her entire body, paying special attention to the places that I've discovered drive her wild. Every touch is sweet. Caring.

Reverential.

My body covers hers. I clasp her delicate hands in mine above her head and slide inside her wet heat.

Foreheads pressed together, our eyes lock as I make love to my sweet girl. Caress every part of her body while we're joined. We reach the pinnacle together and it feels like both a rebirth and a funeral.

This woman holds my heart in the palm of her hand.

I hope she's more careful with it than I was with hers.

Chapter Thirty-Three

Six Weeks Later

Tick. Tick. Tick.

The minutes count down as I wait for the hour-glass to run out.

It's a pivotal moment, a culmination of months of anticipation and dread. As I glance at the time, a wave of nervousness washes over me. Only one hour before we have to leave for court.

Joar swoops into the living room dressed to the nines in a black suit, white shirt, and lavender tie. I'm still in my bathrobe, reclining on the lounger. Trying to find the motivation to get dressed.

He knows the significance of this day, and his mere presence bolsters my spirit.

"Sweetness, we don't have much time." He kneels at my side. "I believe in you. You're a warrior and can face Harrison with truth on your side."

I nod, appreciating his words. "Thank you for standing by me. I can't wait to put this behind us."

Joar takes my hand. "Remember that you're not defined by Harrison's actions. Today, you'll have an opportunity to speak your truth and expose his lies. Let the strength within you shine through."

After the debacle in New York, I flew back to LA and stayed in a villa at the Sunset Marquis for a couple of weeks while Joar finished his business meetings. Although he wanted me to stay here at his place on Wilshire, at the time it was important to me to have a neutral zone for myself. For clarity. Perspective.

We talked for hours every night, but nothing was sexual. Instead, we spent the time getting very granular about our childhoods. Our adulthood. My family. His experience in foster care. Old relationships. Friends. Travels.

Everything.

Neither of us held back and I think it helped us both learn what made the other tick.

We did not discuss our future. He wanted to, but I wasn't ready.

I'm still not fully ready. Not when so much looms over my head.

It didn't occur to me when my insurance provider found out about the voicemails they would delay processing my settlement. It sucks, but makes logical sense. What had been deemed an electrical fire is now a criminal matter.

Seth, who'd been on my shit list in New York for nearly ruining my relationship with Joar, came through with critical and damning evidence which has been turned over to the authorities and my insurance company. Apparently, Harrison found out about my relationship with Joar and lost the last semblance of his self-control.

As horrific as it was to learn he'd deep-faked my voice. It was bone-chilling to find out he'd paid someone to tamper with the AC unit. I could have *died*.

And now criminal charges relating to attempted murder, arson and the AI voicemails have been added to his long list of legal woes. Harrison has years of complicated litigation looming. He's lost everything but Solange, I guess. I suppose she's sticking close in the hopes of not being dragged down into his legal woes. Joar thinks she'll eventually testify against him, write a tell-all after he's convicted and parlay the notoriety into finding her next sugar daddy.

I could care less because right now I have bigger issues. I'm homeless. With the insurance payout in limbo, I can't afford to rebuild or buy something new in Los Angeles. Joar insisted I move in with him because everything I own is at his place anyway. So we're living together. For the time being.

Or so I keep telling myself.

His support and patience mean everything. Yet, unease still lingers. It scares me to lean so heavily on Joar when I want to rely on myself. Memories of isolation, pain and manipulation inflicted on me by Harrison consume my thoughts. It sucks to find myself in such a horrific predicament not of my making.

If that weren't enough, two weeks ago I was subpoenaed to testify before a grand jury assembled to determine what, if any, charges Harrison will face on his white-collar crimes. I'm terrified to face my ex-husband, but I have no choice. Especially after what he did to me.

I take a deep breath and put on a brave face for JJ. "Okay. It's time for me to get the show on the road."

Forty-five minutes later, I emerge from the bedroom, stopping to check my appearance in the floor-length mirror that lines the hallway. I'm wearing a dark-teal suit with black piping. White blouse. Black pumps. My hair is tied back in a slick ponytail. My accessories are simple—a pair of pearl earrings and matching necklace. I look good. Professional.

Then I close my eyes. Breathe. Try to find my well of inner resilience.

As Seth explained, the hour before court is crucial. Once we get to the courthouse, he'll help me gather my thoughts, go over the evidence, and give some time to mentally prepare myself to testify against my ex.

Still, as Joar and I head out, I can't help but feel the weight of my past pressing down on me, when all I want to do is focus on the future.

"I'm scared, JJ." I tug on his hand to stop him before we walk through the doors. "This proceeding. Facing Harrison—it's bringing back memories I'd rather forget. I know that staying silent is not an option. I have to speak up, for myself and for all those he's hurt."

His grip on my hand tightens, offering solace and reassurance. "I'm here, baby." His voice is filled with conviction. "Every step of the way. We'll face this together no matter what happens."

It's just the boost I need.

As Seth takes me through the witness preparation, memories resurface, and emotions run high. Amidst the turmoil, Joar sits next to me. A quiet, supportive presence. Occasionally, he'll offer advice when I ask for it, but he doesn't jump in or take over.

Which I appreciate.

It means he believes in me.

Believes I'm capable of handling this.

The hour of prep passes rapidly. It's worth the effort though. I'm ready to face my ex and, hopefully, reclaim my life.

The courtroom itself is plain but exudes an air of solemnity and order. Positioned on an elevated platform, the judge's bench looms over the room. Just below, three diligent court clerks are busily preparing for the afternoon. Adjacent to the bench, I see the witness stand, where I'll soon take my oath. The plaintiff and defendant tables are side by side. Lawyers flit around with boxes of files. Books. Stacks of documents. You name it. To one side, the jury box stands.

The public gallery is empty, as this is a closed proceeding. The media, however, wait in droves outside. Harrison's troubles are all over the news. I'm in the headlines too, which I don't love, but at least the stories about me are all positive.

So far.

I notice a few cameramen from national news shows have been allowed to set up in the back. When Seth sees me tense up, he assures me they're not allowed to film me except when I recite my oath and again when we depart the courtroom.

I'm glad Joar's most-trusted advisor seems to be—finally—firmly on my side. He's protective of JJ, which I've come to appreciate. My man takes care of so many people, it's comforting to know he has Seth looking out for him.

I hope he's truly looking out for me.

Behind the prosecution bench, I'm seated between Seth and Joar. My hands, which rest in my lap, begin to tremble. There's no hiding how nervous I am. Joar places a comforting palm over mine. Gives it a reassuring squeeze. His presence is a steadfast reminder that I'm not alone. "You've got this, Clover," he whispers, his voice filled with unwavering support. "Remember, you're doing the right thing by speaking up."

The courtroom doors swing open in the back. I take a deep breath, try to steady my racing heart.

Here we go.

The room falls into hushed silence when Harrison enters, flanked by his smarmy legal team. Solange follows, making a great effort to stare me down and toss her head when I catch her eye. My God, their arrogant behavior hasn't wavered one bit, but I refuse to let it intimidate me.

I haven't seen either of them in over a year, but I find the two of them pathetic. It makes me physically ill that I married such a poor excuse of a human being when I was so young, alone, and impressionable. After today, hopefully he'll face the consequences of his actions. My temporary feelings of unease at being here are worth it.

I've come too far, endured too much, to let him—or his lawyers—break me.

Moments later the judge takes the bench, the jury is seated and trial proceedings begin. Aside from a motion Harrison's lawyers file to exclude my testimony, which is denied, I find myself walking up to the stand within fifteen minutes of court being in session.

The prosecutor, a petite woman in a gray suit approaches. She has few questions, but they cut through the air with precision. I try to keep each one of my responses measured and truthful. I'm appreciative when she notices Harrison leering and rolling his eyes at my testimony. He's trying to distract me. Intimidate me.

She expertly positions herself to block him so I can't see, but the grand jury can watch his buffoonery.

Every now and then I catch glimpses of Harrison. His eyes are laser-focused on me, filled with a mix of anger and disbelief as my story unfolds. Probably because he realizes his carefully constructed facade is crumbling. The truth is emerging from the shadows he cast.

When the voicemails are played, it still shocks me at how accurate they sound. I vehemently deny that the voice is mine, and the jury seems to believe me. They look at me with empathetic eyes and barely hide their revulsion every time Harrison's lawyers try to interrupt me or deny my ex's involvement.

At the end of the day, by telling my truth, I'm putting the last parts of my shattered soul together. It's a powerful moment. A glimmer of victory in a battle that's lasted far too long.

Throughout it all, Joar watches me with admiration and wonder. His support is unwavering. When Harrison's lawyers decline to question me, I know I've done well. His lawyers never bothered to depose me, because

I'm sure Harrison told them I was still the young, impressionable woman he could control.

"You were incredible, Clover," Joar whispers when I sit down. "You've stood up to him. Refused to let him define your worth. You're amazing. I'm so proud of you."

When the court takes a recess for the afternoon break, the three of us leave. We're standing in the lobby saying goodbye to Seth when I hear a group of people behind us.

"You always were a useless bitch, Clover." It's Harrison.

"You pathetic asshole." Joar whirls around. "Don't talk to her that way."

Harrison sneers. "Sloppy seconds. That's all you've ever been good for, Jacoby. That fat bitch isn't worth it."

Solange sniggers behind him in her too-tight tan suit and inch-long fingernails.

I couldn't care less about either of them, but Joar's about to blow up. "Hey. Look at me." My voice is low. Definitive. He blinks a few times and then focuses on me. "Not. Worth. It."

By this point, Seth has alerted security, who are swarming around Harrison and his gang of yes-people. They're escorted away and the whole thing is over before it starts.

"You did it, sweetness." Joar's voice is full of pride. "You also kept me in check, which I appreciate."

Tears well up in my eyes, a release of emotions I've been holding inside for a while now. "Thank you, JJ. I'm just glad it's over. I'm so ready to focus on enjoying the holidays. I need some fun in my life."

A week after the trial, Seth calls to tell us that Harrison has been indicted by the grand jury on fraud and numerous other crimes. He's also taking a plea deal on criminal charges related to the arson and attempted murder. The dude who tampered with my air conditioner turned on him, so he had no choice.

Which means I haven't lost everything, insurance will pay for my loss.

I can buy a new house, and I'll never have to see that fucker of an ex again.

It's no wonder I feel lighter. Happier.

Ready to focus on my future, which I hope will be with Joar.

Chapter Thirty-Four

Two Nights Later

It's seven in the morning there, but I have to duck out to the office for a meeting with my team in London. Before I leave, I place a Post-it note for Clover on the vanity mirror above her sink in the bathroom.

Meet me at Bulgari

11 AM

Rodeo Drive

Don't be Late

It's high time we reinstate a hate date.

It's funny. When I so desperately set up that dating profile earlier this year to stop the madness of Clover's own "boyfriend experiment," I never knew it would lead to what we have now.

She's the love of my life. Tonight, I'm going to show her off to the world.

My sweetness is still sound asleep, but I can't resist giving her a kiss before I go. Clover yawns and her eyes blink open when I bend down. "You smell so good."

I press my lips to hers. "I left you a note on your mirror. See you in a few hours."

<hr>

I'm waiting for her outside the Bulgari store when Victor drives up. Clover emerges from the car wearing an oversized sweater over black leggings and knee-high boots. I can't help but feel a surge of joy. This is a monumental moment in our relationship. I'm taking Clover shopping, *Pretty Woman* style, and showering her with the finest things in life.

I'm not taking no for an answer.

"What are you up to, JJ?" Clover takes my hand, interlocking her delicate fingers with mine. The smile on her face is priceless, she's genuinely surprised.

"Today is your day." I lead her inside the grand entrance. "I'm taking you shopping so you'll be the belle of the Carousel of Hope Gala tonight."

"JJ..." She tries to pull away.

I use the momentum to spin her into my arms. I enclose her body and kiss her fully on the lips. "I've suppressed my caveman ways for weeks, you need to let me take care of you today. I want to pamper you. Let me have this, please. Without one more complaint." I boop her nose for good measure.

"I love you." She wraps her arms around my waist. "Okay. Let's do it."

God, she has no idea what she's agreed to.

We enter Bulgari to a warm welcome from Boris, the manager. He's been waiting for us. I see the anticipation—and trepidation—in Clover's eyes, and it fuels my determination to make today truly extraordinary. She deserves everything I have to give, this shopping spree is just the tip of the iceberg.

Boris leads us past dazzling displays of jewelry, each piece radiating beauty and craftsmanship. He leads us into the private room in the back, where a mesmerizing one-of-a-kind necklace is displayed on a black velvet mannequin. Meticulously crafted for Clover

She gasps. "What is this?"

I can't keep the shit-eating grin off my face as Boris describes the piece. It's a collection of exquisite aquamarines, each shimmering with a serene blue hue that evokes the tranquility of the ocean. The delicate strands of diamonds intertwine with the aquamarines, creating a harmonious dance of light and color. The platinum setting is adorned with intricate detailing, showcasing impeccable artistry.

"Did you wear a scoop neck under that sweater like I asked?" I take the necklace off the display.

Clover nods, then shakes her head in disbelief. Sheds her sweater. Turns her back to me so I can place the jewels around her neck. "I can't even..." She turns and gasps when she sees her reflection in the mirror.

"You're beautiful." I openly admire how perfect this necklace is. Every aquamarine gem is the exact color of her eyes, just like I planned. "I commissioned this for you as a symbol of our unique love story. I hope you realize this is an expression of my deep love and admiration for you. I envision this to be one of many cherished family heirlooms that you will pass to our children as a testament to our love."

Hell, I know it's sappy. I know it's a little presumptuous. But, it's how I feel. So, at the very least, I'm being authentic.

Clover is overcome with emotion. "JJ...I have no words. That is the single most beautiful thing that has been said to anyone ever. The fact you commissioned this for me is overwhelming. I love it. I love you."

Boris helps Clover take off the necklace and wraps it up for Victor to take back to the Beverly Hilton hotel, where the Gala is being held and where we'll be staying in the newly refurbished Presidential Suite. We're certainly not going to walk Rodeo Drive with a six-million-dollar piece of jewelry.

We stop for lunch at 208 Rodeo, where we eat lobster mango salads, truffle fries and sip Bellinis, of course. Our next stop is the Armani store, where Clover will pick out her dress for tonight.

"You're spoiling me, and I'll admit, I'm getting into it." Clover's arms are looped through my elbow as I pay for the stunning dress, undergarments, shoes, and clutch she chose.

I gather up the packages and text Victor our location. "You're a quick shopper. We can keep going, or we have a few hours before the gala. How do you feel about a nap?" I waggle my eyebrows.

"You didn't need to spend a small fortune to convince me to ride your cock, you know," she whispers in my ear. I've been semi-erect all day, and with that proclamation I'm straining against my slacks just as Victor pulls up.

I open the door for her and ram my erection into her ass. Whisper in her ear, "Get your sexy ass in there before I yank down these leggings and fuck you right here and now."

***

I wait for Clover at the fireplace in the suite, gazing out through the floor-to-ceiling windows at the Beverly Hills skyline. I have to admit, the pace of life in LA is a lot different than New York but it's growing on me.

She's getting ready in the walk-in closet, where a team of hair and makeup artists primp and prep her. I didn't have as much time as I would have liked to get lost in her lush body this afternoon, but tonight's a different story. I can't wait to make love to Clover wearing nothing but that necklace dangling between her delectable tits.

"Well, what do you think?" Clover appears in the foyer. Holy fuck. She's a vision in a sophisticated black dress embroidered with thousands of black and midnight-blue beads that seem to capture the sparkle of the night sky.

Her necklace hangs delicately against the deep neck-line, which is embellished with crystals and sequins in a refined, elegant pattern. Her hair is curled in loose waves. Makeup is understated, but sultry. She holds a satin clutch with crystals that match her dress.

I've never seen a woman more beautiful. Her taste is impeccable. The combination of the dress, necklace, and clutch is a fashion masterclass in understated yet luxurious sensuality.

"I'm not worthy." I step toward her in my deep-blue tuxedo. "But I'm never letting you go."

As we make our way downstairs and through the check-in to the gala, I hold Clover close. This event is filled with celebrities and famous personalities, but tonight, she's the belle of the ball and I'm the proudest man in the room. I feel like a teenager, giddy at the prospect of introducing Clover to the world at large as my significant other.

This is her *true* public debut, which makes this night unforgettable.

We step into the grand ballroom, which is adorned with elegant decorations. The soft glow of chandeliers cast a warm ambiance and the air is filled with excite-ment and anticipation. "Wow, this is incredible." Clover looks around, absorbing the breathtaking scene before us. "Thank you for bringing me, I'm no stranger to charity balls, but I've never been to such a prestigious event."

"I'm grateful you're with me." I bend down to steal a kiss. "Should we look at the silent-auction items?"

Lively conversations and soft music fill the air as we make our way toward the silent auction area. We approach the first item, a luxurious vacation package to a private island retreat. Clover's fingers delicately trace the description, her eyes widening in awe. "JJ, can you imagine spending a week on the beach together?"

"It would be a dream come true if you'd be in a bikini the whole time." I grin and reach for my phone, where the bids are placed through the app. "I'll just take it at the 'buy it now' price."

She slaps my hand away. "You've treated me enough today. Let me do this." She fires up the app and taps her phone. "Done. Now I'm taking you on vacation and you don't have a say." She sticks out her tongue.

"I know where I want that tongue later." I wrap my arms around her and kiss her deeply.

We continue to browse the array of items, each one more enticing than the last. From exquisite jewelry to once-in-a-lifetime experiences, there will be millions of dollars raised tonight.

For the next hour, Clover and I work the crowd. Engage in light conversation with fellow guests including Kris Blakely, and revel in our first official public outing. It's a celebratory atmosphere, alive with laughter and excitement. I find myself entirely immersed in the enchanting energy of attending an event of this magnitude with the woman I love.

Soon, we're seated at our front-row table with the senior members of my executive team and their dates. One of Isis's clients, John Legend, is the Master of Ceremonies. His charismatic presence commands the attention of the crowd.

Clover and I hold hands throughout the program, enjoying inspiring stories of hope, A-list entertainment, and bantering about which live auction items we want to bid on. I, too, have attended many charity galas throughout my life, but tonight is different. Through Clover's rapt attention, I'm reminded of the importance of supporting this cause and making a difference in the lives of those affected by diabetes.

Although by the time the live auction begins, I'm ready to have Clover to myself. Every time she moves or gestures, I get a little glimpse of her side boob. Only I can see, but I'm hard as a rock just thinking about the time—in the near future—when I pull her top off and suck on those delicious chocolate nipples.

Luckily, it goes by fairly briskly. I purchase five custom barrels of whiskey from Ireland for fifty thousand dollars and raise my paddle for another five hundred grand.

"You're so generous and sexy. Are you ready for your reward for being such a spectacular boyfriend?" Clover leans her head on my shoulder as we wait in line to pick up the certificates for the items we bought.

I cuddle her to me. "Sweetness, tonight's been stupendous, but my cock aches to be buried in your tight little pussy. I've been ready for rounds two, three, four, and five for hours now."

"Ambitious are we?" She laughs.

I nuzzle her ear. "Just stating facts."

Every new experience with Clover is a revelation.

She's my equal in every way.

I want to be with her forever.

One tiny little question remains though.

How can I convince her to move with me to New York?

Chapter Thirty-Five

Later That Night

Joar Jacoby is the finest male specimen on the planet.

To think I nearly wrote him off earlier this year, just because he's a billionaire CEO who dresses to the nines. There is no man who wears a custom-tailored, fits-like-a-glove, luxurious, hot-as-fuck suit—or tuxedo—like Joar.

I'm a convert. One hundred percent.

More importantly, he surprises me with his kindness every day. Not just because of the exquisite jewelry he commissioned. Or the silly, but thoughtful, hate dates. The most telling part of Joar's personality is how big an effort he's made to fit me into his life.

I've never wanted him to change, but I've grown to love the bossy, dominant man that he is. It's fascinating to watch the wheels turn. It's phenomenal to be on the receiving end of whatever crazy plan he comes up with.

I just needed him to tweak how he treated me. I'm not his possession, I'm his partner. It's a big difference. One I wasn't mature enough to demand when I was married, not that it would have made a difference to Harrison. Nearly every day I want to send Solange a letter thanking her for fucking my husband. Losing him was the greatest thing that ever happened to me.

It's made me self-aware. Confident. Capable.

And, it led me to Joar, who I truly believe is the love of my life.

This entire day has been incredible. Shopping spree aside, spending the evening with Joar at the gala gave me insight into the type of leader he is in the fickle entertainment industry. Respected. Coveted. Lauded.

Loved.

It's true. He's so kind and generous with his time. Makes everyone he talks to feel special. He's the opposite of my ex in every single sense of the word. I feel grateful and happy we've stuck together through our shit this year.

I sip a glass of champagne in the living room of our suite waiting for Joar, who disappeared to the bedroom with strict instructions to stay put. Suddenly ambient, romantic music fills the room and he appears in the foyer still dressed in his tux, though his bow tie is missing.

He presses a button on the control panel, which changes the lighting to a gentle glow. The fireplace lights up, adding another touch of sensual atmosphere. My eyes are fixed on Joar, who scans my body hungrily from head to toe and back up again. Power oozes from every pore as he makes short work of the distance between us.

As Joar nears, the sexual tension in the air has my pussy clenching. Holding his hand out to me, he smiles. "Dance with me, sweetness."

When I place my hand in his, he twirls me to him and wraps me in his muscular arms. Moves his hips to the beat, keeping me tight against his body. We dance slowly. Sensually. Our hands run up and down each other's backs as we press even closer together.

When Joar tenderly cups my face between his palms and swipes his tongue through my lips as we move, I can't help it, I'm moaning, lost in our kisses. I want him desperately.

"Did you have fun tonight?" Joar trails his tongue down the length of my neck and he gently suckles behind my ear as he rocks his hips into mine. He doesn't wait for my answer, instead kisses me deeply, more passionately. My sexy, beautiful man presses his erection into my belly. His kisses grow even more demanding and urgent, driving me wild.

"Yes, but *this* is so much more fun," I gasp.

Joar's violet eyes penetrate mine as his hands move up my legs. Lifts my dress to my waist. He drags a finger along my garter strap. "You're so fucking hot. Are you dripping for me yet?"

"Gushing," I whisper.

"*Fuuuuuucck*, Clover." Joar's lips fasten to my neck. He lifts my leg. Hooks it around his hip. Skates his palm from my knee to my ass, grabbing a handful and yanking me against him. Thrusts against my core. "I want to feel. Taste." He lets my leg down then twirls me so my back is to his front. He presses his enormous erection against my butt and pumps his hips.

"I'm gonna come," I cry. My thighs are shaking. He's the master of my body. Just the thought of us fucking can get me all the way there.

Joar pulls the sleeves of my dress—which has a built-in bra—down my arms, exposing my breasts. His cups them. Thumbs my nipples into hard peaks. Trails his hands down my waist and upper thighs to the hem. This time, he lifts my dress up and over my head, leaving me naked except for my thong, garter belt and stockings. "*Sweetnesssss.*" His voice is hoarse with desire.

We rock side to side in a half circle. He nuzzles my ear. "Look. Do you see how hot we are together?"

Our erotic dance is visible in the mirrored wall, I realize. "*So* hot." I sway with him, watching through hooded eyes.

Joar raises my arms and places them around his neck behind me. My lace thong is soaked. My nipples are hard as bullets. His hands roam all over my body. "I need to be inside you." His fingertips dip into my panties. "You're dripping, baby, Can you feel how hard you've made me?"

"Yes. God, yes. JJ, I want you to lick my pussy." I'm shaking with need for him.

"Do you know how much I fucking love you?" He turns me again and kisses me so deeply, tears fill my eyes. I'm overcome with emotion from the depths of my soul. I grab his face with both hands and give him everything I have. I need him to feel how much I love him. How much I desperately need him.

He sweetly wipes my tears with his thumbs. His eyes brim with understanding. "I know, baby. I know."

I reach up to undress him, first removing his jacket, which I throw on the couch. Next, I unbutton his shirt, tipping my lips up for kisses as I work. His breathing grows erratic, a sure sign he's starting to lose control. His shaft burrows into the juncture between my legs, seeking its home.

"All of this has to go." I'm frantic, done with the seduction. It's time to get on to the main event. I rip off his shirt, rewarded with the view of his muscled abs. Strong, defined arms.

Powerful.

Delectable.

He helps me undo his pants. Kicks off his shoes. Removes his socks while I pull his pants and briefs down at once. The thick veins of Joar's cock pulse when I grip him at the root. "God, baby, I'm so close," he groans

I am too. I need him inside me.

Now.

Instead, he turns me around and bends me over the arm of the couch. I hold myself up on my elbows as he kisses my lower back and nudges my legs apart.

"*JJ?*" I question.

"You said you wanted me to lick your pussy." His voice is ragged. Through the mirror, I watch him drop to his knees behind me and peel my thong down my legs. I rock forward when he licks all the way down my slit. Cry with exquisite pleasure when he pushes two fingers into me. Holy crap, he twists his hand back and forth, which detonates an orgasm so blinding and all encompassing, I'm screaming and out of control.

My legs shake and tremble because he doesn't let up. Joar continues to leisurely fuck me with his fingers and laps at my pussy. Each stroke stronger than the last. His mouth is everywhere. Licking my clit. Sucking and kissing my lower back. Biting my ass. Back to my clit. I'm writhing. Keening. Chanting, *"JJ"* like a wild woman.

"Come again, baby." He twists his fingers one last time, hitting that deep spot inside me. I'm completely overcome when the next orgasm rips through my body, causing me to slump forward, breathless and moaning. Joar pets and strokes my lower back, spreading my release everywhere.

Eventually, I manage to turn to my side. Joar's eyes are dilated, still fixated on my dripping pussy—his handiwork. His dick is harder than I've ever seen it. "I need you to fuck me now, JJ."

Growling, he grips my hips, lifts me up effortlessly and impales me on his cock. I lock my feet around his waist and my arms around his neck. He takes a few steps to the couch and lowers us down so I'm riding him, still wearing my garter, stockings and heels. "Is this okay?" His eyes search mine.

"Yesssss." I groan at the intense pressure as his thick shaft finds its way into my body.

I move from side to side, trying to work him all the way in, but he stills my hips. Presses his forehead to mine. I know he's struggling not to ram himself all the way in, but he's always got my best interest in mind. "Relax. Let me get you there." He thumbs my clit. Rotates his hips. That's all it takes. My body loosens and I cream around his cock, allowing him full access. He smiles a slow, seductive smile and starts to move. "Now you're more than ready."

Joar's eyes flick from mine to the wall as we move faster. I look in the mirror at the single most erotic thing I've ever seen. His thick cock is buried inside my pussy. He controls my movements by rocking me back and forth by his hands on my hips. My breasts bounce to our rhythm. Nipples tight. Hair wild and tangled. Skin flushed.

Every one of Joar's taut abdominal muscles ripple with each pass.

"I can go harder, JJ." I lick my lips and grip Joar's shoulders, knowing what he needs. Control. Intensity.

"Fuck, Clover. Take it. *Take it.*" He slams me up and down on his cock, his fingers dig into my hips as he thrusts up to meet me. I'm so lost in the momentum. So full of him. Joar circles his hips. Rocks me. Moves me faster and faster.

My pussy is contracting and squeezing, I'm on the brink when he roars like a beast and, unable to hold off any longer, shoots hot come deep inside me.

Despite how many orgasms he's wrenched from my body already, Joar isn't willing to let up. He presses against my lower back so my clit hits his pubic bone while his cock still jerks inside me. "I know you've got one more, baby. Let me feel it all the way to your toes."

The intense stimulation spirals me into yet another gushing release. I can hardly breathe. My heart races. I can't even scream, I just melt into his strong arms. "I love you," I whisper against his neck as I contract around him.

"I love you too." He squeezes me tighter against him.

A few hours later, after a hot shower and another round, I pad out to the balcony in a fluffy white hotel robe. Joar leans over the handrail, wearing a towel and nothing else. Smiling at my arrival, he hands me a glass of champagne and clinks his to mine. "To a perfect evening."

"To a perfect evening," I agree, taking in his olive skin and muscled torso. I bite my lip. Look up at him from under my hair.

We each take a sip, but naughty grins overtake both of our faces.

Clearly, having the same thoughts.

It's two in the morning. We're exhausted.

Something tells me we're not quite ready to sleep yet.

Chapter Thirty-Six

Christmas Eve

I t's eight in the morning on a crisp but clear Christmas Eve morning.

I wake up before Clover. Usually, I love to let her sleep while I answer email or take care of overseas business. Today, I finalized the arrangements I made for the day.

I've never had someone to spend the holidays with, and I intend on making the most out of any time we have. Create new traditions for the two of us.

The past couple of months have been incredibly busy, and we haven't had more than a week at a time together since the gala.

We spent Thanksgiving in Seattle with Ronni, her husband Connor, and his family before I flew back to Australia for two weeks to finalize the transaction I started earlier this year.

Although Hollywood generally shuts down for the holidays, Clover's in great demand right now, and as the release of *The Boyfriend Experiment* gets closer, she's had a bunch of press commitments and a few exciting auditions to prepare for.

My plan was to stay in LA for the entire month of December, but a last-minute fire drill meant I was needed in New York, so Clover flew here to spend Christmas and New Years with me in Manhattan.

I'm stoked because nothing beats the holidays here, and I intend on showing Clover why. Maybe it will lead to a conversation about our living arrangement, if I'm lucky.

With my surprise arranged, I take out my special Post-it notes and a pen. Write out my instructions for Clover and attach it to the cup o' joe I'm about to bring to her.

Building Lobby

9 am

Wear warm clothes

Don't be Late

She's nestled on her side into the pillow, her black hair fans out around her. Perfect pink lips are open just slightly. Her long, dark lashes brush her cheeks.

Breathtaking.

Every. Single. Day.

I set the coffee cup on her nightstand and rotate it so the note is facing her. Then I lean over and kiss her cheek. Whisper in her ear, "Time to get up, sweetness."

Scooting like hell from the bedroom, I hear her rustle around. "Joar?" she calls out, but I'm already stepping into the elevator.

An hour later, I stroll into the lobby with a couple of breakfast bagels to find Clover waiting in tight blue jeans, black combat boots, a black puffy coat, and a white Jacoby International hat with a pom pom on top. "Aren't you adorable." I kiss her, take her hands and admire the view. "Where'd you get that hat?"

"It was buried in one of your dresser drawers." She puts her hand on her hip. "What do you have planned?"

I tuck her arm under mine and guide us to the door. "We only have one hate date left on the list, do you remember what it is?"

"Uh, amusement park?" She looks at me quizzically. "In December?"

I open the door to the black Range Rover that's waiting for us. "Oh, ye of little faith."

We eat our bagels and Clover spends the next half hour trying to figure out where we're going. It's not that hard for east coasters, but even when we get to Brooklyn she still has no idea. I continue teasing her in between kisses until she notices the road sign.

"Omigod!" She squeals. "Coney Island? I've never been!"

"Are you happy? It's going to be a little chilly, but I still think we'll have fun." I clasp her hand in mine and pull it into my lap.

She presses her lips to mine. "This is the *best* surprise. You're so thoughtful. I love you."

Soon we arrive, our driver parks and we step out onto the lively boardwalk. It's brimming with a vibrant holiday energy. The ocean breeze kisses our faces, the sounds of laughter and excitement envelop us. Clover is clearly delighted, and she doesn't even know my biggest surprise.

Hand in hand, we stroll by the beach, taking in the sights and sounds. The colorful lights of Luna Park beckon and I navigate us in that direction. The park, usually teeming with visitors, is empty today. I've arranged for it to be our private playground. A sense of exhilaration courses through my veins.

The general manager is waiting. "Mr. Jacoby?"

"That's me." I sling my arm around Clover's shoulder.

He holds up a couple of wristbands. "Might as well have the full experience."

"What's going on?" Clover looks from him to me and back again.

"I've shut down the park just for you and me. Merry Christmas." I bend down and kiss the look of shock off her face.

We make our way to the legendary Cyclone roller coaster, its towering structure a symbol of excitement and adrenaline. Clover's eyes sparkle with anticipation as we board the iconic ride. The ascent to the top is filled with anticipation and as we plummet down the tracks, her laughter fills my ears, merging with my own exhilarating screams of joy.

No deal. No acquisition. No business transaction compares to this.

Making my girl happy is my favorite job.

"You're too much, you know that?" We're sharing a funnel cake when she leans into me, bumps my hip. "Everything you do is over the top. I love it."

I point to the carnival games. "Should I prove my love by winning you a giant stuffed animal?"

"Uh, yeah. But, wait for a second." She stops. Wraps her arms around my waist and peers up at me in her Jacoby Media hat. "I used to give you such a hard time. I'm so glad you stuck with it. With me. I'm the luckiest girl in the world. I don't deserve you."

I grip her face and bring her lips to mine. "We've been through a lot in less than a year. Can you imagine where we'll be next year?"

"I know we've danced around it, but I hope you know I see my future with you, JJ. I'm not afraid to admit it." She looks nervous at making such a bold declaration, which is adorable.

Because my heart fills with joy. I've hoped Clover felt this way for longer than I'll admit but, mindful of my steamrolling tendencies, I've learned how to show her how I feel and let her ease into where things are going between us.

"I've hoped you felt that way because I see my future with you too, sweetness." I kiss her nose, unwilling to muddy up the day with a conversation we need to have soon, but not right this minute. "I have an important question for you. Giant unicorn or teddy bear?"

"*Duh*. Unicorn." She whacks my bicep and takes off running toward the games.

Two hundred dollars later, we have the world's most expensive felt unicorn, which Clover carries proudly. "No one ever won me a stuffed animal before, JJ. You're absolutely my favorite boyfriend."

Husband.

The word flashes in my brain and it feels...right.

"I'd hope so. Because you're my first and only girl-friend, and I intend on keeping it that way." I grab her hand and pull her over to the 4D Theater.

For the next few hours, we go on more rides, indulge in a tasting menu of junk food, make out and just enjoy our time alone together. Just as I planned, when the sun begins to set and casts a golden hue over the park, Clover is nestled in my arms aboard the Wonder Wheel.

In between kisses, we gaze out at breathtaking views of the beach. The Manhattan skyline glimmering in the distance. Mostly, I look at Clover, whose beauty and grace makes my life better every day.

"You're my favorite Christmas present, my love." I place a reverential kiss on her lips. Probe the seam with my tongue. She allows me access and our mouths fuse together while our tongues explore and dance. With Clover in my arms, I feel an overwhelming sense of love and gratitude. Excitement for a new year.

One we'll spend together.

"I hope you feel how much I love you," I whisper when we break apart, my voice filled with emotion. "We have such busy lives, it's important for me to make sure you know our connection and happiness are what truly matter to me."

Her aqua eyes reflect the waning sunset, which seems fitting somehow. "This day is beyond anything I could have dreamed up." She strokes my face with her thumb, her voice tinged with affection. "Thank you for making this day so incredibly special. There's nowhere else I'd rather be than with you."

We're at the top of the Ferris wheel when the dusk sky illuminates with a dazzling display of fireworks. She leans into me. I tighten my arms around her. Together, we celebrate the magic of the moment in this enchanting atmosphere, where it feels like we're the only two people in the world.

The only two people who have ever fallen in love.

As we walk hand in hand to the waiting car, I'm filled with a sense of excitement. Clover and I are still at the beginning of our journey together. We're going to have hundreds of days like this in our future.

Back at my place, she's delighted when I open the door and my entire living room has been decorated. A fifteen-foot Christmas tree. Lights. Garland. Poinsettias. The whole shebang.

Clover's gift to me is thoughtful and sweet, a framed picture of her in our elevator in Vancouver BC wearing the pink bustier, black leggings, and a naughty grin. She hired a photographer to take it when she popped up there with Ronni to look at the new set.

I'm even more surprised when she logs me into a private storage account filled with more pics from the shoot including risqué boudoir shots with her nipples peeking out above the lingerie. "For your spank bank when we're apart." She winks.

My heart squeezes when Clover squeals with delight at her present. It takes her a while to open it. It's number ten in an elaborate box-in-a-box package, where she unwraps a big box only to find a smaller one. And so on.

Considering I overwhelmed her with the necklace before the gala, I decided to go for thoughtful rather than extravagant—a new hate date list for next year. Overcome, she throws herself in my arms and we make love for hours by the fire until the clock strikes midnight.

A perfect end to a perfect day.

Except for one thing.

As the love we share grows stronger, I can't ignore we have a huge problem.

I don't want to be apart.

Ever.

My home base is here. Hers is three thousand miles away.

If we get married and have children, we'll need to put down roots.

The question is, where?

Chapter Thirty-Seven

Christmas Day

Yesterday was, quite possibly, the most romantic day of my life.

With Harrison's bullshit no longer hanging over our heads, Joar and I make the most of the time we spend together. It feels like a rebirth of our relationship, at least to me. For most of last year, my life was in turmoil. So many changes to get used to.

I'm not sure I fully comprehended how much I love Joar until I was truly free.

While we haven't been able to spend a ton of time together lately, this trip to NYC more than makes up for it. I'll take Joar Jacoby any way I can have him.

I can't complain. I'm super busy myself. Next year my life will be crazier. We start filming next season in a couple months. I gave in and signed with Isis, and suddenly I'm up for two leading roles in rom coms and one in a thriller, all which film next year. Every major magazine wants to put me on their cover, so I'm constantly booked for photo shoots and interviews.

We're trying to coordinate our schedules, which is getting harder now that my own career is picking up.

If things go as planned, Joar will be in Seattle while I'm filming, which makes it much easier for him to pop up to Vancouver BC when he's working on that deal. He's invited me to Dublin and Sao Paulo, but I can't make any promises yet.

In between, it looks like we'll be bi-coastal.

The thing is, every time we say goodbye it hurts.

I'm not going to think about leaving, though. We have two entire weeks together and my goal is to do something sweet for the man who rocks my world.

"Do I smell cookies?" Joar shuffles into the kitchen wearing only boxer briefs and a boner. He wraps his arms around me. Kisses my cheek. Bites my earlobe.

The counter is filled with two batches of sugar cookies. Chocolate chip are in the oven. "What's Christmas without cookies?"

"I wouldn't know." His eyes twinkle before he snatches a treat and takes a bite of sugary, buttery goodness. "Mmmm."

Over the past few months as we've shared more details with each other about how we grew up, we've realized our childhoods were similar—both of us were forced to fend for ourselves.

My folks saw me as a meal ticket. It's been years since we've spoken, maybe a handful of times since I emancipated at sixteen.

Joar never knew his father. When his mom went to jail for drug trafficking, he was placed in the system as an infant and bounced in between foster care homes the rest of his life.

As adults, we took opposite approaches to cope. He doesn't rely on anyone but himself—except for Seth, who is the son of his favorite foster parent. Unfortunately, in early adulthood I was shaped by the seedy entertainment industry and relied on powerful men to, essentially, take care of me. Until I left Harrison, I don't think I realized I was being exploited the entire time.

I think that's why my career is so important to me now. It's on my own terms. I'm in control. It feels good to take charge of my own life.

"You're lost in thought, sweetness." Joar's on his second cookie. He watches me as the wheels turn in my head.

The timer dings. "Yeah, I think I'm reflecting a bit." I take out the gooey batch and put the next two sheets in.

"Are we going to eat all of these cookies?" Joar pats his belly. "You're making enough for an army."

I throw a dish towel at him. "Not today. We'll put some in the freezer so we have them while I'm here. Come January, I'll be on a strict diet and workout regimen."

"You don't need it. You're perfect as you are." He steps toward me and wraps me in his arms. Cups my breast. Kisses me.

His palms span my hips and he lifts me onto the counter. I'm wearing one of his T-shirts and a thong. He steps between my legs. "JJ..." I moan when he presses his erection against my pussy.

"You're always wet for me." His fingers pull my panties to the side. He shoves his boxers down and drags his tip along my opening. Taps my clit.

I pull off the T-shirt, clutch his shoulders and watch him feed his cock into me. "*Only* for you," I clarify.

Joar fucks me hard and fast on the counter. We climax together just as the oven buzzes. He pulls out, just in time to take the cookies out before they burn.

"You are quite the sight." I giggle. Joar stands naked except for two oven mitts, holding two trays of cookies, and his dick is still hard and wet from being inside me.

———

Later that afternoon, we're snuggled up in cozy loungewear on the couch watching *Below Deck*. Our bellies are full of Chinese food and homemade cookies when my phone buzzes. Joar presses pause while I check it.

Holy crap.

I can't contain my excitement. "JJ, I can't believe how much my career has taken off since I signed with Isis. The offers that are coming in... it's like a whirlwind. Thank you for being such a good boss."

"Well, technically I guess you're my boss since Isis works for you." Joar pulls me back against him. Kisses my temple. "I'm so proud of you, but with all these opportunities, I'll confess...I worry about the impact us being apart is going to have on our relationship."

I've been afraid to bring this up. "I feel the same way. We've worked so hard to get here. I don't want our careers to pull us apart."

"So far, we've made it work. It's just that the more time we have together, the more I want to be together all of the time." Joar's palm caresses my head. His fingers thread through my hair.

His comment makes me sad because, although I feel that way too, I'm not sure how it's possible. "I'm torn. My career is just revving up again. I probably have more flexibility. You're running a multibillion-dollar company with responsibilities I'm only now beginning to comprehend."

"No way. You are not giving anything up for me. This is your time, sweetness." Joar's voice is firm. Unwavering.

I guess we're getting into it. Maybe it's best. I sit up and turn to face him. "Is this where I say, 'My heart is always with you. Distance may separate us physically, but our love will transcend any boundaries.'"

"I've been thinking about this for longer than I've cared to admit." Joar's brow is furrowed with concern. "Do you want to have a family someday?"

I'm a bit taken aback. "I've always wanted a family."

"Do you want to raise a child in Los Angeles? From what I've seen, kids of celebrities..." He doesn't finish his sentence. We both know what he means.

My heart sinks. He wants me to move. Just when things are picking up. I realize I'm clenching my hands. "Aren't we putting the cart before the horse? Shouldn't we just enjoy what we have right now?"

"I'm going to put my cards on the table." Joar leans back against the cushions. Crosses his leg over his knee. "I'm going to be forty-eight next month. I don't want to be an old man with a baby."

I smack his leg. "Aw, JJ. Is your biological clock ticking?"

"I'm being serious." His jaw sets. "A big part of me wants your home base to be with me here in New York. It wouldn't mess up your career. We have the best schools. It would make things so much easier for me. I've been in LA a lot more than I normally am recently...because you're there." Joar rests his head in his palm and rubs his forehead with the edge of his finger as he speaks.

So many conflicting emotions bubble up. Elation. He's asking me for permanence, which I want. Frustration. He also wants me to uproot myself, which on paper makes sense. He's the friggin' billionaire, after all.

While I appreciate Joar's love and his intentions, in the past he's tried to make decisions without consulting me first. I don't want this issue to be an ongoing source of conflict. "It's important for me to advocate for my own life and career," I implore. "We both know moving to New York City isn't the best option for me right now."

Joar's brow furrows. He's disappointed. Determined. "I just want what's best for *us*. Being together—building a life together—is the right path forward."

"Look." I take a deep breath, trying to find the right words to express my feelings without causing further strife. "For at least the next year, I'd like to prioritize my career. Los Angeles is where my opportunities lie, where my agent is, where my connections are. Moving away isn't an option."

His eyes narrow slightly, and I can tell he's wrestling with his own inclination to take charge. "So, that's the end of the discussion?" He sighs heavily. "Clover, I worry about the strain of a long-distance relationship. I don't want to lose you over something we can fix."

"I understand completely." I soften my voice. This isn't just about me. We're both struggling and logistics have always been a factor for us. "Maybe we can take this year to explore compromises, like spending dedicated time together in each city or finding ways for me to pursue opportunities here in New York. It's not like we have to decide today. I'm not pregnant or anything."

Joar looks contemplative, his gaze fixed on me. "I dream about the day your belly is swollen with our child."

My heart swoons. I can't help it. I want that too. I crawl into his lap and straddle him. His arms band around me. I rest my cheek against his chest. "I love the idea of us creating a family together. We can find a way to figure this out. It goes both ways."

"You're right." He strokes my back. "I want us to be equals, in every sense of the word."

A glimmer of hope sparks within me.

This past year, I've been around many strong women.

Some with relationships. Some without.

It's never easy when you want to pursue your dreams. In the past, I just let all of mine go.

Watching my couple friends navigate dueling careers has been inspiring.

If Joar's the right partner for me, we'll find a way to work this out.

Chapter Thirty-Eight

Two Weeks Later

The sun shines brightly overhead, casting a warm glow over the picturesque neighborhood.

Nestled amidst lush greenery, the house stands as a stunning testament to architectural brilliance. Its grand facade exudes timeless elegance, with a combination of modern wood columns, expansive windows, and a meticulously manicured front lawn.

I glance at Clover, whose eyes are wide. A sense of tranquility washes over me when we step out of the car and take in the serene surroundings.

Hand in hand, we walk up the stone pathway.

A feeling of anticipation builds within me, growing with each step. We reach the front door, which is adorned with intricate carvings. When Clover opens it, we move into a spacious foyer, bathed in natural light streaming through the floor-to-ceiling windows.

Marble floating stairs lead both up and down. An incredible custom glass chandelier hangs down the middle from ceiling to the bottom floor, easily thirty feet long.

"It's beautiful. Simply beautiful," Clover murmurs.

I have to agree. The expansive marble flooring gleams like glass, hinting at the opulence we haven't yet seen in person.

"Should we start in the living room?" Beatrice, our realtor, joins us.

Clover's eyes light up. "Yes, that would be great."

The living room is all soaring ceilings and breath-taking views of the backyard through the expansive glass walls. A sense of openness permeates the space, though it also feels comfortable.

"JJ, can you imagine hosting gatherings in this magnificent space?" Clover looks around in awe. "Or decorating it for the holidays?"

I can't help but smile. My girl is a realtor's wet dream, she hasn't been able to control her enthusiasm for any house we've looked at. "Absolutely, my love," I reply.

Although...this place is special.

Beatrice puts on the hard sell. "In my years of selling high-end real estate, this is the most amazing house I've ever seen in Bel Air. It's an organic, modern paradise designed by Tag Front Architect, with ocean and city views." She barely stops to take a breath. "Every finish is museum quality with no expense spared. From the Italian kitchen to the Portuguese Limestone & Calcutta marble throughout. In addition to the master bedroom suite, the house has six en-suite bedrooms, two staff bedrooms, a twenty-seat theater, wine room, spa, and gym." She gestures around the kitchen. "Nothing compares, no need to settle for less."

I want her gone.

"Thank you, Beatrice." I hand her a hundred-dollar bill. "Clover and I would prefer to explore the property on our own. Please give us an hour or so."

Although she's surprised at my dismissal, Beatrice knows where her bread is buttered. "No problem, I'll be back soon."

"I am so hot for you right now." Clover grabs my shirt and pulls me to her. "She probably thinks we're not real buyers. That we're going to have sex in every room."

I bend down and place an open-mouthed kiss on her neck. Suckle her behind her ear just enough to make her squirm. "When we buy this house, *then* I'll be fucking you in every room and on every surface. Multiple times. Today, you get to pick just one place. So, we better get moving if you want to see everything before I rip your clothes off."

This lights a fire under Clover's ass. We stroll through the gourmet kitchen, which is a culinary enthusiast's dream, equipped with top-of-the-line appliances, a center island, and miles of counter space.

Upstairs, are a collection of modern and spacious bedrooms, each with its own unique charm and character.

The master suite is a sanctuary unto itself, featuring a private balcony that overlooks the lush backyard. The en-suite bathroom is a haven of luxury, with a freestanding soaking tub, sauna, a double vanity, and the biggest walk-in shower I've ever seen.

Next, we make our way to the backyard, where a paradise unfolds before us. The expansive patio is perfect for al fresco dining, with a built-in barbecue area and a cozy fire pit. Beyond the patio lies a sparkling curved infinity pool, with a soaking ledge. Across the lawn is a full-sized tennis court.

What impresses me is how secluded and private it is, though it feels open and airy. The meticulously landscaped gardens add a touch of serenity, providing a peaceful retreat from the craziness of LA.

"Well? What do you think?" Clover and I stand side by side on the lawn. Soaking in the beauty of this place that could soon become our home. "I think we could create a lifetime of memories here." My voice grows raw with emotion. "This house feels like a true sanctuary, a place where we can grow and thrive together."

Clover turns to me, her eyes sparkling. "I can already imagine it."

"We have a half hour." I glance at my phone. "Not much time, where should we christen the house?"

She bats her eyes at me. "We're not having sex here today, JJ."

"You had your chance." I pick her up and throw her over my shoulder. "I know the perfect place."

Clover boxes at my ass. "Let me down, omigod."

"Just wait." I slide my hand in the juncture of her thighs and wriggle it around a bit.

We approach the destination that I noticed, but I'm not sure if Clover did. I set her down and point to the wall.

"Is that?" Her eyes widen.

"An elevator?" I waggle my eyes.

I take a step and push the button. It opens. I step in and hold out my hand. "Wanna be naughty with me?"

"Yes." She bites her lip. Her cheeks flush. She steps forward, takes my hand and I pull her inside.

We're on the top floor adjusting our clothes when we hear Beatrice call for us.

I'm not going to lie, there's no way she's not going to know what we've been up to. The hem of Clover's dress is stained with my come, a casualty of our hastiness.

"Be right down," I bellow down the staircase.

Clover tries to brush herself off. "I'm trying to be embarrassed but considering this is my first walk of shame and it's in my soon-to-be own house, I'm surprisingly fine with it."

"You're my dirty, sexy girl. That's why." I give her one more kiss and we practically skip down the stairs.

Beatrice eyeballs us up and down. "I take it you feel at home here?"

"Yes, we do." I look at Clover.

She smiles up at me. "We'll pay asking price, no contingencies except we want all the furniture. All cash. Close in ten days."

"Excellent." Beatrice nods. "I don't see any reason why they won't accept your offer. Let me make the call."

The realtor steps outside, leaving us alone once again.

Clover and I fall into each other. This is monumental. We've just taken the first step toward permanence. We're paying for the house equally, half coming from her and half from me.

"We're going to have the best life here." I sway with her in my arms. "And the best life in Manhattan."

She squeezes me tighter against her. "I'm glad we pulled our heads out of our asses. I mean, I think our entire motto should be 'why choose' from now on."

"As long as there's not another dude involved, I'm okay with it." I laugh. Clover's slowly but surely building her romance collection back up again and seems to be reading a lot more of her reverse harem stuff.

"You're no fun," Clover teases, peppering kisses on my chin.

Beatrice enters the room, interrupting us. She holds up her phone. "We have a deal!"

Clover screams. I pick her up and twirl her around. "I can't wait for us to move in."

Later that night, Clover sleeps soundly.

I'm exhausted too, we made love for hours in celebration of our new home.

We may have been serious for just a few months, but I have big plans for us. The only time I'll have to work on them is when she's asleep, so I'm taking advantage of the opportunity. Things are more urgent now.

Obviously.

For the next two hours, I plot. Scheme. Gather my resources. Get my affairs in order.

If I play this smartly, Clover will fall into my carefully set trap.

This one, I'm certain she'll like.

Clover

Valentine's Day

Production on the second season of *The Boyfriend Experiment* started a week early.

We're in rehearsals, and with Ronni in Seattle for a wedding, I'm feeling a bit blue. Maybe I'm just lonely. It's Valentine's Day, and Joar's in Dublin. The first season drops today and he won't be here to watch it with me. Sure, we saw it together weeks ago when I received my advance screener copy, but it's not the same as when it's out for real.

I hope the public loves it because I think it's incredible. I can't even believe the woman on the screen is me.

My plan is to go to the cast and crew party at the hotel. It'll be fun, we have a great group.

I miss my man, though.

We're not filming yet, so I'm dressed casually in a white T-shirt, jeans, and a blue-plaid shirt tied at my waist. I'm going over the blocking instructions when the door to my dressing room swings open. It's the head of security. "Clover, I need you to come with me urgently." He looks a bit nervous. "We've had a bit of a breach."

"What do you mean?" My heart pounds in my chest.

He gestures for me to follow him. "I don't think it's a safety issue, but there's someone here who says he knows you. He's downstairs on the main floor by the sound stages."

Curiosity piques so I speedily gather my belongings and follow the guard through the bustling corridors of the studio, the familiar hum of activity surrounds us. The elevator doors open. Memories flood my mind, as they always do when I remember the time Joar and I fucked each other silly for eight hours straight in here.

A serendipitous moment that forever changed our lives.

We reach the bottom floor, and no one is there. "Huh." The guard scratches his beard. "Wait here, I'll go see if I can find him."

While I wait, a few crew members pass by and wave. Then turn and snicker to themselves. I glance down at my clothes, checking for stains. Nothing. It's weird, but I'm unbothered.

When the guard doesn't return after five minutes, I decide the crew was pranking me and go back up to my dressing room.

I sit at the vanity. Text Joar about what happened. Scroll TikTok. Decide to make a cup of tea. As I wait for the water to boil, I allow myself to daydream about our perfect new house. How I'm going to decorate. Then my thoughts turn to visuals of Joar and I christening the master, master bath, pool, hot tub...

I shake my head vigorously. I cannot think about us fucking without being sad. Or horny. I'm already missing Joar and video sex is all we'll have for the next four weeks.

Regardless of our temporary separation, I'm excited for our future. Joar and I are committed and moving forward. It's funny, though. We have our living situation sorted out. I'm going off the pill after we finish shooting. But, aside from a few in-the-moment utterances after sex, he's never brought up getting married. Not for real.

I haven't brought it up, either.

Now more than ever, I know my heart. I'm ready to marry him. It's what I want. When he gets back from Dublin, it will be our next serious conversation.

The kettle whistles, snapping me back to reality. I make my tea and bring it back to the vanity.

When I look in the mirror, that's when I see it.

A yellow Post-it note.

My heart races as I pluck it off.

Meet me in our Elevator

9:30 am

Don't be Late

Omigod! Is Joar here?

I grab my phone to check the time. *Crap*. It's 9:45.

I'm late!

Running down the hall to the elevator, I skid to a stop and press the button over and over, hoping to make it arrive sooner. I look at the marker, and it seems to be stuck on the second floor. I stab the button again. Again. Again. Again.

Argh!

Finally, I watch it make its way to my floor. My heart thunders in my chest. I cannot *wait* to see Joar. I shouldn't have doubted he'd find a way to be with me on Valentine's Day—our first as a couple.

When the doors open, there's no one there.

Feeling a bit heartbroken, I step back inside. Notice that the button's been pressed to the top floor.

The floor where JJ's office is.

OMG.

As the doors open when I reach the destination, my eyes widen in surprise. There stands Joar in all his gorgeous full-suited glory, his presence radiating a blend of nervousness and determination. My heart skips a beat as I take in the sight of the man I love, waiting for me with an air of significance. Time seems to stand still as I walk toward him, meeting his gaze.

"Clover," Joar begins, his voice soft yet brimming with emotion. "I've been given the gift of witnessing your strength, resilience, and unwavering spirit. You've brought light into my life and awakened a love in me that I never knew existed."

My heart flutters, and I feel a wave of warmth wash over me. It's as if the world around us fades away, leaving Joar and me standing in this moment.

He takes a step closer, his hand reaching out to grasp mine. Gets down on one knee. Opens a circular, leather box to reveal the most incredible ring I've ever seen—an exquisite emerald-cut diamond, in a classic solitaire setting. It must be at least ten carats. "Clover, I can't imagine my life without you. You are my rock, my inspiration, the love of my life. Will you do me the honor of becoming my wife?"

A mixture of joy, surprise, and overwhelming love fills every fiber of my being. Tears well up in my eyes as I nod, unable to figure out the words to express the depth of my emotions. I throw my arms around him, hoping he can feel how much his very being fills my heart and soul.

"I love you so much, JJ." I flutter kisses all over his face. "You make me so happy. I can't wait to spend my life with you."

We hold each other tightly, whispering words of eternal love and devotion. Our tears of joy flow unashamedly. I have no doubt that saying yes to Joar means a lifetime of love, laughter, and shared dreams.

"I have one more surprise for you today." Joar stands and kisses me deeply. "Everyone has been sent home so we have the entire studio to ourselves.

I can feel my entire body flush. "Must be nice to be a domineering boss," I tease.

He presses the elevator button. Wiggles his fingers for me to take his hand. "You know it."

The doors open. The cab is now filled with fluffy pillows and plush, thick blankets. I cock my head. "You know, I'm never going to be able to go back and forth to set in this thing. All I'll be thinking about is you and me..."

"*Clover.*" Joar wiggles his fingers again.

"*JJ.*" I grab his hand and am nearly blinded by my new bling.

"Get in here." He tugs me and I tumble into his arms. He reaches out and presses the "stop" button on the panel.

The elevator doors closes just as he drops a searing kiss on my lips.

Want more of Clover & Joar scan the QR Code for a Bonus Scene

Look for Kaylene's next stand alone novel The Flirt Alert to be released Fall of 2023. Scan QR code for a link to the book.

Want to learn more about Connor & Ronni scan the QR Code bellow to read their story in the Less Than Zero story Fearless.

For special offers, promotions, news about LTZ and all of my
upcoming releases and all sorts of behind the scenes stuff,

please sign up for my newsletter, by scanning the QR code.

Behind the Scenes

Hello readers!

For those of you who are new to me, I love to share some unfiltered (and largely unedited) thoughts at the end of each book. It's my chance to give you some insight into my writing process, the characters and generally how the story took shape.

Clover Callahan popped up in Fearless Encore in just one scene. Ronni Miller, the brains behind Clover's Netflix series, is the heroine in both Fearless and Fearless encore, which you can get here:

Let's dive into The Hate Date, shall we?

When I was finishing up my Less Than Zero series, I decided that there are so many fun "side" characters throughout, why not choose a few and share their stories. When I came up with the name "Clover Callahan" as the actress in Ronni's series, I knew without a shadow of doubt that she'd be my gal.

I mean, her name. C'mon!

I'm going to share a secret with all of you...ready?

I'm a huge reality TV fan. I live for a reality TV moment. Over the past couple years, two things happened that I knew I had to incorporate into Clover's story. First, Erika Jayne, the RHOBH "pop star," whose music career was funded with the money her husband stole from his clients. You can't make that shit up.

Second...The Scandoval! I've been obsessed. I subscribe to every podcast, wait with bated breath for every episode, read about it. I realize this is a sickness, but I can't help myself. I thought, why not have Clover's husband cheat with her BFF?

Anyway, you see my little references throughout.

Combine the two, and Clover could have been a pretty unsympathetic character. So, of course, I twisted it up. I like my heroines strong and vulnerable and capable of wrangling their strong, manly men without making the man change his personality to conform to her standards. Because, really. Is that a *relationship*?

No, no it's not.

Enter Joar, an ancient Nordic name which technically means "one with the horse" – or, "horse." Fitting, considering Mr. Jacoby is hung like one, no? LOL.

Joar is intentionally mysterious, we get snippets about his life throughout...this was deliberate. Mainly because he's not really used to anyone ever asking about him. Even as a successful, high-profile billionaire, Joar keeps to himself. His background as a destitute foster kid sticks with him throughout his life. He's a brilliant businessman, but doesn't trust easily. In many ways, he's learned how to cope and succeed by saying little and learning a lot. He's a sexy, stealth dude.

I hope you loved to see his growth throughout the book, from taking what he wants hard and fast to really leaning into his feelings. Falling in love and putting someone first for the first time in his life.

Clover, though she also had a difficult childhood with similar themes of abandonment, tried to find someone to take care of her by marrying Harrison. Not used to receiving much, her marriage gave her a feeling of stability. When it was ripped away, she had a moment of reckoning as well.

How can she stop repeating her mistakes and make changes in her life that will bring her happiness. Fulfilment, etc.

Okay, now that the woo-woo shit is over, this entire book was conceived by this idea of a "hate date."

When I met my husband, we had a lot in common but we also have things we like to do that the other isn't such a big fan of. Yet, we've always supported each other and shown up. I thought, wouldn't that be a great premise for a couple to get together?

Voila – Joar did too. He used his relentless pursuing skills to turn things around and show Clover who he really is. Gave himself the opportunity to correct his mistakes and put her first. Their timing was off for a while, but in the end I think these two are a perfect match.

I'll admit, whenever I finish a book, I feel like the characters in the one I just wrote are my favorites.

It's the same here. I love Clover and Joar so much, and hope you did too!

Next up is:

(title to be inserted soon)

If you're looking for more books by me, I recommend my series, Less Than Zero, which follows four devastatingly sexy rockstars and the women who bring them to their knees. I promise, even if you're not a rockstar romance person, you'll fall in love with them as they navigate their HEA's.

Start with Endless here:

Until next time,
Love,

Acknowledgments

Cover/Graphic Designer/Finder of HOTTIES:
Regina Wamba

Editor: Grace Bradley

Proofreading: Beth Carbutt

Formatting: Willow Yanarella

PR: Valentine PR

Publicity: Next Step PR, Xpresso Tours

Website Maven: Sherri Kiarsis, Sublime Creations

My Right Hand: Willow Yanarella

YAY to KAYLENE'S KREW!!!

Beta Readers: Anna Theurer & Beth Carbutt

My Inspirations: My husband, my pup and the entire cast of Vanderpump Rules. The Scandoval kept me captivated this spring and summer!

Dedication

This author thing has taken on a life of its own. When my husband encouraged me to release my first book, Endless, little did he know how deeply I'd fall into this world. I love creating these characters and stories for you, so this book is not only dedicated to G, but to all of the readers who have embraced me. I hope to be around for a long, long time!

About the Author

Kaylene Winter is a best-selling author of steamy, contemporary romance.

Each character-driven novel is filled with snappy dialogue, pop-culture references and enough steam to make you fan yourself. Kaylene weaves authenticity, emotion and angst into a turbulent rollercoaster ride of love, passion and soul-searing romance always ending with a delicious HEA.

Kaylene lives in Seattle with her amazing Irish husband and gorgeous Siberian Husky. She loves creating art of all kinds.

Other Titles